THE NEW DESTROYER:
KILLER RATINGS

BY WARREN MURPHY AND JAMES MULLANEY

The New Destroyer: Guardian Angel
The New Destroyer: Choke Hold
The New Destroyer: Dead Reckoning
The New Destroyer: Killer Ratings

THE NEW DESTROYER:

KILLER RATINGS

Warren Murphy and James Mullaney

TOR®

A TOM DOHERTY ASSOCIATES BOOK
NEW YORK

This is a work of fiction. All of the characters, organizations, and events portrayed in this novel are either products of the authors' imagination or are used fictitiously.

THE NEW DESTROYER: KILLER RATINGS

A Tor Book
Published by Tom Doherty Associates, LLC
175 Fifth Avenue
New York, NY 10010

www.tor-forge.com

Tor® is a registered trademark of Tom Doherty Associates, LLC.

ISBN-13: 978-0-7653-6021-2
ISBN-10: 0-7653-6021-7

First Edition: August 2008

Printed in the United States of America

0 9 8 7 6 5 4 3 2 1

For Mrs. Boegemann, wherever you are.

For the rest of the Foursome from Hell—Bill Chambers, Neil Bagozzi, and Mark Coles.

For www.warrenmurphy.com, where one of us can be reached; for www.jamesmullaney.com, where the other one can.

And for the Glorious House of Sinanju, e-mail: housinan@aol.com

THE NEW DESTROYER:

KILLER RATINGS

Everyone wanted her dead.

The jackals were circling her body and had been for so long now, she had forgotten what her world was like without them. She was not yet dead, not even cold, but the snarling, salivating pack was sniffing around as if it had found a fresh antelope carcass deep in the tall grass.

It had not always been so. She seemed healthy way back at the very beginning although it was so long ago she could scarcely remember now. But even then things were not as rosy as they had seemed. After only one day the bleeding had started. In a week the floor was stained red and the animals that fed off carrion were sneaking in, tearing off pieces of her flesh. Nibbling, nibbling away at a body still standing but wobbling on unsteady high heels.

KITTY COUGHLIN RATINGS DISASTER!
IS BCN ALREADY GROOMING KITTY'S REPLACEMENT?
OUR TOP STORY: KITTY #3 AND FALLING
COUGHLIN'S RATINGS BLEED CONTINUES

Those headlines came at the end of just her first week as the first woman to solo anchor a network evening newscast. The press got worse in her second week. In the third week she stopped reading the reviews and threatened to fire anyone who brought to work any newspaper that dared to devote so much as an inch of column space to the growing ratings disaster. This edict, among many others, further damaged the swelling tide of negative opinion about her among the staff at the Broadcast Corporation of North America world news headquarters in New York.

Naturally, the talk of dissent in the ranks made all the trade papers. It was no secret that the regular news staff hated her. One famous old-timer at the network, an octogenarian who had temporarily held the evening news anchor post until Kitty was wooed to the center chair from a rival network, now regularly fed stories of behind-the-scenes disaster to a hungry print media. A well-known female journalist on a BCN weekly news magazine program, a woman Kitty knew socially and who had been friendly before Kitty became the most famous female news face at the network, would no longer speak when they passed in the hallways. These days it was all icy glares and vile dinner party gossip.

Everyone was waiting for her to fail, longing for the day when the network finally came to its senses and pulled the plug on the ratings bleed over which Kitty had presided.

If the bigwigs concluded that it was better for their bottom line, she knew that even her multimillion-dollar contract would not save her from the unemployment line. At fifty-three she'd be a jobless pariah, damaged goods forced to move out of her tony Park Avenue apartment and into some cold-water skid-row tenement. She made a mental note to wear a more sensible pair of Prada shoes her first day in the soup line.

"Ow. Dammit," Kitty Coughlin muttered as she strode through the gleaming automatic doors at New York's LaGuardia Airport. Leaning against the doorframe, she stuck a finger down inside the tight back of her left shoe.

"Is something wrong, Ms. Coughlin?" asked the nervous young man who accompanied her.

"No, I always stick my hands in my shoes and hop to the plane for good luck, you moron."

She had stopped dead to adjust the shoe and was blocking the entrance so that a husband and wife with two children and an armload of luggage were bunched up behind her.

"There's another door right there, Gomer," Kitty snarled at the man, who until now had been offering a friendly smile. "Go around. Jesus. Idiot tourists."

The man's smile faded and he ushered his wife and kids around a railing to an adjacent door. "So, you still getting hammered in Boston by *Malcolm in the Middle?*" the man queried as he and his family passed Kitty into the building. His wife shushed him but Kitty noted that he was smiling once more as he hurried his family across the busy terminal.

"Does every nitwit in the world know my goddamn ratings?" she growled, tugging her finger angrily out of her shoe.

Her once charmed life was a thing lost in the distant mists of hazy memory. A darling only child, the apple of her parents' eyes; a sorority sister at her exclusive college; an internship at a Washington TV station thanks to her school ties; and up, up, up until she had reached what at the time was the pinnacle of her profession for a woman long on legs and short on talent, cohost of a network morning news and entertainment show. Life had been so easy for so long that her brain could not comprehend adversity, which was why she had taken the job as solo anchor for the BCN Evening News. If she had only had some clue that things might get sticky, that the print press would turn on her, that her coworkers would despise her, that the viewing public could fall out of love with her, she might never have taken the job.

But she vowed that she would not let it get to her. Her therapist had told her she should visit her happy place in times of stress. But the idyllic, sunny field in her mind was filled these days with snakes and on the lake front of her imagination sharks with legs had started scuttling up out of the shallow water. She had spent so much meditation time lately stomping on snakes and kicking sharks in their snub noses that she had given up hope of finding a happy place even in her mind.

Yet all the hatred, the backstabbing, the resentment would not get to her. No way. She would not allow it. She was rock. Unmovable, unassailable. Let them give her their worst, she would not be shaken.

"If only these goddamn shoes fit right, everything would be fine," she snarled at no one and everyone.

Walking was murder in these things but no matter how tight they pinched she would not stumble, especially in a public place like an airport.

In the darkest crevices of her worried mind she might be wobbling, but only in her mind. In real life Kitty could not afford to give even the appearance of physical unsteadiness. Her ratings were miserable, but if she wobbled, stumbled or fell and—God forbid—someone got the image on a cell phone and disseminated it to her enemies, it would be seen as a sign; a physical manifestation of the precarious position she was in at her job. Another headline.

KITTY COUGHLIN TRIPS AS RATINGS DIP!

In this age of the twenty-four-hour news cycle, where anchors not only reported the news but were themselves the topic of discussion on countless panel shows, Kitty would not willingly give the piranhas something to feed on. The pundits would claim even her unconscious knew she was ready to topple. At that point a nudge, perhaps in the form of some supermarket tabloid exposé, and the jackals would have the feeding frenzy they had been hungering after for over a year.

As she walked through the terminal, the prospects of a new round of bad press made her lightheaded.

No. There would be no wobbling, no stumbling. Certainly she would not fall. She would absolutely not give the jackals, the hyenas, the vultures the satisfaction. If she had been a dedicated leftist, she might even have recalled the lyrics to the old labor union song, "We are fighting for our future; we shall not be moved." But in truth, she was not a leftist. She did not really understand political left and political right and such nuances but instead took her political cues from nineteen-year-old bimbo actresses, rock singers with tattooed genitals, and rap artistes whom she liked to interview whenever they were out on bail. Beautiful people all. With beautiful identical ideas of love and peace and brotherhood, which Kitty Coughlin rarely understood but always loudly supported. Beautiful people. And Kitty Coughlin was proud to be one of them and she would hold her head up high and the world be damned before she would show any weakness, especially to the slimy peasants who seemed to infest today's world.

Her high heels clicked with renewed ferocious purpose as she went to check in.

"Washington bureau has a limo all arranged," said the nervous young BCN Evening News assistant who dogged her steps. His short legs had a difficult time keeping pace with her long, certain strides. "It'll be at the airport when you land," he said, panting as he tried to keep up. "They've found someone new for sound just like you asked."

"They better have," Kitty Coughlin snarled. "Last moron

those bozos stuck me with made me sound like Daffy Duck."

Since she was a VIP, Kitty was allowed to skip the line. Ordinarily she was in first class long before the deadweight in the back boarded, but today she noticed that the proles seemed to be moving along faster than usual. For some reason there were not the usual security delays. She only noticed two security officers on duty and they appeared to be arguing with one another, oblivious to the passengers filing through the scanners single file. She saw her own camera crew pass through without having to open their bags of equipment for inspection. At the rate they were moving, the nobodies would all be aboard before her.

"Your FEMA interview is all set for three this afternoon," her assistant said, oblivious to the rapidly moving line at his back. He pulled some 3 x 5 cards from his pocket. "Here's the questions. Mr. Maddox has gone over them and given his okay."

Kitty snorted. "Ah, yes, Uriah Maddox. The great savior of the BCN Evening News with Kitty Coughlin."

"Um . . . yes," said the young man. "Anyway, Washington production staff already has copies. Mr. Maddox had me pass them along. They'll add if they have others."

"Yeah, I know the drill." She snapped her fingers. "Give me those. I don't have all day."

Her assistant handed over the cards as well as her small overnight bag which he had carried from the car. She detected a hint of relief in his shoulders as he turned to leave. He was looking at a whole day in New York without Kitty Coughlin. The rest of the Evening News staff back in Manhattan was probably popping champagne corks already.

She wished her Botox-saturated face would permit her to scowl as she hustled through the nonexistent VIP security, through the connecting air tunnel and onto the waiting 747.

Flying commercial was just the latest indignity she was being forced to endure. When BCN was wooing her away from a rival network where she had cohosted the morning entertainment-news program for nearly two decades, Kitty had been feted like a queen on private BCN jets. But these days corporate never missed an opportunity to remind the news division that they were keeping careful watch on the wounded and bleeding bottom line.

Kitty found her seat at the middle of the first class section of Flight 980, stashed her bag in the overhead compartment and slumped angrily into her seat. She kicked off her uncomfortable shoes and massaged the fresh blister on her left heel.

She ignored the pilot's voice on the intercom. When the stewardess began offering unintelligible advice on the scratchy public address system, Kitty was studying her notes. She was still going through the 3 x 5 cards as the plane taxied, gained speed and then tore off down the long runway.

Uriah Maddox, the executive producer of the evening news and Kitty's nominal boss, had added two handwritten questions about Hurricane Katrina and New Orleans and why the federal emergency management gang had assisted the hurricane in destroying the city.

"Way to stay topical, Uriah," Kitty grunted as the 747 rose into the clear blue spring sky. "Maybe while I'm at it, I'll ask them about FEMA's response to the sinking of the *Titanic*."

The most important questions related to FEMA's preparedness for the global warming crisis. There were seventeen individual global warming questions. There was a question about FEMA and global warming and tornados in Kansas. There was a question about FEMA and global warming and blizzards in the Northeast. Kitty placed on top the card that asked what FEMA's plan was if half of the Antarctic ice sheet broke away thanks to global warming, floated north and lodged in the Gulf of Mexico.

She was tapping the cards back into a neat little pile and wondering if this would be her last interview before the suits came to her office and told her she was finished, when she suddenly became aware of a commotion behind her.

Several people gasped in unison. A woman screamed.

"Stay in your seats!" a voice commanded.

Seat belts unbuckled as people up front craned to see what was going on in back. Kitty fumbled her belt loose but did not have time to peer over the seat.

Several things happened seemingly at once.

First there was hustling in the aisle. A frantic stewardess ran past Kitty's seat toward the cockpit.

"My God, oh my God!" the woman cried.

This was followed by a loud pop and the stewardess was suddenly sprawling forward, a red splotch staining the center of her otherwise spotless white blouse.

More screams. Panic exploded throughout the first class section as three men raced up the aisle, guns clutched in their gloved hands. Each man wore a large backpack. The lower half of their faces up to the eyes was covered with a black mask. Blue baseball caps were pulled down low, leaving only a narrow gap for their nervous eyes to dart around the cabin.

Two of the masked men paused to shove someone into the empty seat next to Kitty. It was her cameraman. His skin had gone pale under his three-day growth of beard. The anxious young man had been collected from the coach section and was now fumbling his camera to his shoulder. He aimed it at the two men who loomed over BCN's star anchorwoman.

"It's her," one hissed to another. He was short and at least one hundred pounds overweight. A moist circle of sweaty drool stained his mask over his mouth.

The second one was much thinner than the first. There were acne boils on the visible skin around his eyes. He shoved a pen and a glossy photograph into Kitty's hands.

"Could you do me a favor?" asked the man with the gun politely.

It was such an incongruous thing given the circumstances that Kitty autographed the photograph out of habit. When she was finished, the skinny man muttered something about auctioning off the signed publicity photo as he snatched it back and shoved it into the pocket of his jacket.

"Thanks," he said, taking off up the aisle.

"Keep filming," the fat man ordered the cameraman.

The two men hustled forward, climbing over the body of the dead stewardess on their way to the closed cockpit door where their comrade was waiting.

Kitty could not believe what was happening. It was a hijacking. An honest-to-God hijacking and she was in the middle of it. This was the sort of thing trained newspeople waited a lifetime for. Unfortunately news reporting in the trenches was not Kitty's area of expertise and the fact that one of the hijackers had asked for her autograph in the middle of it had thrown her completely off stride.

"What should I do?" the cameraman asked.

Kitty pulled out her prepared note cards. "Uh . . . uh . . ." She fumbled through the cards and pulled out the only one that even came close to planes. It was a question for the FEMA director asking what his agency planned to do to respond to the crisis of a diminishing worldwide bee population, a direct result of global warming. She gave up on the cards. "How the hell should I know?" she snapped. "Just point that thing at them and keep shooting."

There was at least one more hijacker in back. Kitty could hear a man over her shoulder barking orders. The men in front were arguing before the locked cockpit door.

"You just blew her away, man," the fat one said. He glanced back at the dead stewardess. His dark mask was stained darker with heavy sweat.

"Shut up," said the hijacker who had asked for Kitty's autograph. "I had a perfect 100 feedback and he blew it. I explained to him that 'near mint' means an album dust jacket might have some corner wear but he's relentless. We do this and he promised to delete it."

"Our seller ratings aren't our biggest worries anymore," the other one said.

Kitty had no idea what their babbling could mean. She watched them stick a small square object to the cockpit door. "What are they doing?" she whispered to her cameraman. But when she looked over she found the man had slipped from his seat and was down on the floor, his camera held over his head like a protective shield. "Get that camera back up here," she hissed. "Wait. They're stepping away from the door. Why are they hiding behind those seats? There's some kind of little lights blinking on that box they stuck to the door. You don't think it could be—"

If Kitty finished her question, the words were swallowed up during the abrupt flash of light and accompanying explosive roar. The explosion at the front of the cabin launched flaming shrapnel back across eight rows of seats. Men and women dove for cover. A prosperous-looking middle-aged man across from Kitty caught a chunk of metal in the center of his broad forehead. There was very little blood as he collapsed dead back into his seat.

A large chunk of blasted metal launched up and embedded in the ceiling. Kitty's cameraman quickly scrambled back to his seat and aimed his camera forward.

The echoing explosion continued to scream in Kitty's ears even as the hijackers swarmed the cockpit. The screaming continued over the sounds of muffled pops. Only when the dead or wounded flight crew was dragged out into the galley and the screaming had not subsided did Kitty realize that the noise was no longer from the explosion but from her own throat. She covered her mouth but the screams still came. At one point her cameraman swung the camera toward her. There was BCN's fifteen-million-dollar-a-year newswoman, face drained of color, eyes like dinner plates, hands plastered over her mouth like a sitcom housewife who had just seen a mouse in the laundry room. And still she screamed.

The plane veered in midair.

Kitty had never felt a large plane move like that. It was wrong. Too fast, too sharp a turn. The plane bucked under her feet like a bronco out of chute.

The cameraman trained his lens on the section of ceiling where the largest chunk of cockpit door had lodged. The sharp five-foot section of metal was rattling. It seemed like the plane was reabsorbing the door. Kitty realized that was ridiculous as soon as the thought occurred to her. But the section of metal was definitely growing smaller, disappearing inch by inch. It was as if it were burrowing its way through the skin of the craft. For a sick moment she swore she could see a sliver of natural light.

The plane banked hard, the chunk of door abruptly slipped like a knife through butter, and a section of ceiling was suddenly missing from behind the cockpit. The ugly rip of metal was overwhelmed by the deafening roar of the wall of air that blasted through the new-formed hole.

Oxygen masks dropped down from hidden compartments and bobbed like a hundred living legs of some monstrous hidden centipede. The wind shrieked through the opening, catching up anything loose in a violent tornado swirl. Papers, coffee cups, and soda cans were blasted backward. Through her own screams, Kitty scraped away an in-flight magazine that had slapped against her face.

A silent flash beside her and something huge briefly darkened the window to her right.

The curved white section of torn-away fuselage slipped

from the window and banged silently against the wing. Through her window Kitty saw it tumbling end-over-end toward the eastern shore of the gleaming black East River.

Some passengers struggled to yank on their oxygen masks although at such a low altitude Kitty managed to suck down so much air that she did not grab at her own bobbing mask. Somehow through her endless screams she had managed to fumble her seat belt back on and now she held on for dear life.

The river grew larger and fell away. An ugly upright block of blue glass loomed into view. Kitty held her breath thinking "This is it." But the familiar facade of the U.N. building, fell away. The plane seemed to struggle to maintain altitude.

Manhattan loomed.

The plane banked right in a loop that brought its shadow over city hall. On the ground the turn appeared lazy, a slow crawl northeast until it was roughly following the choking morning traffic on Park Avenue.

Kitty had never seen the city from this vantage point. Wind thrashing her hair, she spotted familiar landmarks including the black granite monolith that was the BCN building which she had left an hour and a half before.

And then the real target became clear.

In 1972 it had ceased to be the tallest building in New York City when the first World Trade Center tower was completed. But on a terrible September day in 2001 it had regained its former standing in the most horrifying, most unimaginable way possible.

The art deco facade of the Empire State Building was a magnet drawing the plane inexorably forward.

One of the most famous buildings in the world. Soon to be reduced to a pile of collapsed brick and twisted metal.

Yelling at the cabin. Some of the male passengers tried to rush the trio of hijackers who were guarding the cockpit door. Gunshots. Loud pops—loud enough even to be heard over the roaring wind—and the passengers dropped along with the dead stewardess, more corpses clogging the aisle.

The plane rolled. The seat belt cut deep into Kitty's belly forcing the wind from her lungs.

The wings shuddered, rattling the fuselage as the air spilled off the plane's skin. A violent turn.

Faces in windows. Kitty could hardly believe she could actually see the faces of men and women in the windows of the Empire State Building. They looked on in horror as the plane made its last terrible roll.

Passengers not held in by seat belts fell to Kitty's side of the plane. Her cameraman collapsed over her, clunking her in the chin with his camera.

A child. Not more than seven years old. She saw his face distinctly in a sixtieth-story window as the ugly shadow of the wounded plane passed like the angel of death across the west side of the Empire State Building.

And then the plane cleared Manhattan's most famous landmark and began to ascend.

Some last minute change of heart, perhaps a technical problem, maybe the hand of God . . . Kitty did not know why the plane did not slam the building. She only knew that the plane was soon flying level once more and that the hijackers were spilling back out of the cockpit.

Two of the cabin crew had survived the attack. One appeared uninjured but for a bleeding bruise to the side of his head. Another had used his necktie to tie off the bullet wound in his thigh. The men were freed and allowed back inside the cockpit. They did not attempt to engage the hijackers, merely battled through the gale wind back to their stations. The hijackers went to work once more.

More explosive charges. Two doors blown open on the plane. More wind, more screams.

The hijackers fell one by one out the open doors.

Kitty thought she was witnessing some sort of ritual mass suicide. She lost sight of the tumbling men for a few seconds. Moments later she spied them, four dark parachutes drifting toward the Hudson River.

The tension of the next dozen minutes was as nothing compared to the preceding twenty. A heroic stewardess raced along the cabin making certain all passengers were buckled in and braced for the crash that never came.

Twenty-seven minutes after it had taken off, the plane made a textbook landing on its own wheels in a pile of emergency foam at LaGuardia Airport.

The emergency chutes were inflated and deployed and the shaken passengers herded to the exits where they slid down into piles of white foam. Kitty slipped down the chute, skinned her blistered heel on the tarmac as she got to her feet and did not care that she was covered in foam as she stumbled to the mass of reporters that had been herded together behind the row of emergency vehicles. She spied a camera that bore the BCN logo.

"Microphone!" she screeched. In two minutes, mic in hand, she had wiped away most of the foam, smoothed her hair and was staring into the camera's unblinking eye. "This is Kitty Coughlin, reporting live from LaGuardia Airport where many people, myself included, are grateful to be alive."

BCN went live with the story of the hijacking. It was the first day of May, and so the event became known as MAYDAY ON MAY DAY! With Kitty on the scene of the near disaster, offering a firsthand account of the morning's events, BCN's coverage left the other major network news divisions in the dust.

The footage taken by Kitty's cameraman was smuggled from the airport and raced in a satellite news van to the BCN studios before the authorities were even aware it existed.

"They want it, let 'em get a court order, and good luck getting it out of my safe," Uriah Maddox, BCN's executive producer, said. "Till then, it's our exclusive. Our beautiful, solid gold ratings exclusive."

Within an hour the footage taken aboard ill-fated Flight 980 was being packaged in digestible, two-minute bites, and for the first time since Kitty Coughlin's very first night in the anchor chair viewers were flocking to BCN, which had suddenly regained its reputation as the Diamond Network.

A careful viewing of the footage would have revealed that the passengers in some of the camera's sweeping background shots looked somewhat different from shot to shot. That was because BCN had quickly and quietly rented a hangered plane at Newark Liberty International Airport and restaged all of Kitty's reaction shots. BCN could not let the world witness its anchor star crumbling under pressure. Kitty's panicked screams were the first thing to fall to the cutting room floor. In the meantime, men and women were ordered on buses from the offices of BCN *Evening News* with Kitty Coughlin. Clothes were scrounged from the wardrobe departments of BCN's New York-based soap operas and, as best as could be managed, the news employees were dressed to match the clothing worn by passengers in the real footage.

A few strategic snips of the action footage in the editing booth and a few splices here and there of fresh material, and there was Kitty Coughlin, calm and confident, the steel-spined anchorwoman facing down adversity with the calm of an Edward R. Murrow, the wit of a David Brinkley, the steely-eyed gaze of a Howard K. Smith.

For the first time in a fifteen-month-long career nosedive, Kitty Coughlin was sitting pretty on a ratings gold mine.

But Kitty, above all others, should have known that television news was a fickle business.

The next day a story that had been percolating up into the national consciousness from down in Miami exploded onto the nightly network news. During the previous week, several old ladies had been violently mugged by a young thug on an orange bicycle. It had happened again but this time there was videotape. In some grainy footage obtained from an ATM, a young man in a hood and dark sunglasses knocked the walker out from under a ninety-seven-year-old woman, kicked her in the ribs and stole the ten dollars she had withdrawn to buy ice cream sandwiches for her visiting six-year-old great-grandson. Hard news was a thing of the past. Human interest stories were the new bread and butter of the news game so the footage of the little old lady assault abruptly supplanted the story of Flight 980 and the Empire State Building's near miss, BCN's live exclusive became quite literally yesterday's news, and Kitty Coughlin's ratings plummeted back into the cellar.

And in a BCN editing bay high above Forty-third Street, BCN's first solo female news anchor watched some anonymous little punk peddle away on his Schwinn two-wheeler, carting off not only some old bat's ten dollars but Kitty's career as well.

As the old lady rolled in helpless silent tape-recorded agony on the floor of the automated teller booth, Kitty raised her eyes to the uncaring heavens and a thoughtless God that would allow such a terrible calamity to take place and howled, "Why can't I catch a goddamn ratings break?"

2

His name was Remo and he was supposed to kill
the drug dealer before the mugger.

Those had been the explicit orders from Upstairs.
Drug dealer was the number one priority target, and his
elimination was, as far as Upstairs was concerned, the
only reason Remo was being sent to Miami. If Remo
insisted on taking out the mugger while he was in town,
that came second. If at all.

"And I would prefer not at all," Remo's employer, Dr.
Harold W. Smith of the supersecret agency CURE had
said three days before. Over the phone Smith's lemony
disposition became the equivalent of citric acid poured
directly into the listeners' ear canal.

"Then send me after whoever hijacked that plane,"
Remo suggested.

"We're still looking into the Flight 980 matter. There is
something very strange about that situation, not least of
which is the fact that we don't even know what the

hijackers' goal was. When more is known, I may send you in, but for now, you need only concern yourself with the matter of Ramon Albondigas."

"Okay, Smitty. If it's Miami you want, it's Miami you get. But while I'm in town I'm taking out the creep that mugged all those old ladies. That's not open to debate."

"The local police can take care of a mugger."

"They're doing one whoop-de-doo job so far, Smitty," Remo said. "He's up to five little old ladies, one of them just died, and so far the cops still haven't got so much as a decent artist's sketch out there."

"Remo, if you know about these muggings, you already know that his face has not yet been seen."

"I've seen enough of him," Remo said coldly.

Network and local newscasts had made certain that all of America had seen as much of the mugger as possible, although his facial features still remained unknown. A tiny, twenty-second clip of footage from a bank security camera had been playing on the news for days, seemingly on an endless loop.

The film had been taken at intervals of three seconds. On the video, an elderly woman, hunched with age and wearing a housecoat, struggled to get her walker through the heavy door of a bank's glass-enclosed foyer. A quick cut and the woman was pushing buttons at the automated teller. Another quick cut and a young man wearing a dark pullover sweatshirt with hood was inside the foyer, the door swinging shut behind him. Another cut and the man was kicking the walker out from under the woman and grabbing a thin stack of bills from her hand as she fell. The final shot was of the old woman lying on the floor wincing in pain beneath her walker, too shocked even to cry as the young hood made good his escape.

There had been four other such muggings of the elderly in Miami in the past two weeks and the only image the world had seen of the attacker was a thin, nondescript man in dark sunglasses and a hood.

"Remo, you haven't seen him," Smith said. "No one has seen him. He has been savvy enough to obscure his features and avoid cameras as much as possible. Cameras at practically every scene, some on street corners, some in parking lots, record images of him but not one has gotten a clear shot of him yet."

"You know an awful lot of details for a guy who doesn't think I should go after this creep," Remo suggested.

"It has been difficult to avoid. I admit that it is troubling that this thug is loose. But we have a bigger target to worry about than just a mugger. Ramon Albondigas of La Cocina drug cartel is in the United States for surgery. It is a perfect opportunity to cut the head off of his criminal organization."

"You want his head, I'll give you his head. Hell, if you're finally into collecting bad guy noggins, I'll gift wrap his and send it parcel post. But if I'm going to Miami I'm taking out this other mook too."

Smith had long ago learned that in dealing with Remo, his own personal preferences often had to take a backseat to Remo's impulse du jour. The CURE director eventually relented, provided Remo carry out the assignments in order of importance. Remo agreed wholeheartedly that the most important assignment would come first.

"You got it, Smitty. Important one first, mop-up second. Gotcha. Over and out."

"The drug dealer is number one, Remo, and the mugger is number two," Smith warned.

"Sorry, Smitty, you're breaking up," Remo said. He hung up the pay phone he had used to contact his employer and, whistling happily, tore off the receiver and sent it skipping down the street lest Smith get it into his head to phone back and attempt again to go through a dance that, at least for Remo, already had a definite outcome.

In Miami, Remo did not go immediately to the mansion

of Ramon Albondigas as Smith wanted but instead spent the next three nights patrolling the streets, paying particular attention to ATMs in areas that advertised "bottomless cup" free coffee refills, early bird all-you-can-eat buffets and square dancing lessons. But although he saw many elderly people and many young men potentially up to no good, Remo had yet to spot the real reason for his trip to Florida.

It was not quite true that the mugger who had caught the attention of the national media possessed no identifying characteristics. On two occasions he had been spotted fleeing the scene on an orange bicycle with painted flames on the sides. The one thing the newspeople salivated over almost as much as juicy footage of old women lying in pain under their own walkers was alliterative description. When his method of escape became known, the Miami Mugger as he had first been dubbed instantly became the Bicycle Bandit.

Remo would have spied that bike and the slim young man riding it a mile away. Unfortunately all the nocturnal activities he encountered were of the law-abiding variety, a maddening miracle for a city with Miami's criminal reputation. On the third night Remo finally threw up his hands in frustration, abruptly changed tactics and drove to the mansion of Ramon Albondigas.

The gated community was on a small isthmus on which twelve homes had been built, the cheapest valued at just a hair under thirty-five million dollars. Remo parked his rental car down the street from the main gate, shimmied up a palm tree, hopped the wall and, ten minutes later, found himself strolling across the neatly manicured side lawn of one of Colombia's most notorious drug-runners.

Despite millions of cocaine dollars spent on the most advanced private security systems, Remo strode across the grounds undetected. He passed within a whisper of several heavily armed guards, none of whom noticed the thin young man in the black T-shirt and chinos gliding through their midst like midnight fog. At one point near a fountain illuminated in garish yellow neon, a Rottweiler on a leash sniffed the breeze and gulped a frightened snort of air, but that was the only living thing to note Remo's passing. Even the damp grass did not yield a single imprint where Remo's silent loafers fell.

The main building was gleaming white stucco capped with red slate and illuminated by bright floodlights. Every third light was purple and cast a weird shimmering glow between patches of brightly illuminated white.

Remo went to one corner of the palatial mansion where he found some vines deemed by security to be too delicate for a human being to climb. Remo scampered up them with ease, landing lightly on a third-floor corner balcony. He sensed an electronic alarm system wired to the French doors. Rather than mess with a nuisance system, Remo took the easier route.

Drumming fingers tapped the exterior wall, his touch growing more rapid as he completed a large square. Wherever his fingers touched, a thin crack appeared. With another series of taps he divided the main square into four smaller squares. Striking at the center, the stucco surface broke away in four big sheets which he set on the balcony.

The humid Miami air softened mortar imperceptibly. Only one other set of fingers on earth besides Remo's own would have sensed the weakness. Brick below stucco was even easier to manipulate, and soon there was a pile of bricks outside on the veranda and Remo was inside the house and moving through an opulent, air-conditioned walk-in closet and out into a bedroom apparently decorated by blind chrome- and crystal-loving maniacs with a satin and velvet fetish. The room was so large and gaudy it would have shamed Louis XIV.

Soft snores emanated from a huge canopy bed draped in silk curtains. The thin old man beneath the covers was in his early eighties and seemed in good shape, all things considered. His chocolate brown skin had seen far too much sun over the years and was cut with valleys of deep wrinkles. Even in slumber he held his shoulders and spine with the regal rigidity of a man who had created an empire from nothing and would not permit the world to forget it.

A walker was positioned next to the bed. A pair of dentures soaked in a glass of Chateau Lafitte-Rothschild on the dresser. Sunken eyelids were closed and twitching. The old man drooled slightly on his satin pillowcase.

Ramon Albondigas slept the sleep of a rich and powerful man convinced of his utter safety. That certainty was shattered a little after twelve-thirty this humid night when a hand suddenly pressed tight over his sleeping mouth and a voice whispered in his ear.

"Why is it nothing ever works out the way I want it?" the voice asked Ramon Albondigas from the dead of night.

The hand that held the mouth of Ramon Albondigas was attached to a very thick wrist. Standing above was the shadow of a young man with short dark hair and the cruelest face Ramon Albondigas had ever seen. This was saying a lot. Ramon Albondigas had seen many cruel faces in his long life, most belonging to men in his own employ who visited cruelty upon others, courtesy of Ramon Albondigas. But here was a man with a face harder and more deadly than those of any of the paid thugs in the Albondigas La Cocina narcotics empire.

"C'mon, Prune Face, we've got work to do."

The hand released and the old drug runner opened his mouth to scream. But fingers brushed his throat lightly and all that passed his dry lips was a watery gurgle. Albondigas found that if he whispered he could be heard.

"What do you want?" he gasped to the terrifying figure that loomed over his bed.

"I want for things to go my way just once. I had it all planned out. He'd be first, you'd be second. I mean—"

Remo nodded to the walker next to the bed "—it's not like you're going anywhere soon, right? My boss on the other hand wanted it the other way around. You first, him last. Well, no way. I'm still doing it my way. I'm just fiddling with the plan a little. It's going to happen like I want it to happen for a change. What do you think about that?"

Ramon Albondigas dragged the nervous tip of his tongue over his dry upper lip. "Do you want money? I have the drugs, that gives me the money. Lots of money. I give you the money, then you can get the womens. Is that what you want? Do you want the money?"

"Sheesh, haven't you been listening?" Remo asked.

Remo scooped the old man up, tossing him lightly onto his shoulder. He caught the walker up on one wrist. As if carting groceries to a minivan, Remo made his easy way back to the closet, through the hole in the wall, over the wrought-iron rail of the balcony and down to ground level.

Remo avoided Albondigas' private security force as well as the security service that patrolled the half-dozen streets of the larger gated community. In no time he was back behind the wheel of his car, Albondigas beside him and the old man's walker tucked away in the backseat.

Sitting up in the car pained the drug runner's new replacement right hip—the surgery that had brought him to America—and he winced.

"What do you want from me?" Albondigas asked.

"You're plan B," Remo said. "That's B for bait."

Remo drove to an automated teller in the sweltering city near where the last two muggings had taken place. He avoided the security camera by tearing the wall directly beneath the angled camera. He propped Ramon Albondigas and his walker in front of the ATM. The old man looked ridiculous standing at the automated teller at one in the morning in powder blue silk pajamas which hung off his tall, skinny frame and gave him the appearance of a very wealthy, very tan scarecrow.

"I see, I understand," Albondigas said, nodding. "You do want the monies after all. How much?"

"The worm doesn't try to buy off the fisherman," Remo said. "Just do your job as bait and we'll get along fine."

He turned for the hole in the wall.

"You are just going to leave me here?" the old drug runner said, baffled.

"I'll be watching. Just step aside if anyone comes in. Tell them you forgot your PUN or PON or POON number or whatever the hell they call it."

"The first person comes in, I am going to tell I was kidnapped from my bed by a lunatic."

"No, you're really not," Remo said. He touched a spot on the old man's right hip.

Ramon Albondigas could not even gasp.

Once many years ago he had ordered his men to board up the windows and doors of a treacherous employee's home and set fire to it while the man, his wife and their three young daughters screamed in agony inside. Ramon Albondigas had ordered that a tape of the family's dying anguish be made and he played the recording frequently to employees he thought might be wavering in their loyalty.

If the dying anguish of that wretched family, the many other brutal torture deaths he had ordered, the pain of the needle and the agony of withdrawal of his many customers, the misery he had inflicted on thousands, millions of lives were added up into one moment of exquisite torture, it would still barely begin to describe the pain that a single brush of this thin young man's fingers brought to Ramon Albondigas.

Albondigas had never used any of his products before. But in that moment he gladly would have snorted, shot up or swallowed anything that could relieve the indescribable torment. Then the young man touched his newly repaired hip once more and the pain was gone. Albondigas gulped.

"Anyone comes in, you step aside politely and let them

use the machine. Anyone comes in on an orange bicycle—"
Remo smiled "—we'll cross that bridge when we come
to it."

Albondigas could not nod agreement fast enough.

Remo left the old man at the ATM. He dodged the
camera and propped the wall back up so that no one
passing by would even notice it had been disassembled.

Remo went back to his car and watched the activity at
the automated teller.

Remo knew that using Albondigas as bait was not
perfect. So far the infamous Bicycle Bandit had only preyed
on elderly women. But Remo was guessing a skinny old
man leaning on a walker would be too tempting a target to
pass up.

Unfortunately Remo found that few people used this
particular ATM so late at night. A guilty-looking, well-
dressed middle-aged man with a sagging pot belly and a
wedding ring stopped in an hour later. A girl too young
and cheap to be his wife waited for him in his car.

The threat of pain worked like a charm. Albondigas
shuffled politely aside and allowed the man to work the
ATM. Neither man was interested in talking. The pot-
bellied man left with his fistful of cash and his rented
date.

Half an hour later, a sleazy looking middle-aged man
in gaudy jewelry stopped to make a withdrawal. He
seemed to recognize Albondigas but when he asked the
drug dealer a question the old man refused to answer.

The last visitor came a little before dawn. An emaciated
man delivering newspapers stopped in to get cash for gas.
By this point Albondigas was slumped against the wall,
hands clutching his walker as he snored lightly.

That was it. All of the muggings had taken place at
night and Remo and his bait had made it through to dawn
without the appearance of a punk on an orange bicycle.

The hazy red horizon promised another brutally hot
Miami day when Remo went to collect the drug kingpin.

Remo found a nice place for Albondigas to stay during the next day. That night when he went to pick up the drug lord from the ten-by-ten unit at the Store-Away self-storage facility, he found that Albondigas had finished off the water in his bowl but had only eaten half a can of dogfood.

"Num-num, eat 'em up," Remo said, tapping the bowl with the tip of his loafer. "You may be lucky. If the food comes from China, the mercury in it might kill you before I do."

"I do not deserve this treatment," Albondigas rasped. The old man was sweaty and bedraggled after the previous night followed by a hot day sleeping on cement in a locked storage shed. "I am a businessman. I have only ever provided a product. Like the bread maker or milkman."

"No one ever died from snorting bread crumbs or shooting up milk. You're not the milkman or the bread maker. Let's go, Fido."

Another night at another ATM was followed by a third. During the third stakeout Remo heard on the radio that the Bicycle Bandit had struck again. Although infuriating, it gave Remo some hope. The victim this time had been an old man, which meant the mugger was not averse to preying on grandpas as well as grandmas. Unfortunately this latest victim was a tax lawyer who had retired to Florida from New York and not a Colombian drug runner who flooded the streets with narcotics and flouted America's laws. On the fourth night, as Albondigas snoozed at the latest automated teller, Remo was about ready to give up hope of catching the mugger when his sensitive ears detected the squeak-squeak-squeak of a poorly oiled bicycle chain. Eyes narrowing, he spied a figure in black peddling up the sidewalk and into the deep post-midnight shadows across from the ATM.

The orange bike skidded to a stop beneath the awning of a closed and chained pawn shop.

Although the night was steamy, the mugger wore his trademark hooded sweatshirt. The hood was drawn tight, obscuring most of his face. A pair of dark sunglasses helped mask most of what remained. Beneath the glasses was a thin nose and a predator's mouth which curled into an eager smile when, after watching Ramon Albondigas slumped before the automated teller for several minutes, he determined that this was not a trap set up by police.

A knife appeared in his hand from the pocket of his pullover sweatshirt. Breaking from the shadows, the mugger peddled quickly across the empty street. He propped open the ATM door with his bike and hurried up beside the disheveled old man in the dirty silk pajamas.

Even at a distance Remo could have heard the ensuing argument if he so chose. But there was no point. What was taking place across the street was some form of cosmic justice in which Remo was only a facilitator.

The mugger threatened Ramon Albondigas with his knife. Albondigas poked in vain at the ATM buttons, but he was clearly a man out of his element. The wealthy man understood that money was taken from the devices but had never used one himself. Frustrated, the mugger clubbed the drug dealer in the side of the head with the fist that held the knife, raising a bloody welt. Some of the fire of youth returned to Ramon Albondigas and he spat in the face of his assailant.

Bad move. The mugger sank his knife into the old man's heart, kicked at the old man's walker furiously and, as Albondigas toppled over clutching the growing dark smear on the chest of his pajamas, the Bicycle Bandit hopped back on his bike and peddled rapidly away from the ATM.

He was halfway across the street when he realized his bike had stopped moving. A grunt of confusion emanated from the shadows of the hood. The mugger was peddling furiously but for some reason he was making no progress. Assuming he had slipped his chain, he looked down.

He spotted the toe of a loafer near his back wheel. Spinning on his seat, he looked back to find a man casually holding the back of his bike seat with one hand. The rear tire of the mugger's bike spun uselessly. The smell of warm burning rubber on damp asphalt rose to his nostrils.

The mugger grabbed for his knife.

Another hand had gotten there first.

"You're in a lot of trouble, Fishie," Remo said as he snapped the knife blade between two fingers like a brittle popsicle stick and tossed the useless pieces to the gutter. "I had to wait four nights for you to take the bait."

The mugger jumped off his bike and tried to run but Remo snagged him by his hood and, as the man grabbed, choking, at his collar, reeled him back in.

"Stop squirming," Remo warned. "I've already got you in the boat. Fishie's not getting away this time."

"Let me go," the mugger said in a rough voice.

The voice was accented. Remo had pulled the hood off, revealing sweaty black hair. He slapped away the sunglasses. The heretofore faceless Bicycle Bandit was in his early twenties, with darting brown eyes. The smell of fresh fear mingled with the stink of old perspiration.

"You know who that was you just pincushioned?"

"I didn't do nothing," the man snarled.

"You ever hear of the La Cocina drug cartel, Fishie?" Remo asked. The sudden horror in the young man's eyes told Remo that he had. "It looks like maybe you figured out that old codger with the hole in his chest was their numero uno."

The young man gasped. "Albondigas," he hissed. He tried to bless himself at the realization of what he had just done, but Remo, who had been raised by nuns in a Catholic orphanage, slapped the man hard across the face.

"Don't," he warned darkly. He reeled the hood in until the man's face began turning blue. As he carted the mugger and his bicycle back to his car, Remo said, "Some people might think Albondigas was the bigger fish and you're just a little guppy. But the fact is little guppies like you are the ones that always get on the news while big fish like him get ignored. You're an inspiration to every pissant little guppy that thinks it's okay to beat up on little old ladies and steal their Social Security checks. So this time the big fish was bait and he snagged me a guppy. And now, little Fishie, it's time for you to go swimming with the sharks."

Remo stuffed the mugger in the trunk and placed the bike carefully in the backseat.

Remo stopped at a pay phone down the street and pulled from his pocket a scrap of paper on which he had carefully copied down the Miami Mugger hotline number he had seen on his hotel television. Although his anonymous tip was to the police, it was the local newspeople who showed up six minutes later. The cops arrived four minutes after that. Before the police had even arrived, the reporters had identified the latest mugging victim as Ramon Albondigas.

The story went live on local Miami stations in the dead of night and was quickly picked up by the national cable news networks. The ATM security camera footage was broadcast repeatedly with somber warnings that it was too gruesome for the faint of heart. The gruesomeness of the stabbing was not enough to prevent any of the twenty-four-hour cable stations from broadcasting the footage on endless loops.

As Remo had expected, the Albondigas compound was buzzing with activity when he arrived back at the exclusive gated community two hours later.

Remo could hear the noise in the distance as he scampered up the wall of the wealthy neighborhood, bike and unconscious mugger slung easily over one shoulder.

Men shouted and engines hummed beyond the locked gates of the Albondigas compound. Lights sliced up from the ground bathing a swath of the isthmus in false daylight.

On an unseen helipad behind the main building, the rotor blades of a helicopter chopped away slices of thick humidity. Cars rolled in and out of the main gate.

At one point after a Humvee had driven out but before the gates had closed completely, Remo propped the Bicycle Bandit on his orange bike, pulled up the man's hood and stuck on his sunglasses. Slapping the man awake, Remo gave him a good strong shove.

Snorting sleepy confusion, the disoriented mugger rolled through the gates of the Albondigas estate and disappeared beyond the high hedge of well-tended shrubs. The gates closed behind him with a gentle clink of metal.

There was a single surprised shout. This quickly gave way to a chorus of shocked recognition. When the Bicycle Bandit's screams began to rise from the far side of the high white walls, Remo offered a little bow.

"De nada," he said. Clicking his heels with a neat little flourish, he stole off into the warm night.

3

Remo was whistling the Mexican Hat Dance when
he returned to his room at the Miami Grand Hotel early
the next morning. Before he slipped his key in the lock he
sensed two heartbeats coming from the room beyond.
One strong heartbeat he had expected, the other—an
irregular gurgle—he had not. Remo stopped whistling.
Briefly he considered turning around and making a mad
dash for the elevator.

"My son returns, Emperor Smith," a singsong voice
said from the other side of the door before calling loudly,
"Do not loiter out in the hallway, Remo, lest the hotel
staff cart you off with the dirty breakfast dishes. Enter
and bid welcome to our most gracious and generous
emperor."

"Thanks a lot, Little Father," Remo grunted. He sighed
loudly and pushed open the door.

Two men were sitting in the living room of the suite.

The first was a wizened Asian in a golden morning

kimono who sat cross-legged on a sunlit patch of carpet before the suite's balcony doors.

The tiny figure had skin the hue of walnut, speckled with great age. Twin tufts of yellowing white hair clung to the sides of his head above shell-like ears. The hair on his head as well as a thread of beard at his chin danced merrily in currents flowing through the room's cool, recirculated air. The skin was stretched thin, like living parchment, over an otherwise bald skull. Slender fingers ended in long, sharp nails which happily tapped away on a flat square object in his lap.

Remo recognized the woman in the framed photograph which the old man held. Chiun, the last full Korean Master of Sinanju, the original and deadliest of all the martial arts and Remo's teacher in lethal techniques that had originated in an ancient North Korean fishing village, brushed invisible dust from his newly acquired prize. He hummed happily as he fussed like a doting parent over a newborn baby.

Perched on the edge of the sofa next to the old Korean was a tall, thin man in a gray three-piece suit and starched white shirt. His hair and skin tone matched his attire and if not for the green-striped Dartmouth tie knotted around his neck he could have been the subject of a fifty-year-old black-and-white photo album come to life.

A weatherbeaten briefcase was tucked in at his heels. When Remo entered the suite, the gray-faced man stood.

"Remo, what the devil have you been doing down here?" demanded Harold W. Smith.

"I read somewhere, Smitty, that normal people start off with 'Hello,'" Remo said. "Besides, what are you so wound up about? Albondigas is dead."

"I know that. I found out after my plane landed."

"So what's the problem? So I took a few extra days. Big deal. As it is Albondigas came in handy. It's not like I could've used some sweet little old lady as bait."

The smile fled Chiun's face and he grunted disapproval.

Smith's brow furrowed as he watched Remo sink to the floor in the lotus position.

"Are you saying you used Albondigas to lure the mugger into a trap?"

"You bet. We can cross both problems off the list, by the way. Two birds with one stone, more or less. I believe in using every part of the buffalo."

Smith understood what CURE's enforcement arm meant. With a sigh, he reclaimed his seat on the couch. "It was clear to us that Albondigas went missing several days ago," he said, "but the information had not made it out to law enforcement agencies. It was not as if the cartel could phone the police. When you did not return any of my calls, I wasn't sure what to make of what was going on down here."

"What do you mean? You called here?"

Sitting in his splash of sunlight, the Master of Sinanju began humming once more, making a deliberate point to remain apart from the conversation taking place around him.

"Several times. But the phone was out of order in your room so the front desk had to come up here with a cell phone. I spoke with Master Chiun. He didn't tell you I called?" Frowning, Smith glanced at the Master of Sinanju.

Remo, too, turned a bland eye to his teacher.

Chiun hummed more pointedly, seemingly oblivious that he had now become the center of attention.

On the first night when he returned to the hotel Remo had noted the pile of phones that had been harvested from all the suite's rooms and dumped in plastic scraps in the corner of his bedroom. Chiun had already been in a pissy mood before they even came to Miami and Remo assumed when he saw the phones that Chiun had taken preemptive steps to keep from being interrupted during his meditation. However, given the new prize clutched in the old man's bony hands, Remo began to understand the chain of events that had brought Smith here.

"He must have forgot," Remo said. "They say memory's the first thing to go. Right, Little Father?"

The humming abruptly ceased. Sharp hazel eyes, seeming much younger than the old Korean's advanced years, shot daggers at his pupil.

"Of course I told him you telephoned, emperor," Chiun said. "Before I would forget my joy at hearing your voice, the spring flower would forget the first kiss of rain or the life-sustaining nourishment of the sun. I distinctly remember telling him, so if anyone forgot anything, it was Remo who has a long and checkered history of forgetting things. Gratitude for one. He left that somewhere, perhaps at the traveling carnival where he was born. Respect is another thing he misplaced long ago. And kindness. Although, frankly, I suspect he never had that to lose. The thing he has most forgotten is the individual to whom he owes all."

"Not this again," Remo said. "Please. Spare me."

Chiun plowed on as if his pupil had not spoken. "So while it is impossible for the Master to forget a telephone call from you, Emperor Smith, it is well established that Remo would forget his own big feet if they were not attached to his gangly legs. Do not blame me for your sieve-like memory, Remo," the old Asian sniffed.

"Why are you passing this off on me?" Remo snapped in Korean. "You know you never told me he called."

"Because I am not your answering service," Chiun replied in the same language. "No matter what fool's errand brought you to this foul city, this was supposed to be a vacation for me. But scarcely were you out the door when this gray-faced madman began assaulting my ears with that infernal ringing device. I silenced it, of course, as well as the others in each room which were squawking like dying birds. But no sooner had the last one fallen blessedly silent than he was sending runners up to intrude on my peace."

Smith who did not understand Korean could only watch as the world's two deadliest assassins argued until finally he said, "Any time now."

"In a minute, Smitty," Remo said in English. In Korean once more he said to Chiun, "I take it that's when he told you he finally got that for you." He nodded to the photo in Chiun's hands.

The woman in the framed photograph wore a black robe, her arms folded across her chest. Her lips were turned up in a painful contortion that was as much a wince as it was a smile. Her head was capped in a reddish-brown perm. Across the bottom of the photo was written in big looping script, "Behave yourself. Regards, Judge Ruth."

"Yes, and it was about time," Chiun sniffed. "I was promised this boon months ago. He said that he had finally acquired it and that he would mail it to me. I did not trust that it would get to me in one piece."

"So you flimflammed him onto a plane by making him think I'd gone AWOL just so he'd deliver it personally?"

"It is in one piece, is it not?" Chiun said. He gathered up his autographed Judge Ruth picture and breathed onto the glass, polishing away the moisture with the sleeve of his kimono.

"I've got a riddle for you, Smitty," Remo said in English, eyes fixed on his teacher. "How can you tell when a Master of Sinanju is scamming you?"

Smith shrugged and looked blank.

"His lips are moving. And how can you tell when he's not scamming you? He's dead."

"Ah, more elder abuse," Chiun said.

"Don't start," Remo said. "It's not abuse that I took interest in a bunch of old ladies getting mugged."

"It is when you pay more attention to total strangers than you do to your own father. There. I said it, Remo."

"Big shock. You've said it a hundred times in the past week. I pay plenty of attention to you, Little Father. Did it ever occur to you that maybe I respect the elderly more because of you? Maybe it cheeses me off more because they can't defend themselves like I know you can?"

But the old Korean offered Remo his back.

Obviously grateful for a break in their conversation, Smith quickly chimed in. "Remo, I did not fly all the way down here solely because you were taking too long with the Albondigas matter. Something more urgent has come up. The hijacking of Flight 980 in New York last week."

Remo's brow lowered and he tore his gaze from his teacher's bony shoulders. "I thought we back-burnered that."

"That was only until Mark and I could gather more information." Mark Howard was assistant director of CURE and Smith's righthand man. "The outlook looks grim on a number of fronts, not least of which is the damage this stunt has inflicted on the airlines. Air travel in the wake of this event has dropped by almost fifty percent. My flight down from LaGuardia was half empty."

"Ours was kind of empty the day we flew down here too. But they didn't say anything about it on the TV news so I figured it was just one of those things."

Smith's thin lips pursed. "Television news has become an unreliable source of worthwhile information. The near miss of the Empire State Building was major news for a little while and then it got overshadowed by the mugger story."

"Yeah, the news here has been pretty much wall-to-wall mugger. Since the hijacking wasn't on the news anymore and you weren't calling about it, I figured we weren't getting involved." He shot a glance at the Master of Sinanju.

It was not Chiun with whom Smith was upset. A small harrumph of displeasure made clear Smith's attitude toward a news culture that would elevate the criminal activities of a lone mugger above the hijacking of a plane, the crippling of a major industry and the near loss of thousands of lives in America's greatest city. He quickly reacquainted Remo with the broad details of the hijacking including the near miss of the Empire State Building and ending with the extraordinary escape of the hijackers.

"I must have flipped over to *Dragnet* when they mentioned the parachutes," Remo said once Smith was through. "I didn't know they got off the plane. From the hype it sounded like they weren't your run-of-the-mill terrorists, but who listens to TV news hype these days?"

Smith did not point out that it was TV news hype that had gotten Remo so eager to eliminate the Miami Mugger.

"You're right," the CURE director said. "By definition they are terrorists, but obviously this event was unusual in the extreme. There is now every indication that the men who hijacked the planes were Americans. While that does not preclude ties to Islamofascism, it does not seem as if these individuals were motivated by religious fanaticism. They were not overheard speaking of religion, they did not act the part of zealots and, most important, they came to the very edge of succeeding yet did not follow through on what could have been a devastatingly effective attack."

"So if they're not the usual suspects who are they?"

"Unknown."

"They bailed out of the airplane, right? Nobody saw them?" Remo asked.

"Everybody was watching the plane. The hijackers got away without even being spotted."

"Well, what about airport security cameras? They must have been seen arriving at the airport. Aren't they broadcasting their pictures all over the place? Somebody must have recognized them by now."

Smith fidgeted on the edge of the sofa. "There was unfortunately a series of security breakdowns in New

York, which we assume is how they were able to smuggle their guns and explosives on the plane in the first place. The computerized system was being overhauled that morning and several key cameras were down for maintenance. The hijackers apparently passed through during this lapse, so their images were not recorded. The best we have is the footage filmed by the news crew that was actually on the flight. However, that appears to have been tampered with by BCN. I am hoping that when you and Master Chiun view the unedited footage you will detect something in the mannerisms or speech of the hijackers that others have so far missed."

On the floor Chiun was suddenly interested. His neck craned from the collar of his kimono as he turned to Smith. "Where do you wish us to go?" the old Korean asked.

"BCN in New York has the raw footage. It was taken by their nightly news anchor's film crew. But, as I said, only heavily edited snippets have been shown on the news so far. I will arrange for you to view the entire footage."

"Gladly do we accept the assignment from our most generous emperor," Chiun said with a bow of his head.

"Why are you so eager to go gallivanting off on an assignment?" Remo asked, eyes narrowing suspiciously.

"Forgive him, Emperor Smith," Chiun confided, "for although he has attained the rank of Reigning Master he is still young in so many ways." As if speaking to a child, he said to Remo, "Because, Remo, while it is our obligation to serve an emperor, it is a joy to serve one as generous as he who has in his great wisdom contracted our House." And in the same instructive tone, he said in Korean, "Because you are finished paying attention to the elderly who are not me and he is giving us free airfare home. I had to pay my own way down here but he may as well pay our way back."

"I paid your airfare."

"And I had to sit next to you all the way down. Believe me, I paid. Let the lunatic pay. I can bring home my prize and store it safely away with my other great valuables."

"You mean that trunk full of stale saltine packets, matchbooks and toothpicks you used to swipe from every restaurant we ever went to twenty years ago?"

"Of course not. This is a special treasure. It will have a place of honor next to my autographed photographs of Cheeta Ching and Rad Rex."

Remo knew both photos well. Both had been attained at great cost, namely the near loss of Remo's sanity. Cheeta Ching had been a network anchorwoman for whom Chiun developed a great fondness years ago. She had fallen off the national radar a decade before. Rad Rex was an actor on a long-cancelled soap opera called *As the Planet Revolves.* Chiun locked away the pictures of both celebrities and treated them with a reverence generally reserved for consecrated Hosts in a tabernacle. He took the photos out only once a year to polish the frames and clean the glass. Remo was just grateful that the images of Cheeta, Rad Rex and now Judge Ruth weren't lined up on the mantle year-round, surrounded by curling incense and flickering votive candles.

"That is everything," Smith said. "I will make the New York arrangements. Call Mark at Folcroft in an hour and he will give you your flight details as well as who you will be speaking to at BCN headquarters."

Meeting over, Smith gathered up his briefcase and stood to go. Remo ushered the CURE director to the door where Smith paused.

"Remo, I need not remind you that the nation has a large enough problem dealing with the constant threat from radical Islam. If this is a new terror force we must stop it before it succeeds in whatever is its ultimate plan. I find it particularly troubling that the hijackers were American, if that turns out to be the case."

Remo understood what his employer meant. Smith had spent his youth in the OSS fighting Nazi Germany and had slipped into middle age in the CIA's Cold War struggle against the Soviet Union. Now, as head of CURE, Islamofascism was the latest implacable foe Smith had opposed in his long career. The great enemies Harold W. Smith had faced down in his clandestine life always adhered to ideologies offensive to the American ideals of freedom and decency. That these hijackers might be Americans attempting to foment terror in their own nation, a nation they should instinctively love and fight to their deaths to defend, was unthinkable to the coldly logical and fiercely patriotic CURE director. Smith would have had an easier time understanding their motivation if they had come from Mars.

"Don't sweat it, Smitty," Remo said, offering a reassuring smile. "We're on the case."

Smith seemed anything but reassured. "Please call me as soon as you have anything to report."

Smith gave a short bow to Chiun and excused himself from the suite. Remo watched the gaunt old man walk crisply down the long hallway to the elevator, a man who had sacrificed his entire life in service to his country.

"You know, Little Father," Remo pondered as the elevator doors clicked shut on Smith's gray face and pinched, lemony expression, "I know I dump on him a lot, but I'd worry a helluva lot less about this country's future if we could produce just a few more men like Smith."

Chiun cackled at the suggestion but when he saw that his pupil was serious he stopped laughing and shook his head. "The last thing America needs is more lunatics. Madmen you have enough of. What this country needs is more jurists like Judge Ruth to set the rest of you right. Not that I hold out much hope that even she could fix the lot of you for lamentably she is only one woman, after all."

Remo glanced at the unhappily smiling face of Judge Ruth then up at his teacher's wise visage.

"Should I thank God out loud or to myself?" Remo asked.

4

Their flight back to New York was only half full and the flight attendants seemed lost with so few passengers. They wandered up and down empty aisles like the last barmaids in a ghost town saloon. Remo knew that before long the airlines would be forced out of necessity to cut back on staff, then on the number of flights. Before long there would be another round of airline bankruptcies, which seemed to come every few years, with more money lost and more men and women out of work.

When their plane landed at LaGuardia, Chiun insisted that before they go to the BCN offices they first go to their home in Connecticut so that he could drop off his autographed Judge Ruth photo.

"I've got a better idea," Remo suggested. "How about I skip it across the East River? If the wind's with me I bet I can reach the Bronx in five skips."

Chiun suggested that if his precious autographed

photograph somehow wound up in the water, it would not go swimming alone. Remo did not feel like going for a dip, but neither did he feel like schlepping all the way to Connecticut and then all the way back down to Manhattan.

"C'mon, Little Father, let's split the difference and get New York out of the way while we're here. Smith already set up some meeting with some BCN mucky-muck."

Chiun stroked the thread of beard that clung tenaciously to his pointed chin. "I could probably skip you to the far shore in four skips," he mused. "Although, Remo, you have been paying so much attention to elderly who are strangers to you recently that you have no doubt failed to notice that I have gotten old myself. At my advanced age I cannot promise that you would make it more than halfway to the far shore."

"Okay, how about this," said Remo. "How about I tell Smith you scammed him for the picture and then you double-dipped and scammed him for the plane fare home?"

Chiun's eyes narrowed. "You wouldn't."

"Maybe I wouldn't if you weren't on this tear about me abusing the elderly when what it really comes down to is jealousy that I was paying attention to someone over sixty-five who wasn't you. And maybe if you hadn't blamed me for not calling Smith back I'd be in a better frame of mind. But you are and you did, so I would. Where's the nearest pay phone?" He glanced around the airport.

"You are a sneaky and manipulative man."

"I learned from the best," Remo said.

It was spoken as a true compliment and so the Master of Sinanju merely shook his head and muttered his standard imprecations against ungrateful whites.

The compromise which Chiun grudgingly accepted was a cab ride into the city and entrusting the two trunks he had brought with him to Miami to a security guard in the lobby of the Broadcast Corporation of North America world headquarters. Remo peeled five one-hundred-dollar bills from a roll in his pocket, tore each of them in half and handed the five right halves to the guard.

"You get the other half when we get back," Remo said to the guard, whose face was the very picture of disappointed avarice as he watched the half-bills disappear in Remo's pocket. "But make sure those trunks don't have a scratch on them. One ding and we'll both be swimming back from Governor's Island."

Chiun kept his Judge Ruth photo in hand as they rode the elevator up to the thirtieth floor.

"You could have left that with your trunks."

"That palace guard already proved himself untrustworthy when he accepted your bribe. For your promise of paper money he will now keep watch on my trunks and ignore the duties for which he has been employed. If someone waves more scraps of green paper before his nose he will run off with them and abandon his station and my trunks. I would not dare risk leaving this, my most precious possession, in his greedy hands. Besides, did you not see the covetousness in his eyes when he beheld the countenance of Judge Ruth? Given half an opportunity he would have abandoned my trunks and your paper money and run off with my prize. Trust me, I know of what I speak. You whites are all the same."

"The guard was black, Little Father," Remo pointed out.

"Was he American?"

"Yes," said Remo, knowing where this was going for he had heard it many times before. "And I know that makes him white as a Christmas snowflake to you. But I doubt he cared one hoot about that photo of yours. The picture probably just gave him the heebie-jeebies. She looks like she just ate a raw baby for lunch. When we get home we can hang it on the front door to scare away burglars."

"Really, Remo," Chiun said, tut-tutting as he shook his age-speckled head. "This covetousness is unbecoming. But since I see how badly you now wish you had asked Smith to get you one of your own, others will surely react similarly." The old man slipped the framed photo inside a kimono sleeve, out of sight of would-be thieves.

"My eyes thank you," Remo said.

The elevator doors opened and, side by side, the two Masters of Sinanju stepped into the lobby that was the main hub of the BCN Evening News.

The desk on the first floor had called ahead. Waiting for them was a thin man with perfect blond hair, well-toned muscles and a glowing tan that had just gotten its weekly fresh coat that morning. He flashed perfect white teeth in a tight smile that did not agree with his gloomy eyes.

"Uriah Maddox, executive producer of the BCN Evening News with Kitty Coughlin," Maddox said, in a tone so rich and perfectly modulated he could have been any one of the hundreds of on-air reporters in his employ. "You must be the gentlemen from the Department of Homeland Security."

Remo offered the appropriate identification. He had a stack of phony IDs supplied by Smith for virtually every situation, but these day the Homeland Security one seemed to open the most doors with the fewest questions.

"Remo Welch," Maddox said, reading the name on the badge. "And you're some sort of consultant, I'm told?" he said to Chiun. "Well, I can tell you both I'm not happy about the strong-arm tactics you people used to get to see our footage." He produced two pieces of paper which he handed to Remo and Chiun. "I have confidentiality contracts here for both of you to sign agreeing not to reveal in print, broadcast or any other medium anything that you might witness on the Flight 980 tape. You can sign on the bottom line."

Remo tore the contract into ten even strips and stuffed

them in Uriah Maddox's breast pocket. Chiun folded his
into an origami dove which he sailed into the nearest
wastebasket.

"That wasn't very nice," complained Maddox.

"Sure it was, Richie Rich," Remo said. "My first impulse
was to stuff it in your mouth."

Whatever blackmail chip Smith had dug up on Maddox
to get them this meeting must have been damning.
Maddox stewed for a moment, shook his head and turned
on his heel.

"Follow me," he said through tightly clenched teeth.

They marched down a hallway lined with pictures of
BCN news personalities past and present. Remo recognized
nearly all of them and liked none of them.

They passed an eight-by-ten-foot photo of an elderly
man whose face was one large, wrinkled frown capped by
a tousled tumbleweed of white hair. The photographer
had airbrushed out the bristly cat's whiskers that jutted
from his ears. The old man was famous for the weekly
commentary segment he had been doing on a BCN Sunday
newsmagazine program for the past forty years. A typical
segment had the old man sitting behind a cluttered desk
complaining about loose change in the sofa cushions or
how he had a desk drawer full of pens, none of which
worked. In the last segment Remo had seen, the old man
brought in a month's worth of belly-button lint in a
sandwich bag to complain about how the doctor who had
delivered him ninety years before had given him an innie
rather than an outie and that as a result he was constantly
picking bushels of fluff from his navel. He closed out that
segment wishing he could rent a time machine so that he
could go back and tell the doctor to give him an outie.
Remo and much of America would have lined up to rent
the same time machine to go back even farther, to try to
convince the commentator's mother to join a convent
prior to her ill-fated dalliance with the commentator's
future father.

"I have seen this imbecile," Chiun said. "He speaks always of toothpaste and paper towels."

"Just don't go asking for an autographed picture," Remo said. He turned his eyes away from the photo of the wrinkled old man with the bushy, caterpillar eyebrows. "Can't you people scrape up even one non-jackass to put on the air?" he asked Maddox.

Maddox glanced at the photos on the wall as if he had never seen them before.

The largest picture of all was that of Kitty Coughlin. The aging face of BCN's anchorwoman, already playground to a plastic surgeon's scalpel, had been airbrushed nearly to the point of being unrecognizable. An ordinary woman of fifty-three would have had at least one wrinkle. The woman in the picture had not so much as a single forehead crease or crow's foot. Remo might have mistaken the photo as belonging to someone else if not for the fact that this woman was flashing Kitty Coughlin's trademark smile, which consisted of twin rows of perfect caps and gums wide enough to park cars on.

"It's more difficult than you'd think to find on-air talent that clicks with the viewing audience," Maddox said. "Right now we're still finding our groove with Kitty."

"Two years since you hired her?" Remo said. "I think Stella's groove has grown over."

"Fifteen months. And I didn't hire her," Maddox said quickly. "I was managing the sports division when Kitty was hired. They brought me aboard when . . . well, when the ratings took an unanticipated turn in a less than upward direction. I'm here to help turn things around for the news division."

"I've got a suggestion," Remo said. But when Uriah Maddox spun to him with a desperately hopeful look on his tan face Remo didn't have the heart to say what he was originally going to, which was set fire to the building, collect the insurance money and turn the 6:30 time slot over to *Munsters* reruns. "Never mind," Remo said.

"No, please," Maddox said. "We've got to start learning to be responsive to our consumers like we are over in the sports division. I keep telling these news-people that all the time. Do you have any suggestions how we can improve our newscast? Anything at all?"

"You're kidding, right?" Remo asked. "Aren't you people supposed to know this stuff? Don't you do focus groups or market research and then eventually just copy whatever they're doing over on ABC?"

Before Maddox could reply, the Master of Sinanju cut in.

"It should be in Korean," Chiun suggested. "And the pretty person who reads the news moments should be Korean too. A Korean from Korea, not some American of Korean ancestry who is practically white. Preferably North Korean, although not from Pyongyang because you would end up with a pickpocket or a prostitute and no one likes to get their news from pickpockets and prostitutes. You could get your reader from one of the smaller villages on the West Korean Bay. I can make you a list."

"I'll warn you now it'll be a short list," Remo said.

"Interesting suggestions," Uriah Maddox said slowly. "Probably not quite what we need."

Chiun, having given this idiot free ratings salvation, shrugged indifferently. "Then do whatever you want. Have a Frenchman or Thai read the news. I care not."

"Actually," Maddox said, "you needn't be upset. We did have a Korean anchorwoman years ago. She didn't work out."

"Yeah, whatever happened to ol' Cheeta Ching?" Remo asked. "Didn't you lose touch with her, Little Father?"

"She became too demanding after I helped her and that dreadful husband of hers conceive their child," the Master of Sinanju said. "She was constantly pestering me which, although a trait common to all females, was unrestrained in Cheeta. I stopped returning her messages years ago."

"You people knew Cheeta Ching?" Uriah Maddox said. He glanced around. "You wouldn't happen to still have her number lying around, would you?"

"Don't tell me you're really desperate enough to even think about rehiring that Korean barracuda," Remo said.

Maddox's shoulders tensed as he dared consider the unthinkable, then relaxed as hope drained away. "No," he said with a heavy sigh. "No, Cheeta is damaged goods. She had a cable show a couple of years ago. Did you know?"

Chiun looked along the wall of news celebrities for a picture of Judge Ruth, his new love, indifferent now to the recent career choices of the woman he had once adored.

"Never heard of it," Remo said.

"I'm not surprised. Ratings were worse than ours, if you can believe that. She made a real fool of herself there. On the last episode she got drunk on the air and sang 'Makin' Whoopee' on top of a grand piano. When she tried to slide off—loaded off her ass, remember—she knocked over a candelabra and set fire to the hem of her gown. The last image the world has of Cheeta Ching on live TV is of her piano player screaming like a woman while the stage crew beat Cheeta with sofa cushions trying to put her out. I'm told it was all over the Internet for weeks afterward. No, after that stunt there's no way we'd hire Cheeta back for network."

A shrill voice suddenly cried out from the open office door they were walking past. "What the hell did you say?"

Maddox winced as a woman came storming out into the hallway, sharp high heels clicking angrily with each furious footfall. She wore a skirt far too short for a woman well into middle age. Her strong legs were long and tan.

Remo noted that in real life Kitty Coughlin was more airbrushed than her promotional photo.

"Did I just hear you say you were hiring Cheeta Ching?" Kitty demanded. If she could have grabbed Uriah Maddox by the tie and twisted until his head popped she would have. As it was, her Botoxed eyes flamed at Maddox with killer rage.

"Of course not, Kitty," Maddox said, squirming.

"I heard her name," Kitty snarled. "Don't tell me I didn't hear what I know I heard. Are those corporate SOBs buying out my contract? They're the ones who dragged me over here from mornings. I wouldn't have left if I'd known they weren't committed. I'll sue for breach of contract. I'll sue every last one of them, starting with you, Uriah."

"Kitty, please," Maddox begged. "These gentlemen just happen to be friends of Cheeta's, that's all. Her name just came up in conversation."

Kitty sized up Remo and Chiun from head to toe. "You're friends of Cheeta's?" she snarled.

"If you stretch 'friends' to include people who can't stand the sound of her harpie voice," Remo said.

"You're not her agents?" Kitty asked. She tried to narrow her eyes suspiciously, but the botulinum toxin injections made it impossible to squint.

"Alas, pretty lady, no," Chiun said. "Our enchantment with that fair Korean maiden ended many years ago."

"You better not be working for her," Kitty warned.

"No, no. These are the Homeland Security men I told you about," Maddox explained.

"Oh, them," Kitty said, voice flat. Her expression did not change but Remo got the impression she was trying to scowl. "Well, if you're going to be watching that raw footage I'd better go with you to supply context."

Kitty fell in beside Uriah with Remo and Chiun taking up the rear.

The news department was buzzing with activity, as Remo would have expected from one of the Big Three networks. He noticed that none of the men and women they passed made eye contact with Kitty. Wherever she walked came glances of hatred or terror. Several men dove into offices when they saw her coming. When Remo glanced into the open doors, he saw knees and neckties peeking out from under desks.

"This isn't exactly Santa's Happy-Time Christmas Village, Little Father," Remo said, his voice low so that Kitty and Uriah could not hear. Up ahead, a production assistant jumped into a broom cupboard.

"I am not surprised everyone is miserable," Chiun replied. "This woman with the face that does not move is unpleasant even by white standards. People who do not even know her cannot stand watching her on television. It stands to reason that those who work with her, those who know the true face beneath the tightly-pulled mask, would like her even less. Forget my Korean suggestion. That is obviously far too ahead of its time. The people who run this television station should stick to putting on pretty men with stiff hair to read the day's events like everyone else. Why they put this white woman with the plastic teeth and large gums in Cheeta's old seat is beyond me."

Up ahead, Kitty failed this time to hear Cheeta Ching's name. She was arguing with Uriah Maddox.

"It's ridiculous, hopping me all over the country. There's got to be something we can try right here," she said.

"We've already tried everything," Maddox insisted. "Kitty, we've got to face that we've got more than a ratings bleed going on here. Now, the other networks have shown an uptick in ratings when they send their anchors out of town. We've got a whirlwind tour for you. We've got you hitting a whole slew of markets. You pique local interest, get the local stations in on the deal, maybe you can bring those viewers back with you when you come home."

"You make it sound like a political campaign."

"Now you're getting it," Maddox said.

Their little group entered a long room at the end of the main hall, used for editing tape for the nightly news.

A warning had come down the line that Kitty was accompanying the Department of Homeland Security men so everyone else had fled and inside the room was only one glum editor at one lone editing bay. The young man looked up as Maddox led Kitty, Remo and Chiun into the BCN editing facilities. "Where is everybody?" Maddox demanded.

"Gone to lunch," the young editor said.

Maddox was clearly displeased but seemed to understand what had happened. The executive producer said nothing.

"There's your problem," Kitty snarled. "Everyone's always running off to lunch around here. It seems like practically every room I go into is empty. It's nine-thirty in the morning, for God's sake. If we're last in the ratings it's because you're not enforcing discipline with these skeevy little clock-punchers, Uriah."

The skeevy little clock-punching editor, a nice young man with a wife and two daughters who would not earn in his entire life what Kitty made in three months and had to commute to the city from New Jersey every morning because he could not afford to live in Manhattan on his salary, clenched his teeth and swiveled his chair to his booth.

The editor brought up the raw footage that Kitty's cameraman had taken on doomed Flight 980. It had been converted from tape to a crystal clear digital image.

"I don't know what you expect to see," Maddox said, glancing at a suddenly quiet Kitty. "I've viewed it dozens of times and there's nothing that could possibly lead you to the hijackers. They were pros. But this footage has not been seen outside of this editing facility so I expect that you will keep quiet whatever you see here."

What Remo and Chiun saw was BCN's million-dollar anchorwoman screaming herself hoarse.

On the screen Kitty blanched when the hijackers first appeared, which was not so bad. But when the explosives went off the screaming began. She screamed at the blast, she screamed when the hole tore open in the ceiling of the cabin and she screamed when the doors were blown out and the hijackers jumped out of the plane.

Beside Remo, Kitty held herself stiff as a board as she watched her on-camera performance. She braced herself for laughter or worse. "I can explain that," she said.

"Explain what?" Remo said.

"That stuff that sounds like screaming," Kitty said. "Our sound people say it's a problem with the audio on the original tape. It's probably a faulty camera."

"Lady, we're not idiots," Remo said.

"We, white man?" Chiun interjected. The editor had restarted the footage and the Master of Sinanju was leaning over the screen peering intently at the hijackers.

"Obviously that's you screaming," Remo persisted. "Big deal. You were on a hijacked plane with nuts with guns and bombs. That's a normal reaction. I'd think there was something wrong with you if you didn't scream."

Watching the footage again, Chiun tipped his head. "These men do not want to be here," he told Remo. He tapped a sharp fingernail against the screen. "Hold the picture there," he commanded.

The editor froze the image on the screen. The hijackers were setting the explosives on the cockpit door. One of the masked men was glancing back at the camera.

"See?" Chiun aimed a bony finger at the screen. "Those are not the eyes of a zealot with a cause. These men were coerced into performing this act."

Remo nodded. "You're right, Little Father."

"Of course I am," Chiun sniffed.

"Are you kidding?" Maddox said. He squinted at the screen but all he saw was a sweaty man in a mask who had failed to sustain high ratings for more than two nights.

Remo turned to Kitty who was also looking for signs of coercion in the freeze-frame eyes of the hijacker.

"Did they say anything that might have indicated what they thought they were accomplishing here?" Remo asked Kitty.

BCN's million-dollar anchorwoman shrugged.

"Did you recognize any regional accents that might pin down where they were from?"

BCN's million-dollar anchorette shook her baffled head.

"Did they say why they didn't crash the plane?"

BCN's million-dollar anchorbabe frowned confusion.

"Great reporter instincts you've got there, kitten," Remo said. "Now I see why BCN stole you away from that morning show. You were wasting your talent sitting on that couch for twenty years yapping about fall fashions and brownie bake-offs with that fatso weatherman."

Kitty's jaw dropped. "What did you say?" she demanded, eyes wide. She wheeled on Uriah. "What did he just say?" She wheeled back to Remo. "How—how dare you? Why, you pathetic, underdressed, thirty-thousand-a-year government bureaucrat."

"She is right, Remo," Chiun said. "You do dress poorly." He looked to Kitty. "I have tried to get him to wear a kimono but he refuses."

Kitty ignored the Master of Sinanju. "Who is your supervisor? I demand to know who your boss is."

"Demand a little more and I might forget to keep my mouth shut about your in-flight panic attack," Remo said. "And I might forget and wind up mentioning that the footage I've seen on your airwaves doesn't match what I've seen here and looks like you restaged it for the air." Remo smiled.

Kitty seemed about to scratch the smile off his face. Instead she growled like a furious animal and kicked an empty swivel chair which went spinning into a wall.

"Kitty, Kitty," Maddox said, his voice soothing. "You really should leave for Pennsylvania soon. Your flight—"

"Back off, Uriah," Kitty snapped.

Remo was back examining the video footage. The editor had hit play again. The hijackers had just blown the door and were parachuting out one by one.

"That's it," Remo said with a sigh. "I don't see anything else. How about you, Little Father?" His teacher shook his head. "Weird the camera caught it all on tape. I can't figure out why they didn't stop the guy from filming."

"Stop him?" Kitty scoffed. "Guess you don't know everything after all, smart guy. They're the ones who dragged him and his camera up to first class."

"Why would they do that?"

Kitty laughed bitterly. "Welcome to the twenty-first century. Everyone's media savvy these days. All these wackos love to play to the cameras. I only wish they'd had big families. With all their moms and aunts and second cousins once removed watching maybe we wouldn't be getting hammered by *What's Wrong With Raymond* reruns every night."

"That doesn't make sense," Remo said. "If they planned to crash the plane, then they'd have to know that there's no way the videotape would survive."

"Unless they never planned for it to crash," Chiun said.

Remo nodded. "Seems like that was the plan all along. Whatever the hell the plan was. I'm stumped."

Near the door, Uriah touched Kitty's elbow. "Kitty," he said, tapping his watch and nodding to the hall.

"All right, all right," Kitty said. She held out a warning finger with a painted nail that nearly touched the tip of Remo's nose. "No one else on the planet outside this room has seen that footage," she threatened. "One word gets out about this, I'll know it was you."

Offering Remo and Chiun her back, she marched from the room. Uriah nodded to his two guests and hustled after her.

"You work with that every day?" Remo asked the editor once the three of them were alone.

"Just until I hear back from Fox News on my résumé," the young man sighed. He was scrolling back through the footage. "And I wouldn't sweat her coming after you. About two hundred thousand people have seen this footage so far."

Remo frowned. "The restaged stuff you put on the air?" The editor shook his head. Still sitting, he wheeled his chair over to the door and glanced up and down the hallway. Swinging the door shut, he wheeled back to a computer in the far corner. "You know about MyTube?" he asked as he signed online.

"More toothpaste," Chiun said. "This entire place is consumed by toothpaste."

"I'm guessing it's not a brand of toothpaste," Remo said.

"It's a video-sharing Web site," the young man said, pulling up a directory and clicking on a URL. "Someone— not me, and I'll swear to that in court—but someone who hates her guts around here loaded it online. Here it is."

Remo saw a small screen-within-a-screen on which played a miniature version of the same footage they had just watched. Below were comments posted by viewers to the site.

1.) U go Kitty! Grate lungs! LOLN!
2.) I ciould ont stan her whenever she wuz on in the moring bu tthis is funn y stuff!!! Keep it up!
3.) I gist wet my pants laffing!!!!!!!!!!!!

According to the statistics on the main page, there were over three hundred comments posted and from what Remo could see of the grammar, spelling and punctuation the nuns who had taught him strict rules of English at St. Theresa's Orphanage were spinning like tops in their graves. A counter on the page kept track of the number of people who had accessed the video. The page had been viewed 213,998 times.

"She's more popular on the Web than she is at 6:30 on the network, and she doesn't even have a clue," the editor said, allowing himself a rebellious grin.

"I don't understand this Internet crapola," Remo said. "Won't someone here make them take that down?"

"Probably would, if anyone in management saw it. I'm sure Kitty hasn't seen it 'cause it's been up a week and we're all still alive. Maddox hasn't either or he would've put the lawyers on it by now. I don't think either of them log online for anything but e-mail, and Kitty probably doesn't even do that 'cause it'd mostly be hate mail these days."

"What is that?" the Master of Sinanju asked.

There were several small static images stacked to the right of the screen. One was labeled "Drunk Cheeta." The frozen image was a blast from the past for Remo Williams. It was a picture of Cheeta Ching in a silver gown.

"These are just related videos," the editor explained, clicking on Cheeta's face. "People share files and shift them around. Newswomen making fools of themselves got lumped together. This one was huge a year ago."

The video was short, just under two minutes. Cheeta Ching was older and thicker than the anchorwoman Remo and Chiun had encountered a number of times years ago. Her eyes were glassy from too much drink. Cheeta rolled around in her glittery gown on top of a grand piano while attempting to sing. "Attempting" was the operative word since there was not a single note that did not manage to elude Cheeta by at least three full tones. After an excruciating minute, Cheeta rolled into a candelabra which dripped wax from three burning candles. Over went the candles onto the hem of her dress which went up like a roadside flare. Remo had a hard time telling exactly when the singing stopped and the screaming started. On fire, Cheeta flopped to the floor where several stagehands attempted to smother the flames while her panicked accompanist screamed and hopped beside her.

By the end of the video Remo could see that the bloom was truly off the rose for the Master of Sinanju. Chiun had given up on the video halfway through and without comment had pulled his picture of Judge Ruth from his sleeve.

"What about that one?" Remo asked the editor once the Cheeta video was over. He pointed again to the row of small images on the right of the screen. The third one was labeled "Here, Kitty, Kitty."

The editor laughed. "Cheeta had an excuse for screaming. At least she was on fire. And even then she wasn't as panicked as Kitty was on Flight 980. But that plane wasn't really fun because you couldn't really see her face, you just mostly heard Kitty screaming. You want to see a real meltdown, get a load of this."

He dragged the mouse over and clicked on the image.

The footage started immediately. There was Kitty walking through a zoo. BCN's anchorwoman passed a paddock where distant zebras trotted a dusty enclosed landscape.

"We're all aware of the global warming crisis," Kitty said, in her serious newsreader tone, "but there is one group that is already suffering the effects and who do not have our ability to give voice to their fears. Scientists say that zoo animals give us a glimpse into our own dark futures."

Kitty walked in front of a cage filled with cavorting chimpanzees. They screeched loudly as they played, nearly drowning out Kitty's last scripted line. Aware of the problem, Kitty lowered her mic in frustration and snarled at someone unseen off-camera, "Can we shut those damn monkeys up?"

A pause as someone muttered something incomprehensible off-camera. "How the hell should I know? Tranquilize them," Kitty said.

Another pause. "Who says? I don't care. Smother them under a damn pillow if they don't like it." Kitty turned to the screaming monkeys. "Shut up, you damn dirty apes!"

The chimps reacted to her taunts with delight as if they thought this yelling human was joining in their fun. Kitty did her best to ignore them, but when she began reading her introduction a second time, something splattered the back of her head. She gasped and grabbed for the source only for her hand to return smeared brown.

Remo watched the comic slow burn as the realization of what exactly had splattered her hair sank in.

"Get a load of this," the editor said, leaning forward gleefully. "She's just figured it out."

Kitty turned to the chimps and furiously flung the feces back at their cage. The chimps responded like Richard the Lionhearted's best trained archers. A dozen chimpanzees hauled back and hurled brown globs. The chimps cheered as Kitty was showered in handfuls of chimpanzee waste.

Kitty screamed. Kitty cried. Kitty threw her mic at the delighted chimpanzees. The chimps threw the mic back along with another volley of ordure. The cameraman held the image as Kitty, in tears now and shrieking, ran back up the zoo path, the whole time pelted by globs of chimpy-doo.

"Can we break for lunch now?" a laughing voice asked on the tape before the image became shaky and cut to black.

Next to Remo, the seated editor slapped his knee and wiped a tear from his eye. "I've seen it a hundred times and it's still funny."

"Did that go out live?" Remo asked.

"No, unfortunately. It was taped six months ago. BCN killed the segment after that disaster. It never went to air."

"So that's not supposed to be online either," Remo said.

"No way. But stuff manages to find its way out there anyway. God bless the information age. But Kitty's fans—all ten of them—would never see it. TV evening news is dinosaur news. Only grandmas watch at 6:30 these days. But what a meltdown that was. No one who saw that would be surprised she reacted like that on that plane. The real shame is that Daisy O'Toole isn't on mornings anymore."

"Daisy O'Toole?" Remo asked. "What does that no-talent load have to do with this?"

A few more mouse clicks and Remo was treated to a close-up image of an overweight woman's face.

Remo knew more about Daisy O'Toole than he wanted to. An alleged comic who had briefly hosted two television shows, Daisy was equally famous for her outrageous conspiracy theories, her rudeness and her live-in girlfriend.

On the computer screen, Daisy's mouth was hanging wide and there were words printed inside the cavernous opening. The menu categories included "Daisy's Thoughts," "Daisy's Gigs," "Daisy's Archives" and "Pretty Kitty." The editor brought his mouse to Daisy's mouth and clicked on the last item on the menu list.

And there was an image of Kitty once more, covered in chimpanzee scat, and with her mouth hanging open wide in a frozen scream.

Remo scanned some of the text Daisy O'Toole had typed in next to Kitty's picture.

—kitty prooves herownself "newswomen of the sentry yet_again with monky shit.
—u r a notalent an we all no itt_kitty i hate u die die die!!!!!!!

"Can't anyone on this box spell?" Remo asked.

"No," the editor answered truthfully. "But what kills me is that Daisy doesn't have a show anymore. She hates Kitty's guts. Rumor has it she came on to Kitty once years ago. If Daisy was still on, I'd bet you Kitty's fifteen million bucks a year that Daisy would be playing that monkey crap footage every day. And the Flight 980 hysterics would be right up there too." The editor sighed. "As it is, it looks like it's going to be relegated to Internet obscurity."

He backed out of Daisy O'Toole's Web site.

Apparently Kitty had left the BCN building for the call had gone out that the coast was clear and men and women began to filter back into the big editing room.

"Thanks," Remo said to the editor. "Let's go, Chiun."

As Remo and Chiun were leaving the room, the young editor restarted the MyTube zoo video. BCN employees gathered around the screen to watch and guffaw at the footage they had seen many times already.

"That," the editor confided to his colleagues. He pointed to the screen just as the first glob of chimp waste struck Kitty in the head. "That's my screen saver at home." More laughter as Kitty began screaming. And as he watched her in her most miserable moment, that moment replayed to the delight of fellow employees who despised her, Remo was introduced to an emotion he thought he would never feel. He actually felt sorry for Kitty Coughlin.

5

The ivy-covered brick building that was Folcroft Sanitarium was settled amid woods and well-tended grounds where the gently frothing waves of Long Island Sound met the shoreline of Rye, New York. Inside a private office in the back of the private mental health and convalescent facility, Mark Howard watched the endless scroll of news digests and tried for the dozenth time that morning not to check the digital clock on his computer screen.

But it seemed the more he tried not to look at the clock, the more he felt his eyes drawn to it.

Dr. Smith would not approve. Mark's employer would say that his assistant was wasting time worrying about something over which he had no control and as usual Dr. Smith would be right. But that would not stop the worrying.

Mark had lately felt a growing concern about the health of CURE's director. There was nothing specific.

Smith was not ill and indeed had come through his last physical four months before with flying colors.

"Dr. Smith, you're doing remarkably well for a man your age," the examining Folcroft doctor had said.

"For a man your age." It was a phrase that weighed heavily on Mark Howard.

Dr. Smith was already not a young man when Mark had come aboard the agency seven years before. A good chunk of another decade had passed since then.

Smith was not like Chiun. The Master of Sinanju seemed ageless, locked in some miraculous bubble where the ravages of time broke around him like water from the prow of a ship. Smith on the other hand had grown older. The CURE director's hair had grown thinner and seemed more brittle, and the battleship gray was surrendering to white. Mark could see the occasional effort Smith made just to push himself up out of a chair. In the past year Smith had lost focus during their regular morning meeting, as if uninterested in his CURE duties. It had only happened two or three times but it was significant in that it had never happened before. The last time was the worst, a month ago.

It had been a sunny spring day and Smith had swiveled his old leather chair so that his assistant, sitting before his desk, could see only the top of Smith's head. Behind Smith's broad desk, a big picture window of one-way glass looked out over Long Island Sound.

"I've confirmed that Ramon Albondigas is flying into Miami for hip replacement surgery," Mark said that morning a month ago. "When I prepared that report for you on priority drug and Mob targets back in November, Albondigas was top of the list. We won't even have to send Remo to South America since this monster's going to be in the country anyway. I don't think we should let this opportunity pass, Dr. Smith. The Feds don't have anything to directly tie him to La Cocina so once he gets his new hip he'll just walk."

Mark was not surprised that Smith did not chuckle at his wordplay. The emotionless CURE director was not known for his sense of humor. What Howard had not expected to hear was snoring from the other side of the desk.

"Dr. Smith?" Mark asked.

When no reply was forthcoming, Mark got up from his plain wooden chair and stepped hesitantly around the desk. He found the CURE director's head pressed against the chair's back, his eyes closed and his mouth slightly open. Smith's hands rested on his belly, fingers interlocked. The hands rose and fell with each deep, dozing breath.

"Dr. Smith?" Mark repeated. He gently shook his employer's shoulder.

Smith snorted awake. His gray eyes were clear and came into immediate focus. There had been no disorientation, not a moment where the CURE director had thought he was waking up in his own bed at home.

"I'm sorry, Mark," Smith said with a sigh. Removing his glasses, he rubbed his eyes with tired fingers.

"Are you all right?"

"I'm fine. I don't think I have caught up yet on the sleep I lost during the Mustafa Mohammed crisis." Smith noted the look of concern on his subordinate's broad face. "Mark, I told you I am fine. There are merely—" Another deep breath and long exhale "—merely certain physical realities that eventually become unavoidable over time." The CURE director replaced his glasses. "You will understand them better a good many years from now. Now, what were you saying about Ramon Albondigas?"

The remainder of that meeting continued like all the other morning meetings the two men had shared over a good portion of the past decade, and there had not been a similar incident at any of the meetings since. Mark mostly put Dr. Smith's advancing age from his mind. Except on mornings like this one.

Smith was late for work, and it was partly Mark's fault.

Mark had volunteered to fly down to meet with Remo in Miami the previous day, but Dr. Smith insisted that he himself would go. Remo could be difficult to handle, and the fact that he had been ignoring Smith's phone calls likely meant that he was in a more difficult mood than usual.

"It's a long haul back and forth in one day," Mark had said the previous morning. "That's assuming he lets you find him. If he rabbits on you, you could be stuck there a few days before he comes back. Why don't you let me go?"

Smith detected the concern in Mark Howard's voice. Looking over the tops of his rimless glasses, Smith gave his assistant a stern look.

"Mark," the CURE director warned. "If there is one thing I have learned in this job that I wish to impress on you more than anything else it is that the work you do here is not made any easier by worrying about things over which you have no control. I told you before that I am fine. Master Chiun said that Remo will be back this morning. This will be a simple trip down and back. I will be back in Rye early this evening. Besides, while I'm there I can give Chiun that photo he coerced us into getting for him."

It all sounded good but Mark knew that despite his advice Smith had spent a lifetime worrying about things he could not control. Before he let the CURE director leave he forced a promise out of his boss. If Smith insisted on flying to Miami and back in one day, the CURE director would take a few hours off the next morning to recover from the long flight.

"Sleep in, play golf, whatever. I'll hold down the fort here at Folcroft," Mark had said.

There were some arguments that Smith was willing to let his assistant win. Smith was at his core a logical man even, and perhaps especially, when it came to his own advancing years. Mark assumed it was a testament to the faith he had in his assistant, as well as a reluctant accep-

tance of the fact that Mark was right, that Smith had
agreed. And so it was this morning that as ten o'clock
came and went and Dr. Smith had still not arrived at
Folcroft, Mark, like a worried parent on prom night, had
begun sending an occasional creeping eye to the clock in
the lower righthand corner of his computer screen.

10:13 a.m.

To Mark's shame, his concern for Dr. Smith was
motivated partially out of selfishness. The longer Smith
stayed at his post as head of CURE, the farther away was
that eventual day Mark Howard would take over as head
of the supersecret agency. Even after all these years at
Folcroft, Mark still did not know how Smith had handled
the demands of his job for so many decades. Mark could
not imagine a more lonely, difficult post in the world than
director of CURE. When the day came that he had to
accept the position he would do so with grim dedication
but until that time came he was more than content to
remain Smith's number two.

More than merely self-interest, Mark worried about
Smith's health because unlike nearly everyone who had
ever met the taciturn CURE director, Mark Howard
genuinely liked his employer. Perhaps that was due to the
secret daily burden they shared. Out in the field Remo
and Chiun witnessed the ugliness of their business up
close, but they still only saw it in spurts. The two Masters
of Sinanju would often go months between assignments.
At Folcroft on a daily basis, Dr. Smith and Mark Howard
viewed a steady stream of violence, depravity and threats
to the country as it passed across their respective computer
screens.

That data stream had been flowing long before Mark
settled into his small office in Folcroft's administrative
wing. Dr. Smith had been monitoring its flow for over
four decades now. It was work without end, and Mark had
no idea how Smith had managed it alone for so long.

Still, Mark would do his best not to burden his employer

with his concerns. There were some things best worried about in private. Besides, Dr. Smith could have another good decade in him. Mark had a childhood neighbor back in Iowa who lived to ninety-seven and who until his last winter chopped wood and climbed onto his roof to shovel off snow.

Mark took one last look at the clock. 10:18 a.m.

Time was slipping away. For all of them.

Forcing the clock and its psychological implications from his mind, Mark turned his attention to his computer.

Dr. Smith had asked Mark to look into a specific aspect of the Flight 980 hijacking, namely how the hijackers had been able to sneak weapons and explosives onto the plane. So far there were no absolute answers, but what authorities had been able to ascertain was deeply disturbing.

It was discovered within an hour of the near-disaster that a series of security breakdowns had left the terminal from which the hijackers had boarded the flight wide open to terrorists. Several key cameras which left a clear path from doors to boarding gate had been removed. The cameras were taken down as part of a routine security upgrade.

When the cameras were removed, the computerized system for the entire terminal was taken off-line. Communications were effectively shut off between stations.

Minutes before the boarding announcement was made for Flight 980, several key security personnel left for a regularly scheduled morning coffee break. When questioned after the hijacking, the two who remained at first claimed that understaffing left them overwhelmed at their stations. However, eyewitness testimony confirmed that the two men had been talking to one another and had permitted passengers to board without inspection.

Several passengers claimed that metal detectors seemed to be disabled and that they had managed to carry through items that should have set off an alarm. It was only because of these statements that airport officials eventually admitted that the metal detectors through which the Flight 980 passengers were screened had been shut down as well, another part of the overall security maintenance taking place in the terminal that morning.

An unbelievable series of events had contributed to what should have been a certain catastrophe.

It was unknown as yet if this cascading series of failures was part of a sinister organized effort or were merely terrible coincidences. Absent proof of the former Mark was, for the moment, inclined to believe the latter. Airport security had been federalized and unionized post-9/11, and was now run with all the streamlined efficiency of the Department of Motor Vehicles. It was a major miracle that planes were not being hijacked every week.

Tapping his keyboard, Mark pulled up the latest FBI data. Of particular interest now were external cameras, particularly those from airport parking lots. Since no images of the hijackers had been taken inside the terminal, there was hope among law enforcement that the exterior cameras might have picked up something.

Mark scanned the latest report and was unsurprised by its conclusions. With such a busy airport, with so many people coming and going at every minute of the day, the FBI was finding it impossible to sift through all the faces collected outside the terminal. Only a handful of Flight 980 passengers even showed up on the parking lot cameras. Most had chosen not to leave their cars at the airport and had taken cabs and shuttle buses or had gotten rides in to LaGuardia. With the terminal cameras down, those who had been dropped off at the doors might as well have been ghosts.

Another FBI report noted that now, a week later, the cars in the near lots had all been traced to owners. The hijackers had not left vehicles at LaGuardia only to collect them after their remarkable escape from Flight 980.

For Mark it was one frustrating dead end after another.

Alone in his small office, Mark Howard attacked the problem logically.

If the security difficulties at LaGuardia were not the result of a series of unfortunate coincidences, the next sensible conclusion was involvement of airport staff. Mark had already spent the week poring through detailed files of everyone from upper management to lowly baggage handlers. Of particular interest to Mark, as well as to the FBI, were the two men who had allowed the hijackers onto the plane.

Calvert Stuart and Edward Nole.

Stuart was in his fifties, Nole in his thirties. Both were married, Nole for three years, Stuart nearly twenty-five. One child for Nole, five for Stuart. Neither had ties to any radical groups. In fact, it seemed that each had only one extracurricular activity. Stuart was an Elk and Nole was an active trader on the iBay Web site. They were, frankly, two very boring men unlikely to be involved in an act of terrorism.

Mark closed out Stuart's and Nole's files for what seemed like the hundredth time that week and reached under his desk, pressing a recessed stud near his knee. The computer screen and keyboard sank below the scarred surface of the oak desk. He stretched as he got up.

Out in the hallway, Mark headed for the door. On his way downstairs he glanced out the stairwell window expecting to see a familiar battered old station wagon pass through the stone columns at Folcroft's main entrance, but Dr. Smith's car was nowhere to be seen.

On the first-floor landing he caught up to a matronly woman who was heading in the same direction.

Eileen Mikulka, Dr. Smith's secretary, was carrying a cafeteria tray on which was an empty plate dusted with toast crumbs and an empty juice glass. In all his years at Folcroft, Mark had never seen Mrs. Mikulka eat at her desk.

"Those aren't yours, are they, Mrs. M.," he said, nodding to the dirty dishes. It was not a question, but a statement of fact.

"Oh, good morning, Mr. Howard," Mrs. Mikulka said. "No, they're not mine. I had to sneak in to get them just now. Dr. Smith told me he did not want to be disturbed when he snuck in here first thing this morning. But the cafeteria staff run the breakfast dishes through the dishwasher at around eleven, and I wanted to get them down before then."

Mrs. Mikulka did not know why Mr. Howard, usually such a polite young man, turned around without so much as a how-do-you-do and darted back upstairs. But, then, the assistant director of Folcroft was becoming so much like her own boss it was getting harder and harder to tell them apart these days, despite the many years that separated them.

Clucking her tongue and shaking her blue-permed head, Eileen Mikulka continued down the stairs.

When the door to his office opened without a knock, Smith peered up over the tops of his glasses.

"Good morning, Mark," Smith said when his assistant marched into the room. He turned his attention back to his computer screen. Smith's desk was a broad onyx slab with a subterranean monitor visible only when one was seated behind the desk. A capacitor alphanumeric keyboard lined the desk's edge. Letters and numbers flashed small bursts of light with each strike of Smith's arthritic fingers.

"I thought you were taking the morning off," Mark said. "When did you get in?"

"My usual time."

"Dr. Smith, you don't—"

Smith stopped typing and raised a silencing hand. "Please take a seat." With reluctance, Howard sat in the plain wood chair before his employer's desk. "I know you wanted me to take the morning off, but there was no need. I came in this morning, Mark, because there is nothing wrong with me to prevent me from coming to work. I have tried to explain to you that your concern is unwarranted. I will accept the fact that you won't stop worrying if you agree to accept the fact that as long as I am able I will continue to do my job. Agreed?"

Exhaling, Mark nodded.

Smith allowed a sharp nod of his own. "Now, as long as you are here, what news about 980?"

"Zip," Mark said. "I was leaning toward those two security guys, but they're both clean as a whistle. Not so much as a parking ticket between them. It may be, Dr. Smith, that the hijackers lucked through a security window."

Smith steepled his long fingers at the tip of his patrician nose. "I've seen coincidences in my life, but it's unlikely here. I cannot accept the premise that the hijackers miraculously stumbled through a security breach that had only opened that morning. No, they knew. A broader net must be cast. We're going to have to sift through all airport personnel who would have knowledge of the security overhaul scheduled for that day."

"That'll take days," Mark warned.

"For now it is all we have," Smith replied.

A soft beep emanated from the CURE director's hidden computer. He leaned over the screen to check the report the basement mainframes had flagged. When he glanced up at his assistant, there was something approaching a grim smile on the older man's thin lips.

"We may not have to go through airport personnel records again," Smith said. "Perhaps we can find out what we want to know from one of the hijackers himself."

6

The body had been discovered on the roof of the Weehawken, New Jersey, warehouse.

"It was just lying here when I came up," the overweight, middle-aged building owner explained for the tenth time. "Here, there, everywhere. Smeared all over. Big mess. I don't feel so good."

Behind him a roof sign thirty feet long advertised Steinmetz Rugs and Remnants of Weehawken, Inc. The letters had once been painted so brightly red they were visible from boat decks on the Hudson but they were now so faded that they were barely legible from the street below.

The fat man tried not to breathe the reeking air as he held a cheap linen handkerchief over his mouth and nose.

"You didn't find it until today?" the detective asked.

"Do I have to repeat this to everybody?" the building's owner said. He tried not to look in the direction of the biggest chunk of body. A dozen men surrounded the main lump of the corpse. A smear of brown like a gruesome runway dragged across the faded tar to the rotting body.

"Please, sir," the detective said, his tone bored and professional. He held a notebook and pen and did not look at the building's owner as he spoke.

"I told the other officer I don't come here much. We rented a corner to a furniture refinisher, but he moved out a year ago. The place has been completely empty since then. I check in every week or two. I thought something was wrong with the roof fan this morning. I could see from the lot it wasn't moving. I got inside and I could smell it. I thought it was a dead raccoon or something. I got up here and—"

The wind off the Hudson shifted and brought the stink of decaying corpse to the building owner's nose. Gasping, he ducked over the edge of the building and launched his breakfast to the weed-filled parking lot three stories below.

"So you're the only one with keys, Mr. Steinmetz?" the detective asked, unmindful of the stench even as the fat man retched his guts out over Weehawken.

"What is all this twenty questions business?" Steinmetz gasped. "I found a dead body. I got keys I leave at the house but no one else uses them. What, you think my wife comes up here in secret to meet the poolboy? Fat chance. If it's not a beauty parlor, she's not getting off the Barcalounger. Plus she hasn't walked upstairs since Nixon was president. I got kids have never seen this place. They couldn't tell Weehawken from Warsaw and they couldn't get up here if I told them there was gold on this roof. Not if it meant they'd have to pry themselves from their PlayStations or the credit cards I get stuck with paying every month. You want to know what happened here, look at that." Steinmetz waved a pudgy hand at a pile of cloth that had wrapped around the corner of the Steinmetz Rugs and Remnants of Weehawken, Inc. sign.

Half the parachute was wadded at the metal base of the

sign. The rest was spread out across the roof and was rolling lazily back and forth in the strong breeze.

"I saw the news last week," Steinmetz said, mopping his mouth with his sweaty handkerchief. "This is one of those hijackers jumped from that plane. Can you believe it? Figure the odds Herschel Steinmetz is the lucky one who has one splat on his roof. I should play the lottery. That's it. I'm done. I don't know anything else, I can't help you anymore, I'm sick of repeating myself to every Tom, Dick and Harry, so I'm leaving. I've got to call my insurance agent about all this. Then I'm calling my real estate agent."

"Thank you, Mr. Steinmetz," the detective said. "Someone will be in touch if we need anything more."

"Yeah, thank you," Herschel Steinmetz muttered. "We're all so goddamned polite, aren't we?"

As the detective went to the body, the fat man turned and waddled hastily in the other direction. On the way through the rusted roof door, Steinmetz met a pair of men coming up the stairs from the third floor.

"What is this, Grand Central? Gonna sell the place," he announced loudly to the new arrivals. "I already wanted to but my mother says no. 'Keep it in the family, Herschel.' . . . 'Your father's blood is in that building, Herschel.' . . . 'Your father would die if he thought you were going to sell, Herschel.' Well, my father's been dead for twenty years, the discount rug business went belly-up twenty-five years ago, and now bodies are dropping down onto this rat trap from out of the sky. That's it. Herschel Steinmetz takes his signs from God serious. I'm selling. Either of you fellas wanna buy a building cheap?"

"No," Remo said.

"How cheap?" asked Chiun.

"Fuhgeddaboudit," Steinmetz said. "Figures. Who'd want this dump anyway?"

Grousing all the way, the fat man hustled past Remo and Chiun and waddled down the dank stairwell.

"You did not even ask him the price," the Master of Sinanju complained as they stepped out onto the roof and into the hot midday sunlight.

"You don't need a New Jersey warehouse, Little Father. You've already got more closet space back home than you know what to do with, and I'm not driving you all the way to Weehawken every time you want to change kimonos."

"Perhaps you are right," Chiun said, crinkling his nose. "I doubt I could get that odor out of my precious kimonos."

The wind shifted once more and carried to their sensitive noses the wretched stench of week-old corpse.

"Yeah, silk does tend to soak up the stink of rotting flesh," Remo agreed.

"I was talking about New Jersey," Chiun replied. With a thin smile, the old Korean breezed past his pupil who had been raised in Newark only a few miles away and headed for the knot of policemen.

Remo flashed his Homeland Security ID at the detective who tried to stop them. The detective, a captain who was in charge of the investigation, eyed the identification with undisguised irritation.

"You guys got here fast," the captain grunted, clearly annoyed that the Feds had sniffed out his crime scene. "I figured FBI would be the first to show up."

Remo ignored the cop and nodded to the parachute. "It's one of our guys, Little Father," he said to his teacher.

"A couple of abandoned chutes have turned up on both sides of the river," the captain said. "Bastards jumped out pretty low, but it looked until today like they all got away. Guess it's no surprise that one of them wouldn't be so lucky. Odds were against them. Just stay back. We're— Hey. Hey, get away from there."

The Master of Sinanju had stepped past the captain and slid between the plainclothes officers who were examining the body. Chiun stooped over the decaying corpse. The confused investigators glanced from the old man in their midst to their captain.

"I said get outta there," the captain said. He tried to grab the old man's arm, but found himself grasping air.

Although the hijackers' faces had been covered in the BCN video and this man's face was not masked, there was something familiar around the dead man's eyes.

"Isn't he that guy you froze-framed on the video?" Remo asked.

The Master of Sinanju nodded. "Yes. This is the one with doubt in his eyes."

The captain threw up his hands. "Sure, why not," he snarled. "Pull up a couple of lawn chairs, why don't you? So you're saying you know this guy?"

Remo explained about the video that they had seen at BCN headquarters in Manhattan.

"So you never saw his whole face?" the cop said.

"Nope."

"And you only saw him one time on video?"

"Yep."

The captain flashed a deeply skeptical frown. "I think we're going to play it safe and not declare this one solved just yet." Shaking his head he turned to his men.

The body had hit the roof hard and at an angle. The parachutist had jumped from the plane too low, had failed to compensate for distance and had lost control of his chute. His chest had shredded in the long slide from point of impact to his eventual resting place, wedged into the rusted roof vent. An arm had torn off en route when the dead man slammed an ancient chimney. Several bricks had broken away and scattered, along with ancient mortar, to the roof surface.

The impact looked to have turned part of the torso inside-out. Wearing rubber gloves, the detectives felt around inside the goo for pockets. There was no wallet, keys or even a comb. But the search did turn up one item.

It had been slipped into a thick plastic bag to protect it

from fingerprints. The bag was torn and part of the object within had been shredded and was smeared with dried viscera. But enough of it had survived the crash.

"What the hell?" the captain said.

Remo and Chiun examined the item.

It was a publicity photo like the Judge Ruth photograph Smith had secured for the Master of Sinanju. But rather than Judge Ruth's stern visage, the woman in this photo flashed white teeth and an inch of pink gums. The photo was signed.

> To my #1 fan. Thanks for watching!
>   Love, Kitty Coughlin

Remo noted that "thanks" was underlined twice.

"That narrows the search," the captain said. "She's only got—what?—about eight viewers left these days?"

Smirking, he glanced to the Department of Homeland Security men. The two men were no longer beside him. When he looked back over his shoulder he spotted them ducking through the roof door and heading back downstairs. The young one wore a face that was an angry, dark mask.

"Guess they're not all bad," the captain grunted. "By the looks of it they're not Kitty Coughlin fans either."

Shaking his head, he turned full attention back to his grisly crime scene.

7

The first colonists to drag the first buckets of black anthracite from the green and fertile ground of eighteenth-century Pennsylvania had no way of knowing that they were pioneers of an era that would see the end of their agrarian way of life and the rise of a flame-fueled and smoke-belching mechanized age that would transform the globe.

Back then it was shovels and pickaxes, with oxen and carts to haul the coal to small home fireplaces. Soon came the kiln and the blacksmith's forge. Quick on their heels came the powerful furnaces that began the iron industry.

The Industrial Revolution witnessed great changes in the methods of production, its furnaces fed by the hard black coal chipped from beneath the hills of Pennsylvania.

Chimneys sprouted up where trees once grew, and the home workshop was replaced by the factory. As industry swelled so too did the worldwide demand for coal. In southwestern Pennsylvania, farmers abandoned their plows, horses and barns for hard and dirty lives below ground.

The iron age met the age of steel. Steam engines led to automobiles and airplanes; crude oil was refined to power the internal combustion engine; the power of the atom was harnessed; and eventually around the world demands came for newer sources of energy, for cleaner fuels. But even as towers rose to harness the power of the wind and solar panels began popping up on rooftops, even as wealthy Hollywood celebrities decried the burning of fossil fuels as they boarded private jets to fly from L.A. to Cannes, men still climbed into grimy elevators and descended into shafts drilled deep into the bowels of the earth to chip loose the same chunks of black coal by which the pre-Revolutionary colonists had warmed themselves two hundred and fifty years before.

Pennsylvania coal country was a land of sadness and illness but a land as well of history and strength. And it was to this land rich in human as well as natural resources, on a sunny weekday afternoon, that a sleek black limousine came, followed closely by a white van painted with the BCN logo. The logo, like a pair of tipped-over parentheses encircling a blue dot, resembled an unblinking eye.

Kitty Coughlin, whose eyes these days had their own difficulties with blinking, slipped two long, bare legs out of the back of the limo and wobbled up on spike heels. She wore a pair of sunglasses that completely hid her eyes. Her head moved in one long, slow arc as she took a single panoramic look around the bleak landscape.

In the far distance a hint of treetops peeked over a bluff that had been gouged from a hillside. The sliver of trees was the only sign that she had not stepped into some inhospitable alien world. As it was the area looked as if a giant had reached down one mighty hand and scooped up a mile-wide stretch of earth. Heavy loaders moved

mountains of coal from cavernous holes. A constant stream
of trucks rumbled in and out of the man-made valley while
to the east a locomotive on one of three sets of tracks
trailed a seemingly endless line of heavy loaded cars.

Kitty watched the train thunder off to parts unknown,
she watched the trucks roll off, she saw hundreds of dirty
men moving like ants in and out of holes in the ground in
a tradition of back-breaking hard work that stretched
back generations.

All of this did Kitty Coughlin take in and when she
had absorbed it all she pulled off her sunglasses and gave
her Upper East Side opinion of every dirty little corner of
the world, be it Pennsylvania coal country, the entire
southern United States or her Guatemalan maid's
Brooklyn apartment.

"What a shithole," complained Kitty Coughlin, who
hated it when the peasants dwelling in the slums of talk
radio called network news personalities "elitist."

Kitty nearly climbed back into the seat and ordered the
driver to return her immediately to Pittsburgh, but she
was too late.

"Ms. Coughlin!"

A well-groomed man in his early thirties was hurrying
over from the small cluster of permanent trailers that
served as location headquarters for the mining company
to which Kitty's limo had come. The trailers had been
white at some point in the distant past but like everything
else in coal country were now covered in a thick coat of
black grime.

"I'm going to kill Uriah Maddox when I get back to
New York," Kitty muttered, slamming the limo door.

The young man hustled up to Kitty's side. He wore
slacks, dress shirt and tie but no jacket. His shirt was
immaculately white and the hand he offered Kitty had
suffered calluses only after too many hours on the golf
driving range.

"Arthur Welt, vice president public relations the

Weltsburg Coal and Mining Company of Weltsburg, Pennsylvania. Hello. Hello. Hi, there," he added with a bright smile as Kitty's production crew came up from the van. The glum men hauled cameras, lights, cables and boom microphones.

"Let's get this over with," Kitty demanded.

Welt's smile wavered. "Oh. I guess you must be on a tight schedule. Well, you wanted to interview real live miners as they worked, so you're the boss. This way."

Kitty and crew were ushered into a van which drove them along a rutted, unpaved road to the nearest open wound in the side of Weltsburg's rolling hills.

Kitty was surprised at the telephone poles that brought electricity down into the mine, as well as the wide opening more than large enough for their van to drive through.

Kitty had once been brought down into a Russian missile complex. It was back during the 1980s, at the Cold War's end and the height of the U.S. military buildup that had toppled the Soviet Union. New to her morning network job and eager to unmask the American administration as warmongering "xenophobes"—a word she had just learned but which she had been assured meant "hated peace-loving people"—Kitty had allowed a Soviet spokesman, a Red Army colonel who had once shot two scientists dead for the crime of being Jewish, carte blanche to propagandize on behalf of peace-loving Mother Russia for two whole bottom-of-the-hour segments broken only by the weather and local station identification. This coal mine in Pennsylvania reminded her of that old Soviet missile complex.

The well-lit tunnel angled down and the van stopped in front of an industrial-size elevator that had been built into the wall of solid rock.

Kitty and her team were issued hardhats by mine workers and Arthur Welt ushered them onto the elevator.

"My great-grandfather founded the Weltsburg Coal and Mining Company," Welt said. "The town of Weltsburg was established for the laborers who came here to work the mines. Many of them originally came from Pittsburgh, but as the—"

"What about mining deaths?" Kitty interrupted.

Arthur Welt was trying not to blink in the harsh light that was angled down at him from over Kitty's camera. She held a microphone out to him although it was unnecessary since a boom mic on a pole above his head picked up his every word.

"Well, of course accidents happen," Welt said. "I won't tell you that coal mining isn't dangerous work because it is. In Pennsylvania, more than fifty-five thousand men have died in mining-related accidents in the past two hundred and fifty years. However, modern techniques have minimized the risk and we are constantly working to improve even more. We're proud of the innovations we've made, innovations which recently caught the attention of a Chinese mining—"

"What do you tell those concerned about the effects of coal use on the global warming crisis?" Kitty demanded.

"Excuse me?"

"Isn't the burning of coal public enemy number one for releasing carbon into the atmosphere?"

Welt had been instructed not to look directly into the camera but to keep eye contact with Kitty. It was hard to keep from glancing at the camera or either of the two microphones that hovered around his head, inanimate objects that seemed to be silently awaiting an answer to a question he knew would come but which he had assumed the BCN anchorwoman would casually build to.

Fortunately circumstances saved Arthur Welt before he was able to tell Kitty that cows and sheep belching and farting caused more environmental harm than all the engines in all the countries of the world.

They were a hundred feet down and still descending when Welt heard a muffled boom.

"What was that?" Kitty asked.

"I'm . . . I'm not sure," Welt said. He looked between his own feet. The floor of the elevator was comprised of welded grates through which could be seen the mine shaft down which the elevator was rapidly descending. The shaft below was dimly lit at regular intervals, but in the far distance below all the staggered lighting seemed to meet at a single point, blending into an indistinct amber blob.

As Arthur Welt looked down, a black pinprick appeared dead center in the soft focus light. The single black blotch began to expand rapidly upward as lights from below flickered off level by level.

"What's wrong?" Kitty asked, noting the stunned expression on her tour guide's face.

Before Welt could answer there came another boom, this one louder and closer than the first. The first rumble had not yet dissipated, and the two sounds seemed to combine into one single noise that rolled up from far below their feet. And when the leading edge of this single boom enveloped the rapidly moving elevator, the car in which they were descending began to rattle, then shudder. Loose metal clattered. The BCN news team dropped various equipment and grabbed the car's welded railings. One-handed, the cameraman struggled to keep his lens aimed at Kitty.

"What's happening?" Kitty asked, feeling the first familiar flutter of panic grip her chest.

Even as she asked the question, the full force of the explosions slammed up hard into the elevator car.

The tomb of earth through which they were traveling became a living beast, furious at human intrusion. The walls around them shook violently, slamming the car against solid stone in a hail of bright yellow sparks.

The elevator fell. Ten feet, twenty feet.

Kitty's spiked heels went out from under her and she was flung to the metal floor of the car. Microphones, batteries and hardhats bounced as men grabbed on for dear life. Welt lost his footing and landed hard on Kitty's shoulder.

The wave of black erupting from deep within the earth passed over the car. The wall lights flickered out and would have plunged the elevator into total darkness if not for the camera lights.

Emergency brakes kicked in, slowing the car's rapid descent and sending up a fresh wave of sparks. Metal screamed against metal, nearly drowning out the human screams that were coming from within the elevator car.

Kitty thought that the terrifying shrieks were coming from the elevator shaft. She did not realize they were coming from her own hoarse throat. Flat on her belly, she clutched the floor grate with her fingers and held on for dear life as the elevator bucked inside the dark shaft.

A burst of cool air belched up from the unseen distance below, carrying with it a thick cloud of black dust.

And then the cable pulled tight like a rubber band that had been stretched to its utmost and the car jerked to an abrupt stop. More chaos as Welt was flung from Kitty and hurled into a corner of the car. He got up panting as the emergency lights flickered on inside the car.

"I think that's . . . I think it's over," Welt hissed. His white shirt was covered in black grime. "Ms. Coughlin?" Somewhere far above them a metallic creak. Voices shouting. The car bounced gently and began to rise, a jarring return to normalcy after the previous minute.

"Ms. Coughlin?" Welt asked. Coughing, he tried to offer Kitty his hand but she remained glued to the floor, fingers clutching the grate, lungs screaming fear.

And through the screaming and the kicking and the white-knuckled terror, Kitty's cameraman kept his unswerving camera aimed squarely at BCN's star anchorwoman.

Remo and Chiun arrived in Weltsburg to find a town under siege.

National as well as local Pennsylvania news media had descended on the small coal town in a crush of vans, cars and helicopters. Cables and satellite dishes choked the modest town square as gaggles of reporters talked to cameras in serious voices. The media feeding frenzy grew worse the closer they got to the Weltsburg Coal and Mining Company. The roads were so clogged that Remo finally had to abandon their rental car a mile from the company's main headquarters.

On the walk in, Remo snagged an eager young reporter who had flown in from Philadelphia.

"What happened?" Remo asked.

"You're kidding, right? Haven't you been watching TV?"

"Not since they cancelled *Bonanza*," Remo said.

"There's been a big mine collapse. Nineteen mine

workers are trapped down there. It's on all the networks. I just got my first national spot on NBC. Can you believe it?"

Obviously, the potentially fatal tragedy for nineteen men was nothing when weighed against national network exposure. The reporter was positively giddy.

"So I guess you're a 'glass is half full' kind of guy," Remo droned.

"What?" the oblivious young man asked. "Oh, wow, I've got to make a call. NB-freaking-C." The reporter skipped off down the street to tell his mother the good news.

As they walked along, Chiun eyed the turmoil with distaste. "Civilized nations used to put their lunatics in asylums. America puts them in front of television cameras."

"Yeah, this place is a zoo," Remo agreed. "I don't think her boss knew about the mine collapse when I called him. He just said Kitty was down here interviewing some miners. This must have happened after we left New Jersey."

"Do not remind me of the opportunity you lost me."

They passed through the main gates of the Weltsburg Coal and Mining Company.

"Don't start that again," Remo said as he scanned the crowds for Kitty Coughlin. "You're still just pissed that I was worried about some old ladies in Florida getting mugged."

"Why shouldn't I be? When was the last time you gave so much thought to me? Not that I care. I do not. What I care about is my building which I now do not have thanks to you."

"You didn't really want a warehouse in Weehawken, you just want another excuse to beat me over the head."

"Do not tell me what I do and do not want. Besides, did you forget the lesson of Lok-Hoo?"

"Lok-Hoo," Remo repeated. "He the guy in the Dark

Ages who passed on Ireland?" He pointed to a crowd of reporters. "C'mon, it looks like all the excitement is over there."

Chiun padded along beside his pupil. "For a service to the English crown, Master Lok-Hoo was offered Ireland at a discount but he did not even ask the price. How could the Master of Sinanju who is an assassin not an emperor hope to govern a barbarian land at the edge of the world so far from Sinanju? And Lok-Hoo suspected that the English king merely wanted Sinanju to tame this land so that he could send his own English troops in after the Master had gone, for the king knew that the Master of Sinanju could not stay away from his village forever. Ultimately Lok-Hoo passed on the chance to own Ireland mainly because he did not want to wade knee-deep in Irishmen to claim it. Did you ever try to evict an Irishman, Remo? Toss him out the front door and he just staggers back in the back. But it was still folly of Lok-Hoo to pass on Ireland for it would be worth much today, even filled with Irishmen. And you may have just repeated that folly for who knows what my warehouse would have been worth one day?"

"It's in Weehawken, Little Father. If it's worth a buck today it'll be worth ten cents ten years from now." He pointed deep into the cluster of reporters. "There's Kitty."

As the only reporter on the scene at the moment tragedy struck, Kitty Coughlin was the biggest news celebrity in town. Local BCN affiliates from across the country had spent the past half-hour interviewing her, and for the second time in a week there was talk of a big ratings score for BCN.

Kitty, her cheeks brushed black from her ordeal in the mine, glowed in the limelight like a lump of red-hot coal.

During a lull between affiliate interviews, Kitty excused herself ostensibly to heed the call of nature. Alone, she ducked behind a trailer and squatted down in

her miniskirt to scoop up a handful of black dust. She
was applying fresh streaks to her face to maintain her
image of gritty field reporter when a voice chimed in
behind her.

"If you start singing 'Ol' Man River,' I'm calling Jesse
Jackson."

Kitty jumped, smearing her forehead with a too-thick
glob of coal dust. When she saw that it was Remo who
had startled her, she exhaled angrily.

"What the hell are you doing here?" she demanded,
struggling to stand in her miniskirt and heels. She tried
dusting the excess dirt from her forehead.

"Apparently you weren't as forthcoming back in New
York as you should have been, Al Jolson." He nodded to
his teacher. "Chiun."

Kitty barely acknowledged the Master of Sinanju as he
padded up beside her. "Listen, I don't know what you think
you're doing here, but I've got interviews up the yin-yang—
pardon my French, Charlie Chan—so if you'll excuse me."

She tried to stomp past Chiun but as she passed the
Master of Sinanju the old Korean reached up and pinched
her earlobe. Kitty stopped dead in her tracks. She gasped
at the white-hot pain in her ear.

"Did you know the hijackers?" Remo asked.

"What? No. Of course not. You're hurting me."

"Then why did one of them have an autographed
picture of you when they found his body?"

"They found one of them?" Kitty asked. Chiun applied
more pressure to her ear and she squealed. "I signed it for
him," she hissed. "He stuck a pen and picture in my hands
and asked me to. But I didn't know him. I didn't know
any of them. I swear it."

She was telling the truth. No one lied when in Chiun's
grasp. Remo nodded and the old Korean released Kitty's
coal dust-smeared earlobe.

"Those maniacs hijacked your plane and you still
signed it 'love Kitty'?" Remo asked.

"That's how I've signed all my autographs since my morning show days." Kitty rubbed her injured ear. "I must have done it out of habit. Hey, don't give me that look, bucko. I was under a lot of pressure."

"Yeah, I've seen how you react under pressure. Your pot lid's not exactly screwed on tight if all it takes is one crap-flinging monkey to knock it off."

Kitty's eyes opened wide despite the injections that paralyzed her forehead. "How do you know about that?"

But Remo wasn't listening. "So he must have known you'd be on that plane," he mused.

"Hello?" Kitty said. "I told you they brought my cameraman up to film them."

"I mean before you even left the ground," Remo said.

Ace girl reporter Kitty Coughlin crinkled her nose in confusion. "Hnhh?"

"Dumb as a cabbage," Remo said to the Master of Sinanju.

"Hey," Kitty said.

"This surprises you from a job that requires only that one be able to read in a slow voice?" Chiun replied. "This one has risen to the pinnacle of her profession with skills possessed by every schoolchild in this nation."

"You obviously haven't been in a public school lately, Little Father." To Kitty Remo suggested, "Maybe you should have stuck to interviewing George C. Looney about the evils of capitalism or the evils of America or the evils of everyone who isn't marching in lockstep with George C. Looney and left real reporting for people with at least a brain stem."

She had crossed her arms and was quietly seething at the two Masters of Sinanju. "I suppose you're going to tell me what you mean by that crack?" she snarled.

"The hijacker must have known you'd be on the plane before you ever boarded because I doubt anyone's running around with a publicity photo of you suitable for framing in their pocket. Least of all a guy whose pockets are otherwise completely empty which this guy's were. So he had to know you were going to be on that plane before the hijacking."

Kitty chewed the inside of her mouth as she contemplated Remo's words. "I don't know. I guess . . . maybe."

"Okay, so moving right along . . . who knew you were going to be on that plane?"

"Beats me. Tons of people, I suppose. The airline. Uriah. His staff, my staff. Everybody in the BCN news division. They keep track of whenever I'm out of town. I know they're throwing parties the minute I'm out the door."

"So basically everyone in the free world," Remo said, disgusted. "C'mon, Chiun, this ditz isn't in on it."

Kitty stood there for a wounded moment, annoyed once more at this man who had the nerve not to treat her with the reverence that her teleprompter reading skills required. A thought suddenly occurred to her.

"Wait," she called, chasing Remo out to the front of the trailer. "I did hear one thing. The hijacker, the one who made me sign the autograph, said something about how he was going to auction it on iBay."

"iBay?" Remo asked. "Is that pig Latin, Onkeyday Umsgay?"

"No, it's from that Internet they have. I've never been on that thing myself but we did a whole bunch of stories on it when I was on the morning show. Millions of low-class people go on there and buy and sell all kinds of stuff. Old records, knickknacks, concert tickets. Anything. We had one guy on who got in trouble for trying to sell his kidney."

"So your hijacker pal was one of millions," Remo said. "Hardly narrows it down." He was peering into the distance.

Arthur Welt had just appeared out the door of the Weltsburg Coal and Mining Company trailers. He ushered a group of women, shaking and pale, to a roped-off area a few dozen yards from the collapsed mine. Some of the women guided children before them, a few in their teens, most under ten. Several held babies in their arms and at least two had bellies swollen with child.

The next phenomenon to take place Remo had only witnessed before in nature documentaries. As one, the press seemed to catch a whiff of the women. Noses lifted, heads turned, necks craned. In a pack the collected media stampeded toward the small cordon, shouting and hauling cameras and microphones.

"How does this make you feel?"

"Have you told your children the truth yet?"

"What would your last words to him be?"

Kitty noted Remo's lowered brow. "The widows," she explained. "I mean wives. Technically, I guess. For now."

"I figured," Remo said. "You really are some kind of Bad-Luck Sally. At the scene of two disasters within a week. That must be some kind of record."

"Maybe my luck has finally turned around. Remember that coal mining disaster a couple of years ago? That was a huge ratings boom for all the networks. We covered it on my old morning show. And this time Kitty Girl is right in the thick of it. The sun must finally be shining on me. Can't say the same thing for those women though. I heard the PR guy talking to the company president. They're not going to get those miners out before they run out of air. I broke the story twenty minutes ago. That exclusive should be good for at least another million viewers to-night. A real tragedy."

"You know when warm-blooded people say that word they usually don't smile," Remo said. "Let's go, Chiun."

Behind them Kitty touched her needle-numbed skin, unaware that she had been smiling. Forcing on a serious news anchor expression befitting the coal dust smudges on her face, she hustled off in search of a camera.

"What do you think, Little Father?" Remo said as they circled the far fringe of the crowd.

"I think by your tone that you are thinking of doing something stupid," the Master of Sinanju replied.

"If Kitty's right, they're giving up those guys for dead. If we can help, we can't just leave here without doing something."

Remo was looking at the frightened children. One little boy of about eight had caught his eyes. The boy was trying to be tough for the sake of his mother, as his father had taught him. His back was straight but his jaw trembled ever so slightly as his eyes, wells of infinite sadness, gazed toward the entrance to the mine.

"We are assassins, not gophers," Chiun said. "If these men chose to burrow underground for their livelihoods their predicament is not our concern. However, I see by that cow-eyed look that you will not be dissuaded, so I will maintain the premises up here."

"You mean, mind the store?"

"Exactly. And if you find any loose diamonds lying around, they are mine. For minding the store." He smiled hopefully.

"You got it, Little Father. See you in a little bit."

Remo left the Master of Sinanju to watch the proceedings from above. He followed the edge of the crowd, then slipped away from the last lingering fringes. Roads had been carved through the hills. Remo found a rutted path that led to an old road that looked to have been abandoned a dozen years before. Brackish water stood in grimy puddles.

At intervals as he circled around the hill, Remo would periodically stomp his foot. An observer would think this thin man in the dark T-shirt had a thing against ants. Remo was actually feeling the vibrations of the earth, sensing hollows through the solid ground, and when he was at the far side of the big hill he found what he was looking for.

An old abandoned tunnel cut into the hillside. A few hearty weeds grew in thin soil near the dark tunnel mouth.

Remo slipped inside.

The air was cooler than it was outside, and the sounds of human activity that had continued to filter to his sensitive ears on his trek around the wide hill slowly faded away as Remo walked deeper into the Pennsylvania earth.

The ambient light began to fade the farther he traveled away from the surface. Remo extended his senses. Tunnels stretched here and there from the main path. Remo ignored these, allowing instinct born of training to guide him.

There were few dust particles in the air, indicating a mine long abandoned. The old dust stirred up by hardworking miners had long settled to the ground. But as Remo walked deeper into darkness he began to encounter more airborne particles. The world had long plunged into total blackness when he followed the thickening airborne dust down a side tunnel and stopped at the very edge of the earth.

Remo sensed the nothingness before him. The toes of his loafers touched empty air. The vertical shaft cut deep into the earth. Even Remo could not sense how far down was the bottom.

Ordinarily he would have been forced to climb the walls of the vertical shaft, but fortunately the Weltsburg Coal and Mining Company of Weltsburg, Pennsylvania, had left him a gift. Five feet out was a gently swaying chain that had once lowered and raised an old elevator.

In another day, when he was new to training, he would not have believed that a man could somehow stand in total darkness yet still see the world around him. As his training progressed and his senses began to unlock the hidden, dormant abilities of mind and body, he sometimes wondered how he could do the things he did. Now, so many years since those early, uncertain steps into the perfection that was Sinanju, he no longer gave such matters thought. Remo could do what he did

because that was who he was. Which was why, after
reaching down to the floor and dusting his hands like an
Olympic gymnast, he could step into the nothingness and
trust his body to do what it had been trained to do.

Remo plunged into the black of the abyss. Wind
whistled past his ears. Falling faster, faster still.

Thirty feet down, reaching out. Palms of dusted hands
brushing rusted chain. Joining it, becoming one with it.

Remo's hands slipped over gummy globs of ancient
grease; felt every rusty bit of corroded metal.

He gave no weight to the chain as he allowed it to slow
his descent. He allowed the chain's own dangling unseen
end far below to tell him where it stopped and when he felt
the end of the line coming and sensed solid earth racing
up to meet him, he gripped a little tighter to cut his rate of
speed, tensed his calf muscles and released the chain.

The soles of Remo's loafers touched the ground in
silence and he strolled away from the gently-swaying
chain.

Remo let his breathing tell him where to go. The dust
cloud raised by the collapsed mine brought him along a
horizontal shaft that carried him toward newer excavations.

He kept his breath shallow, not allowing the harmful
coal dust into his lungs.

Remo sensed machine activity through the solid rock.
Heavy equipment, but still at a distance.

He was retracing ground he had covered on the
surface, closing back toward the mining company's main
entrance, when his ears pricked up to the sounds of
heartbeats.

He was surprised to find two concentrations of life
signs. The first and nearest was through the wall up
ahead. Blocked behind solid rock, Remo detected the
telltale signs of nineteen men. The miners were still alive.

The second collection of heartbeats is what came as a
surprise to Remo. They were out in the open and came
from down a side tunnel, away from the trapped men.

There were three of them. Nervous, jumping erratically. Remo thought at first the men might be rescuers but men used to working so deep underground would not display such fear. One wore a heavy aftershave that assaulted Remo's nostrils.

The darkness was absolute. Remo could not see the men who breathed heavily and stayed hunkered down, seemingly afraid to move. Remo sensed that their attention was focused in his direction. But more than that, Remo sensed the familiar pressure waves of a camera lens aimed his way.

Before Remo stepped into view their attention was directed on the wall beyond which the miners were trapped. But once Remo appeared, three pairs of eyes as well as a camera lens turned sharply toward him. As Remo moved from left to right across the open mouth of the tunnel, he felt human and mechanical eyes slowly tracking him.

It was apparent that despite the total darkness these hidden men could see him. Remo decided that the polite thing to do would be to introduce himself.

"Hi-diddly-ho, neighborino," he called. He waved at the trio of men who sucked in a collective gasp of air.

The men panicked. The moment Remo waved, bright bursts of light erupted at the far end of the tunnel, accompanied by multiple explosions. Remo felt the pressure waves that preceded a dozen, then two dozen hurtling bullets.

"This town's welcome wagon leaves a lot to be desired," Remo called as he danced unharmed through the volley of lead.

A cartwheel over three zinging bullets and Remo came up with a chunk of coal in one hand.

"Next time you might want to try a muffin basket," Remo suggested. The shard of coal snapped from his fingertips.

His eyes could not see, but his ears knew that his aim was true. A crack of plastic followed by a wet thud and one of the trio of hearts stopped beating. The gunfire ceased.

"Holy Christmas," a voice gasped.

Remo heard stumbling and tripping as the remaining two men ran off into an adjoining tunnel. He was about to go after them when he heard the soft sound of pebbles dislodged by bullets rolling down at his back.

Beyond the wall, nineteen thready heartbeats. At a distance machines still rumbled too slowly to be of help. Far above, unseen but unforgotten, anxious wives and children awaited news of trapped husbands and fathers.

Remo turned his back on his fleeing attackers.

The next several long minutes Remo spent tapping the wall of rock, gauging strength and weakness, and when he was satisfied that he had located the weakest spot, he attacked. Hands became pistons, fists pounding, pulverizing stone. A declivity formed, then a cavern, and still Remo dug. Boulders loosened, then broke free to be hurled down a side tunnel. Sudden weakness in stone risked collapse. Remo moved instinctively to the right, around the danger zone. Hands pounding still, but strength ebbing.

Sinanju at its most basic was breath and the harmful dust forced Remo to keep his breathing shallow. Coupled with the heavy work of moving tons of rock by hand and the strain of monumental effort, fatigue soon crept in. A leadenness seeped into Remo's arms. Beads of perspiration formed on his brow.

As he burrowed through stone the sounds of struggling heartbeats grew louder, then louder still. Then the final wall of rock came down, but this time it did not need to be rolled behind, it fell forward, and Remo was rolling with it and he found himself inside a dimly lit cavern.

The air was thin and fetid. The nineteen trapped miners were lying on the floor of the mine. Only one man appeared to be injured. Dried blood ran down his face. Two more—older than the rest—had slipped into unconsciousness. But the remaining men seemed fit of limb. When the wall came down they looked up with expressions of disbelief.

"I knew I should've taken that right turn at Albuquerque," Remo announced.

Remo was quick to avoid the lights that bounced across the tomb walls. Before flashlights could settle upon him he had already ducked back inside his tunnel.

"Break time's over," he called, now a disembodied voice to the men who were struggling to their feet.

Too exhausted to cheer, the sixteen healthy men dragged their three injured and unconscious comrades through the newly excavated hole to the adjacent abandoned tunnel system.

"Where's the equipment you used to dig this hole?" a baffled voice asked from behind Remo.

"Rock was loose already. Didn't take much to knock it in," Remo said vaguely, his voice drifting like an echo back to the miners. "Are you coming or what?"

Remo remained always ahead, a darting shadow among shadows as he led them back to the elevator shaft down which he had come.

Remo tapped one young man on the right shoulder and when the man looked around to the right, Remo reached around to the man's blind left and tugged the flashlight from his hand.

"I'll be needing that. Now why don't you go get help?"

"You mean you're all alone?" the miner asked the shadow whose face none of them had seen. But Remo had flicked off the flashlight and already faded into the darkness.

An old metal ladder was affixed to one side of the vertical shaft. From a distance Remo watched the young man begin his long ascent to the surface. Once he was sure the miners were on their way to rescue, Remo left them. He waited until he was far from the men before he turned on his flashlight. The light played off the low ceiling and somehow made the cavern feel smaller than it had in darkness.

Remo followed the sounds of heavy equipment and when he reached his tunnel he turned left.

He found the body of the man he had killed behind a pile of rocks at the end of the short tunnel. The scent of aftershave he had detected earlier hung heavy in the air but did not come from the corpse.

The man wore a pair of gray coveralls that looked as if he had bought them that morning. Aside from a few dirt marks on knees and elbows, his outfit was immaculate. A shiny yellow hardhat without so much as a single scuff had been knocked off when the man fell. It sat in a corner where it shone like a brand-new display model in the window of the Abercrombie and Fitch Coal Miner Outlet Store.

There was no sign of a videocamera.

Flashing a beam of light over the face, Remo found the night vision goggles as he had suspected. Near the body, Remo found a small box with a toggle switch on its surface. Wires ran from the box. He followed them up the length of the tunnel, pausing for a moment to duck in the hole he had pounded through the wall of rock.

He came back out a moment later with a handful of tools—shovels, picks, sledgehammers and crowbars—which he scattered on the ground around the newly-dug hole.

After he had arranged the tools, Remo followed the trail of wires through a maze-like series of natural and man-made tunnels until he reached a massive pile of collapsed rock. The smell of explosives confirmed his suspicions.

He retraced his steps back to the body of the dead man Remo now knew had set off explosives and sealed the mine.

It was an easy matter to follow the scuffing footprints

of the dead one's partners. Two hundred yards along, the tunnel began a sharp upward climb and twenty minutes after leaving the body Remo found himself standing in sunlight.

The mouth of this shaft was a natural cave which opened in an inhospitable area of the Weltsburg Coal and Mining Company grounds. Remo was halfway up a steep hillside that looked out over a thick forest. An access road that appeared to be rarely used disappeared into the trees.

Remo hustled down to the road.

He found fresh tire tracks in the mud but that was the only sign of recent human activity in the desolate area. The two remaining gunmen, who had sealed nineteen men in an underground tomb, were gone.

"Better hope we don't meet up again in some dark tunnel," Remo warned the empty road and swaying trees.

Leaving his threat to drift away on the soft breeze, he turned and began the long trek back to civilization.

Dusk was falling by the time Remo ambled back through the gates of the Weltsburg Coal and Mining Company.

A celebration was in progress. Wives cried tears of joy and children laughed and played as the last of the rescued miners were loaded up in waiting ambulances. The men waved, healthy and whole, as the ambulance doors were shut.

Arthur Welt stood to one side, beaming, baffled and shell-shocked as he tried to answer reporters' questions.

The atmosphere stood in stark contrast to the funereal pall Remo had left in late afternoon. Everyone in the crowd, from the oldest Weltsburg citizen to the youngest child, seemed delighted. Everyone, that was, except the press. The quick and happy resolution had torpedoed any chance of turning the drama in Weltsburg into a two week-long tragedy, from initial death watch to the nineteen dramatic funerals that would now not take place.

Most glum of all was Kitty Coughlin, whom Remo spotted berating her crew as she climbed into the back of her limo.

At the edge of the crowd, hands clasped behind his back and taking in the entire scene, was the Master of Sinanju.

Remo sidled up to his teacher.

"Hola, amigo," Remo said.

"I see by your empty hands that you did not find any diamonds," Chiun said as he watched the cables being rolled up and the cameras being packed away.

"Sorry, Little Father, didn't see any. Only coal."

"Coal is good," Chiun said. "Sort of like you. A diamond waiting to happen."

"How nice," Remo said. "I'm touched."

"Of course, coal—being smarter than you—doesn't have your bad habits."

"That's right. Spoil our Kodak moment."

Remo saw Kitty, sitting in her limousine, as she stabbed one hard finger into the chest of her cameraman. Even at a distance Remo could hear her screeching but he did not bother to focus on what she was saying. Let Kitty scream at her staff. Remo had done a good thing, he felt good, and no nasty anchorwoman worried about her collapsing ratings could dampen his spirit.

Kitty slammed the door and as the limo peeled away Remo noted that the cameraman wore an odd expression for one who had just received a tongue-lashing from BCN's evening news diva. The man was smiling as he gripped his camera.

But why not? Everyone should be smiling this night of happy endings, even members of the piranha press whose mission it was to broadcast death and misery every night at 6:30, Eastern Standard Time.

Chiun noted with disapproval the smile on his pupil's face. "Why are you wearing that idiot grin?"

"I'm high on life, Little Father," Remo said.

Remo spied the eight-year-old boy he had seen earlier in the day. Earlier, the boy had been holding back his fear. Now his face radiated pure joy. His mother could not hold him back as he skipped for the bus that would take the miners' wives and children to the hospital.

Beside Remo, the Master of Sinanju clucked his tongue as he watched the press dismantle their makeshift village.

"See you, Remo, a nation in decline. The Romans had their bread and circuses so that the citizenry would be distracted and not notice that their empire was crumbling. You people call your games news, but like the Roman hoi polloi you lose interest the moment the blood stops flowing. Still I must give the Romans some credit. At least they gave away bread." He shook his head. "No diamonds, no bread, no nothing. In every way this was a wasted trip."

Still shaking his head, the old man padded away.

Alone, Remo watched the delighted little boy hop up the bus steps followed by his exhausted but joyful mother.

"Can't say I agree," Remo said softly. Still smiling, he trailed his teacher through the mining company gates.

9

The rusted blue Toyota Celica turned into the parking lot of the Stop 'N' Start convenience store.

"Is he looking? Does he see us?" Noah Sherman asked the man in the passenger seat who leaned over to try to get a glimpse of the Pakistani who had been working at the Stop 'N' Start when they stopped in for provisions earlier in the day. The dark-skinned man's back was to the front windows as he filled a rack with potato chips.

"No, he's not looking. Still not looking . . . still not looking . . . and . . . we're clear."

Behind the small, one-story brick building Noah and his passenger hopped out of the car and darted behind a Dumpster. They peeled off their stiff new coveralls, revealing simple button jerseys and Dockers. The men stuffed both sets of coveralls, as well as two handguns that were in their pockets, deep in the Dumpster under some Styrofoam trays of rancid hamburger. A swarm of angry flies lifted off and resettled on the green meat. Less than a minute after turning into the lot the two men were heading back out onto the main drag of Weltsburg, Pennsylvania.

"Any cops back there?" Noah asked, the stress causing his high-pitched voice to crack.

Noah's passenger, an overweight man who had been waging a losing battle against acne for three decades, was sitting sideways in his seat and watching the road behind them.

"No cops. No nobody. Everybody's still across town at the mine. I think we made it."

Noah did not entirely trust his passenger. The man's name was Wayne Dwyer and the two of them had only met two weeks before. But as Noah watched the rearview mirror and saw no sign of flashing police lights, he began to feel the tightness in his chest ease slightly, although his heart still pounded and his fingers still tingled. Noah's tongue was thick with the tang of stomach acid. He fished in his pocket and peeled a Tagamet from a tinfoil card.

The instructions said to take the acid medication with plenty of water and Noah Sherman was generally the worst sort of stickler for rules, especially medical ones, but after the week he'd had, he no longer cared.

In what would have been a daring move for Noah just a few scant weeks ago, he tossed back the little white pill and swallowed it dry.

They drove through two small towns before stopping in the parking lot of a little strip motel that was settled back against a copse of pine. Noah and Wayne had been the only customers that morning, but this evening the lot was nearly full.

All the hotels and motels in the area had been unprepared for the flood of reporters who had begun pouring into the region an hour after Kitty Coughlin hit the BCN airwaves to break the story of the mining disaster. But the juiciest part of the story in Weltsburg was over and the press that had descended in droves expecting to be in the area for days was already packing up to leave.

Wayne hunched down in his seat and picked nervously at a pimple on his chin as Noah wended the car through the knot of people and vehicles.

No one paid them any attention as they parked the Toyota and hustled inside their room.

Noah pulled a suitcase from under the nearest of the pair of twin beds and took out a laptop computer that was packed carefully inside a soft knot of T-shirts. He sat on the edge of the bed and set the laptop on his knees. Noah booted up and quickly signed online.

The familiar triangle logo of America Internet Connection appeared on the screen, along with a window listing the current major news stories. Noah noted with a sinking sickness in his stomach that the mine collapse was the number one story in the country according to AIC. There was a picture of two of the miners, grimy but healthy, waving and smiling outside the Weltsburg Hospital emergency room. The caption read, "Pennsy Mine Tragedy Avoided."

Noah could not bring himself to look long on the faces of the two miners and with a click, he closed the news window.

Another small rectangular box appeared in the upper right corner of his screen at sign-on. At the top was the legend "My Pals." The My Pals box was an AIC innovation that alerted members of the Internet service when friends were online at their computers. One need only enter the online name of a person into the system and the network automatically kept permanent track of that individual.

Noah had several AIC addresses, but this one, which he called in a bit of ironic whimsy "Noah Man's Land," was used by only a single individual. Under the Noah Man's Land My Pals listing was a single name: WingerDinger.

Of course WingerDinger was online. He was always online. Sometimes there was a "Gone Away" note. This was the short message that could be typed in by someone on the My Pals list when they stepped away from their computer for a few moments. Most people would type in a polite "away from computer" or "be back in a minute." WingerDinger's Gone Away messages usually consisted of "get bent, homo" and "you R gay."

But today there was no Gone Away message. Today, as Noah Sherman expected, WingerDinger was online and waiting.

Noah clicked on the name and typed out a personal message. "Im here. U there?"

He pressed Send, knowing that the instant he did so electronic impulses would whisk his words far away and that a little box would almost instantaneously appear on WingerDinger's computer screen. Noah had no idea in what city, state or even country his little box would open up. If the past year was any indication he would not be surprised if it was in one of the lower levels of Hell.

A little reply box opened up on his screen. When the computer beeped, Wayne sat next to Noah on the bed and crowded nervously in to read the Instant Message text. He breathed shallowly to avoid Noah's too-strong aftershave.

Like most online messages, the IM was typed with a lazy eye toward punctuation and grammar.

WINGERDINGER: Coarse Im here asshole.

Noah took a deep breath before typing his next words.

NOAHMANSLAND: Blew mined too fast. Kitty not below. Waited 2 see if she come down after colapse like you said but no show. did not film her

WINGERDINGER: Thats cuz U are screwup. U screw up plane you screw up mine. U R M-O-R-O-N. Someone else did you're job. Check this out

An Internet address appeared in the IM box. Noah copied the URL with his mouse to the search bar at the top of the page and hit Enter. He was brought to a MyTube page.

The video started at once. There was the camera

holding steady on Arthur Welt of the Weltsburg Coal and Mining Company as, off-screen, Kitty Coughlin asked him a question. A distant boom. The next moment the elevator was bouncing in the shockwaves produced by the underground explosions and the camera had bobbed over to Kitty, latched to the metal floor grate and screaming in stark terror. She was still screaming when the elevator stopped and the video ran out. The word "Replay?" appeared on the screen.

Noah did not restart the video.

"Does this mean we're off the hook?" Wayne asked, picking at his chin zit. "Ask him if this means he's letting us off the hook."

With shaking hands, Noah typed.

NOAHMANSLAND: U have video. We dun now. No more problems? Wat about r ratings?

There was an agonizing pause as the two men waited for the reply to appear on the screen. When it finally did, their hearts sank.

WINGERDINGER: Will think aboutit. Meantime 3 of u get out of their

Noah glanced at Wayne before he typed a response.

NOAHMANSLAND: 2 of us

A pause, then, WINGERDINGER: ???

NOAHMANSLAND: SamEyeAm dead.

Noah was not surprised by the unsympathetic reply.

WINGERDINGER: How did fag screwup get himself killed?

Noah tried to think how to describe what they had seen down in the coal mine. How to best tell about the man who had come out of nowhere, the stranger who had no special equipment to see underground yet who had spotted the three hiding men. How they had tried to shoot him and how in pitch blackness he had avoided every one of their bullets and managed to kill Sam, whom they had only met three days before, and who they knew only by his online name "SamEyeAm."

Finally, Noah simply typed: Send snail mail addy. Will send you tape we took

The address that WingerDinger sent back was not from Hell, Noah was surprised to discover, but it was almost as close. Noah tore a page from the Bible in the nightstand and jotted down WingerDinger's Los Angeles suburb street address in the margin. Once he had the address copied down, he returned to his keyboard.

NOAHMANSLAND: U see this tape U fix rating and leaf us alone?

WINGERDINGER: Dont be such a whiny fagot u fagg. Send tape.

A little away message appeared in the My Pal box, signifying that their Instant Message conversation was over and that WingerDinger had left his computer. When Noah clicked on it it read, "NOAHMANSLAND IS A FAGGOT."

As Noah shut down the Instant Message box, Wayne pointed a shaking finger at the phrase. "That! That right there violates their stated terms of service! Why don't they kick him off, for God's sake? Why doesn't anyone ever ban him?"

"He's been banned a million times," Noah said, rubbing his exhausted eyes. "He just signs on as somebody else. He files complaints, wears them down. He wears everybody down. What'd he do with you? Department of Homeland Security?"

"Yeah. He was going to get me on a terrorist list. You too?"

"No. He said he was putting me on the child molester warning lists. Predators. My life'd be over. He nails us all with his complaints about what we're selling online and then he sneaks in and ruins our lives. Come on, let's get this over with and get out of here."

By the time the two men checked out of the motel most of the press had already left. There were coffee cups and doughnut bags all over the parking lot. The elderly motel owner was out with a big plastic garbage bag cursing under his breath as he picked up the mound of trash the press had dumped all over the ground. Two full bags were already piled near the office door.

Noah and Wayne collected their videocamera from the trunk of the Toyota. They drove around until they found the nearest OverNite Express office store. Noah carefully filled out the address the man he knew only as WingerDinger had IMed him, stuffed the mine tape inside the envelope and brought it inside to mail.

When he came back outside five minutes later, Noah saw Wayne hunched down in the passenger seat of the Toyota tearing at the bloody mess he had made of his acne-ravaged chin with stubby, shredded fingernails.

Wayne Dwyer was a completely pathetic figure, frightened of his own shadow. Noah was self aware enough to know that Wayne saw the same thing when he looked at Noah.

Noah sniffled. "Why did I put that Monty Python album up for sale as near-mint?" he asked the cruel heavens. "That let him into my life."

Trying desperately to hold back tears, Noah hustled across the sparsely filled parking lot to his waiting Toyota.

10

Smith had taken his small black-and-white television down from his office shelf and set it at the edge of his desk. Although his computer monitor could function as a TV screen, he needed the monitor to do the work of CURE.

Smith detested network news coverage, which was packaged as syrupy treacle designed to make the viewer feel good, overhyped medical scares designed to make the viewer feel frightened, human interest dramas designed to make the viewer feel compassion, and scandals—either corporate or governmental—designed to make the viewer feel angry.

The very idea that what passed for modern news was presented in such a way as to steer the viewer into a particular emotional box was abhorrent to the emotionless Smith. The news should be a dry recitation of the day's events with all emotion removed, thus allowing the viewer to make up his or her own mind about what they should feel, or whether they should feel anything at all.

Smith would not have set the television up at all if not for a report out of Weltsburg, Pennsylvania. A single, strange story late in the afternoon claimed that a mysterious figure had saved nineteen trapped miners from tragedy.

Remo had called earlier in the day to say that he and the Master of Sinanju were flying to Pennsylvania to question Kitty Coughlin once more. The mining accident had occurred while Remo was en route, and it was not much of a leap for Smith to figure out what had truly happened in Weltsburg.

Smith had breathed a sigh of relief when the one early story of a shadowy savior had been supplanted by a tale of more conventional heroism.

Once rescuers had gone down the shaft the miners had used to climb to safety and discovered the miners' own tools near the freshly dug tunnel, the one initial report had been overwhelmed by an avalanche of human interest stories about the plucky nineteen miners who had not waited for help but rather had saved themselves by using hand tools to dig through solid rock. Indeed, when the press caught up with two of the miners outside the Weltsburg Hospital emergency room, the story had obviously arrived before the reporters, most likely via cell phone or emergency room television. Confronted with the tale of their own heroism, the men had accepted the praise with humble nods as if they'd had a hand in their own miraculous rescue.

The miners were now being called the Weltsburg Nineteen on all the networks, and the earlier tragedy packaging of the story that was meant to make viewers feel bad had done a side shuffle worthy of Fred Astaire and had morphed into a series of feel-good news segments on what had now become an inspiring tale of human survival.

In his private office in Folcroft Sanitarium, Dr. Harold W. Smith alone knew the truth.

He was glancing at the small TV screen when the blue contact phone jangled to life. Smith grabbed the receiver on the first ring.

"Smith," he said, his voice tart with displeasure.

The CURE director's unhappiness was evident in one syllable and Remo said, "I guess good news travels fast."

Smith could practically see the smile on the face of CURE's enforcement arm. Smith reached over and turned the volume on his television all the way down.

"Remo, your actions in Weltsburg were irresponsible. You should never have involved yourself in that situation."

"Who says it was me?" Remo asked.

"It was him," Smith heard the Master of Sinanju's singsong voice call out.

Smith heard some rattling over the phone, then Chiun's voice, loud and clear as if he had just yanked the telephone from Remo's hand. "It was Remo, Emperor Smith. I tried to tell him that as Khufu did not halt construction of the Great Pyramid for the sake of a handful of trapped slaves, so too you would not want Remo distracted from his sacred mission to save a few sloppy laborers who got themselves stuck in some diamondless hole in the ground. But as usual my entreaties on your behalf fell on deaf ears."

Smith heard Remo in the background. "Speaking of deaf ears, Chiun, what were you saying before about reimbursing Smith for our flight from Florida?"

A frenzy of high-pitched Korean ensued, after which the Master of Sinanju fell silent and the phone clattered as if it had been dropped on the floor.

"Okay, Smitty, yeah," Remo said into the phone once the old Korean's tirade was over. "I saved those miners. So nineteen women aren't widows tonight. So what?"

"So including Florida that is two major news events you have involved yourself in this past week," Smith said.

"If you're about to harangue me about secrecy, I know the drill, Smitty. But has the mugger turned up in Florida yet? No. That's because Albondigas' goons have probably fed him to some alligators by now. Nice and neat and the bad guys do our work for us. As far as Pennsylvania's concerned, if you saw the news you saw that those miners are being credited for saving themselves. From here out they'll just chalk anything else up to hallucination and if they don't who'll listen to them? Again, nice and neat with a big pink bow on top. And for the cost of air fare I get to feel good for once. We may as well get something out of this trip, 'cause the Kitty angle was a bust."

Smith frowned. "Coughlin wasn't involved with the hijackers? What about the autographed photo?"

"The guy had it on the plane. He's the one who gave it to her to sign while they were storming the cockpit. Apparently she signs them for all her viewers. They're having a fan club meeting in a phone booth on Forty-third Street next week if you want to bring the dip."

Smith removed his glasses and placed them atop his gleaming desk. "If she did not supply the photo to him, clearly the hijackers knew she would be on that plane. The fact that the dead man had that photo is evidence enough."

"I said the same thing. But according to Kitty half the known world knew she was going to be on that plane. And thanks to that whackdoodle Internet the other half probably got i-mailed about it that morning."

"E-mailed," Smith corrected.

"Don't care," Remo said.

"But why would they stop in the middle of a hijacking to get her autograph? None of this makes sense."

"It makes even less sense," Remo said. "She says the guy was planning on selling it at some Internet outfit where geeks sell all kinds of different crap to other geeks. Ibbidy-bibbidy-bay or something equally stupid."

"Was it iBay?"

"Yeah, that was it. Is there a law that only stupid names are allowed on that World Wide Whatchamacallit?"

Smith replaced his glasses and gave them a push back up to the bridge of his nose. "This could be helpful, Remo," he said as he turned to his keyboard. "If the dead hijacker intended to sell the autographed photo on iBay, then maybe he had an account with them."

"You mean people really would waste good money on an autographed photo of Kitty Coughlin?" Remo asked. "I was hoping that was some big joke the world was playing on me."

Smith was at the main page of the iBay Web site. He crinkled his nose when he saw the number of categories listed. Although Smith was one of the pioneers of the electronic information age long before the terms Internet or World Wide Web had come into common parlance, this was one corner of the electronic ether that had thus far eluded him.

"Apparently you can purchase almost anything here," Smith commented as he read the list that included cars, jewelry, home furnishings, movie memorabilia and a hundred other categories. Rather than select a single category, he typed in "Kitty Coughlin" and "autograph" in the search bar on the main page. The answer came back instantaneously: # of auctions: 0.

"There are no Kitty Coughlin autographs currently up," Smith said.

"Chalk one up for sanity," Remo said.

"One moment, Remo." Smith removed Kitty's name from the bar and searched only for "autograph." The search results listed over fourteen thousand individual auctions for baseball cards alone. Thousands of other autographed items were listed in subcategories such as movie posters and books.

"It is likely he is here," the CURE director said in frustration. "His account would still be active after only a

week. But without more information to go on it would be
impossible to sift through all of these accounts. We do not
even know if he's auctioning other celebrity autographs.
He could be selling fish tanks or salt and pepper shakers."

"What about out in the real world where normal people
live?" Remo asked. "There's no leads on the parachutist?"

"Not yet. The FBI has taken over the investigation, but
their initial fingerprint analysis turned up nothing. Until
we have more to go on I'm afraid he's a dead end."

"So you're just going to let these guys walk?" Remo
said "Smitty, they almost knocked over the Empire State
Building."

"Remo, I'm not going to let anyone walk. But for right
now, we have nothing more to go on," Smith explained.
He leaned back in his chair, feeling every day of his
eighty-plus years in his tired joints.

"There's got to be something," Remo said. "I mean,
they didn't just drop out of the sky. Except at the end, when
they actually did drop out of the sky. Just go on those
computers of yours and find me somebody to whack."

"It's finished, Remo. At least for now." Smith allowed a
protracted sigh to slip from between his thin lips. "And
maybe there was nothing here all along."

"What do you mean?"

"It's possible this was an isolated group of maniac
thrill-seekers with no larger goal than an adrenaline rush.
Hopefully this is not the next step from hang-gliding off
volcanoes or bungee jumping from bridges. But if it is,
then maybe the presence of Kitty Coughlin's cameras on
the flight presented a showboating opportunity too great
to pass up. After all, they did not crash the plane. And it's
been over a week since the event and there has been no
claim of credit or terrorist chatter in the usual places."

"They killed a bunch of people," Remo pointed out.

The shadows on Smith's face lengthened. "Yes," he
said, clearly unhappy with the entire inexplicable situation.

It was Remo's turn to sigh. "I guess maybe it'd be nice

for us to luck out of the heavy lifting just once," he said. "So we can go home?"

"Yes. The whole matter stays open. Mark can continue to look into it. Perhaps there is a connection to Coughlin that she herself does not know."

"Oh, speaking of idiots with cameras, I almost forgot. Something weird happened when I was down that mine."

Remo went on to tell the CURE director about the three armed men with the camera that he had encountered in the deep coal tunnels below Weltsburg.

"You weren't filmed?" Smith gasped when he was through.

"Calm down, Smitty. You know how we can do that thing to make it so cameras can't see our faces. But it was weird. Anyway, I guess they haven't found the body yet or it would have been on the news. It was down a side tunnel and behind some rocks, so they could easily have missed it. Tell them to just follow the stink of man-perfume. One of the shooters must bathe in the stuff."

Smith's fluttering fingers found his keyboard and he began issuing circuitous commands to the proper authorities. "I will alert the FBI and local police to the body," Smith said. "Is there anything else?"

"Just the two guys who escaped. I didn't see them, so I can't ID them. They made some marks in the mud on an old access road. Maybe they can lift the tire marks and track them that way. That's how Barnaby Jones used to do it."

"Very well," Smith said, finishing typing with a flourish. His arthritic fingers fled the edge of his desk and the pulses of light from his keyboard faded to black. "The information is in the pipeline."

"I hope they get the scumbags. The guys must have been disgruntled mine workers or something. Only reason I can think of for them blowing the place up like that. But the one I whacked was the cleanest coal miner you've ever seen in your life. His fingernails were practically

manicured and it looked like he ordered his overalls from
L.L. Bean."

"If he was an employee of the Weltsburg Coal and
Mining Company, someone there will no doubt recognize
him."

A flickering image at the edge of his desk caught
Smith's eye. The evening news had just started. On the
small screen Kitty Coughlin stood next to her traveling
anchor desk in Pittsburgh, a sheaf of papers in her hand.
On a large screen over her shoulder was a still image of a
rescued miner embracing his sobbing wife. Superimposed
over the image was a caption that read, "Miracle in a
Mine."

"Hmm," Smith mused as, with the sound still turned
down, he watched Kitty read the day's events from the
BCN affiliate station in Pennsylvania.

"Something else, Smitty?" Remo asked.

"It's just odd," Smith said. "Kitty Coughlin has been at
the scene of two major news events in a single week. The
odds against that happening must be astronomical."

"So have I, but you don't hear me bragging about it.
Talk to you soon."

When the dial tone buzzed in his ear, Smith reached
over and dropped the blue phone back into its cradle.

Frowning, he watched Kitty Coughlin for a few more
seconds. She stood there with her fake smile, somber nod,
horse-like gums and a skirt far too short for a woman her
age. Beyond the surface distractions there was something
about the woman, even in silence, that irked Smith.

Finally, he shook his head. "Good night, Ms. Coughlin,"
Smith said.

Harold W. Smith reached over and like hundreds of
thousands of evening news viewers across the country at
that very moment flipped to another station.

11

The driver stopped his truck in front of the dropoff
box outside the OverNite Express at the small strip mall
just outside downtown Weltsburg, Pennsylvania. Wearing
blue short pants and matching short sleeve jersey, the
driver hustled down from his cab, a large plastic bin
under his arm.

Unlike the U.S. Postal Service, where a regular day's
delivery schedule could mean receiving Tuesday's mail
any time between 10:20 a.m. Tuesday and nine o'clock
Wednesday morning, OverNite Express held its drivers to
a strict schedule and by mid-morning the special packing
envelope mailed in Weltsburg had reached a regional
clearinghouse in Pittsburgh, and two hours later was on a
plane to California. An evening of processing at another
regional center in Los Angeles and by ten o'clock the
following morning a white truck with red and green
writing identical to the truck that had picked it up in

Pennsylvania pulled to a stop in front of dilapidated little house with a rusted chain-link fence.

The driver hustled through the gate which had been twisted on its hinges when it met the bumper of a car that turned around in front of the house. The fender bender had happened fourteen years before and the gate had been wedged open ever since.

The front lawn had little grass, many ceramic garden gnomes and far too many mismatched flower pots, only half of which contained flowers, all of them plastic.

The driver left the package inside the screen door, rang the bell once and darted back down the cracked cement front walk.

"You're supposed to wait for me to answer the door!" an angry nasal voice yelled at the driver just as he settled back behind the wheel and started the engine.

The driver was used to this customer. This had been his route for the past two years and he had delivered many packages to the tumbledown bungalow. From the cab of his truck he smiled and shrugged as if he did not understand. Waving to the customer, he quickly sped off.

"Slob," he muttered when in his sideview mirror he caught a glimpse of the figure in pajamas waving his fist on the crumbling cement steps.

The OverNite Express truck sped around a corner. Standing on his steps, express package in hand, the man in the pajamas seethed. Before turning for the door he noticed a young woman on the sidewalk across the street.

She was pretty, in her early thirties and was helping push along a tricycle on which sat an adorable little boy of about three. The woman scrupulously ignored the pajamas man.

There was a For Sale sign on her neatly tended lawn even though she and her husband had purchased the house across the street only six months before. Although they otherwise liked the neighborhood, they were selling so soon because of a problem with the pajama man nutcase across the street.

"Stop pedaling that bike on the sidewalk!" the pajama man shouted at the woman and shook his fist. "You're getting my flowers dirty!"

He turned on a mangy slipper and stomped inside, slamming the door so hard it shook the tiny bungalow.

Package in hand, he marched through the kitchen, its sink filled to overflowing with dirty pots, and clomped down the creaking cellar stairs.

The basement had been converted to a cheap rumpus room back in the 1970s, with plastic paneling, ugly yellowed suspended ceiling and painted cement floor. Eight computers, no two of them matching models, were lined up on a long shelf which consisted of a piece of cheap pressboard laid across stacks of cinder blocks.

He dropped the overnight envelope to the makeshift desk and slumped into a chair behind the Dell computer.

When he moved his mouse, the star field screen saver disappeared and Daisy O'Toole's massive face filled the monitor. He had been checking for updates on Daisy's "Pretty Kitty" page, but the erstwhile comedienne had not yet bothered to update her Flight 980 observations.

His pudgy fingers pulled up the OverNite Express Web page from a list of "Favorite Places." He went to the Help page, found the Comments section and typed out a note. Unlike his sloppy, hastily typed instant messages, he was careful with spelling and punctuation.

I am very unhappy with the service I have received from your company, particularly the cretin driver who delivers to my home. I have told this moron repeatedly that I do not want him to abandon packages on my step, but he is too stupid to get it. I want my packages delivered INTO MY HANDS, not left out where any passing thief can steal them. I expect to hear back from you promptly on this

matter and at this point the only satisfactory
conclusion for me would be for you to fire this
retard and hire somebody who understands PLAIN
ENGLISH.
Also I have told you before that I do not think
you should call your company OverNite Express
when packages like this one take two nights to
get here. Mexicans on siesta are more efficient
than you incompetent idiots. Rest assured I will
be in touch with the Better Business Bureau over
this matter.

He typed "sincerely" but rethought it, deleted the word
and merely typed his name: Orville Wilbur Feldon.

Feldon filled out the other required lines on the form,
which included his address, package tracking code and a
daytime telephone number where he could be reached,
and when he was done he pressed Send and watched the
latest in a line of thousands of irate notes—and one of
nearly fifty he had sent to OverNite Express—disappear
into the electronic ether. Only when he was finished did
he turn his attention to the package from Pennsylvania.

Feldon tore open the perforated strip at the envelope's
edge and shook the videotape into his palm.

One wall of the basement was lined with shelves
loaded with hundreds of videotapes. A dozen television
sets were arranged before the wall of tapes. They sat on
tables, plastic milk crates and on one upended wicker
laundry basket. The oldest dated back to the late 1970s,
the newest and biggest had been purchased just two
months before.

The corner of the basement looked like the elephants'
graveyard of broken television sets. Junk TVs of various
sizes were stacked eight deep and nearly reached the
suspended ceiling. A furnace repairman, stunned by
the sheer number of TV sets, had once tried to count the
number of dead televisions but had only gotten up to

twenty-eight before he was caught by Orville Wilbur Feldon who, after calling him a "lazy, nosy pedophile" had sent a nasty note to the repairman's company which resulted in years of jokes at Feldon's expense at the small company's headquarters and an edict from the owner that none of his furnace repairmen would ever answer a call from Orville Wilbur Feldon again.

Five of the televisions were turned on and tuned to different channels. Feldon waddled to the nearest working television and slipped the tape into the VCR that sat on top.

He could not imagine what Noah Sherman thought he had taped down in that mine. The fact that he had taped anything was amazing to Feldon.

Feldon had found the old Weltsburg Coal and Mining Company maps online on a history buff's lonely little Web site which was devoted to Pennsylvania coal mining. The mines were abandoned, but were in close enough proximity to the working mines that the explosives Feldon had supplied would do the trick and bring down the ceiling of the active vein. But the old mines were virtually forgotten and the mining company's equipment and personnel were a mile away aboveground, so the likelihood of anyone finding their way down to those old tunnels was virtually nil.

Feldon had ordered Noah Sherman and the others to stay put after the explosion knowing full well that they would have nothing to do. It was a little test Feldon had, a personal joke to see how long the morons would sit alone in the dark before finally giving up and coming up for air. The thought of the three of them crouching terrified in that lost mine had given Orville Wilbur Feldon a rare moment of joy. And now Noah Sherman had taken that joy away by leaving the mine two days earlier than Feldon had anticipated and by telling Feldon that one of his companions was dead.

"This better be good, you stupid son of a barley

harvester," Feldon said as the VCR clicked and whirred and the word "Play" appeared on the screen.

At first there was nothing. The special night-sensitive camera turned the black walls and floor of the cave to shades of white and gray. Feldon was already plotting revenge against Noah for wasting his time and was leaning forward to pop the tape from the VCR when a person appeared on the screen.

Like the caves, the stranger's clothes were a weird, washed-out white. Feldon leaned further toward the screen to try to see the man's face, but there was something wrong with the VCR. The face of the man on the tape was an indecipherable blur.

The man's body was perfectly visible, the lines sharp and distinct from the background. It was only when one got above the neck that the blurring started. Feldon assumed it was a problem with the camera. He was already composing a letter of complaint to the Japanese company from which he'd purchased the device when something happened on-screen that made him momentarily forget about e-mailing the Nishitsu Corporation.

The ghostly figure with the blurry face turned and waved to the camera. Nearby, the audio picked up gasps from Noah and the other men. The cameraman did his best to hold the videocamera steady during the chorus of gunfire that ensued.

The ghostly stranger did not die. He picked up something, hurled it toward the camera, and the world suddenly went crazy. The camera bucked, sweeping crazily from ceiling to floor. For a flash Feldon saw the body of SamEyeAm@AIC.com, a gaping hole clear through both night vision goggles and face. And then he heard WayneThePain8 gasp "Holy Christmas," the camera went crazy once more, and all Feldon saw was feet and a bouncing backward view of the tunnel as the two remaining men ran for all they were worth to the surface.

Orville Wilbur Feldon failed to see what was so special

about the man on the tape. It was just some guy who could throw a rock hard. So he had good aim, so what? Baseball players could throw hard and fast. Nothing special there. And so what if the three men had been such lousy shots they failed to hit him? If Noah Sherman, who ran like a little sissy-pansy girl at the first sign of trouble, thought that there was something miraculous about the footage that would convince Feldon to let him and that worthless WayneThePain off the hook, he was even dumber than his Yahoo profile let on.

Feldon popped the tape from the VCR.

The instant the VCR stopped running, normal TV function resumed. The television was tuned to BCN. Feldon had expected word on Kitty Coughlin's firing by now, as well as coverage of nineteen dead miners. Instead he had neither.

The regular BCN morning show was playing. A young blond woman was interviewing two ordinary housewives who had started a business making aprons from old wedding dresses.

"We figured you might as well get some use out of them!" one of the ordinary housewives, now a millionairess, exclaimed as her partner shrieked with laughter. The interviewer shrieked in delight as well.

Feldon punched down the volume so violently he snapped the panel on the front of the TV.

He waddled over to his Compaq computer. This computer, like all his others, was constantly online. He noted that there were nearly one hundred e-mails since he last checked an hour ago, all with subject lines like, "Please, won't you PLEASE stop?" and "I refunded money! Leave me alone!!"

Feldon ignored the mewling e-mails. He pulled up the latest MyTube Kitty Coughlin footage.

There was Kitty, the fifteen-million-dollar-a-year anchorwoman, losing her cool yet again. And no one in the dinosaur news had even noticed. In fact, for the past two nights the BCN Evening News had broadcast footage of Kitty ostensibly recorded down in the mine before the explosion. But that footage had obviously been doctored and restaged, just as had been done to cover up for her Flight 980 panic attack. The Kitty on broadcast television was not screaming; she was not lying on the floor of the elevator. She was every inch the professional anchorwoman, and when the sound-effects explosion came, Kitty Coughlin was calm and cool in the face of adversity.

Thankfully Kitty had ticked off another cameraman. Feldon had traced this latest MyTube account back to a BCN employee in Pittsburgh. If not for yet another irate underling, this footage would probably have been buried forever. Not that its presence on MyTube mattered to the fossils of network news, whose only knowledge of the Internet was that it had been created by the candidate they had endorsed for president back in 2000.

"Obviously I've got more work to do," Feldon said. He pulled up Kitty Coughlin's globe-trotting itinerary for the coming week from the BCN News main Web page, thought better of it, and set it temporarily aside. "But first things first," he grunted.

Feldon had some e-mail notes to write. The first to JVC to complain about TV volume controls that cracked at the slightest touch, the second to gripe at Nishitsu about their defective night vision videocamera that somehow blurred out the faces of perfectly ordinary human beings.

12

"The worst was those damned stuffed seals," the sailor at the end of the Anchorage, Alaska, tavern confided in a boozy whisper. "I don't know who started that. Greenpeace, PETA, those Sierra Club bastards. They used to send 'em to me by the bushel. They get these cute little stuffed seals, see, and then they pour motor oil on them. Then they put them in Ziploc bags and send them with notes like 'Seal Killer.' These are environmentalists, mind you. You tell me, is that good for the environment? A whole bunch of stuffed toys dripping with WD-40? My bosses had a hell of a time just disposing of them. By that point they all had their piggy little eyes on us, so we couldn't just toss them in the Dumpster. They were hazardous waste. Damned stuffed seals."

The sailor hunched over his whiskey muttering unintelligible curses.

"Well, I think you got a bum rap, captain," said the man on the green nylon barstool with the taped-up tear.

Robert Eaglemeyer's back stiffened at the use of his old rank. "I haven't been a captain in twenty years."

"That's an outrage, captain," insisted the new best friend of former captain, now lowly second mate, Robert Standrill Eaglemeyer. "That cover of *Newsweek* where they called you Environmental Enemy #1? Outrageous. And that was right after Chernobyl, wasn't it?"

"Damn straight," Eaglemeyer slurred. "But you gotta remember that the Russkies could do no wrong. They drain lakes, create deserts, dump tons after tons of nuclear waste in the Arctic Circle and then top it off with the biggest radioactive disaster in history. There's reindeer still glowing in goddamned Norway and nobody says nothing about the damn Russians. But me? I slam one dinky little oil tanker aground in Chignik Bay, dump a few thousand gallons of crude on a few miles of deserted coast, and I'm the bad guy. Thank God for Hazelton and the *Exxon Valdez* with their bigger spill. If it wasn't for him they'd still be pillorying me."

"It's an outrage that they won't let you captain another ship," said former Captain Eaglemeyer's sympathetic friend. "Here, let me buy you another drink."

Eaglemeyer decided that he loved his new friend. This was a great man. Pasty, tubby, twitchy, and with a bad case of acne, sure, but still great. He understood. Really understood.

Eaglemeyer's new friend understood through another whole bottle of whiskey poured on top of an already active evening of boozing. And he understood when the Chugach Tavern became a murky, spinning haze from too much drink. He understood with another bottle for the road, and he understood when the van stopped and a stranger Eaglemeyer had never met along with his new best friend pushed the staggering ex-captain into the back. And then Robert Eaglemeyer didn't really much care who understood anything because he lay sprawled on a pile of beeping electronic gizmos, and blacked out for the night, cursing the army of little stuffed white seals dripping black goo that came to him in his nightmares.

When consciousness at last returned, it was the all-too-familiar pounding of an ill-spent night that roused Robert Eaglemeyer from his drunken coma.

It was morning.

Eaglemeyer opened his eyes on the ugly white sunlight of a brand new day. His bloodshot eyes felt huge and rough. It hurt to blink. His brain felt too big for his head. The right side of his chest and his right shoulder were damp.

Groggily, Eaglemeyer pulled himself up to a sitting position. He had passed out on the floor again. But for some reason the floor of his Anchorage apartment was metal and he was damp because there was vomit on his uniform.

He did not remember changing into his old uniform. It was the one he had worn that fateful day twenty years before, the day of Chignik Bay, the last day his employers at Motiv Petroleum had allowed him to dress in captain's livery.

The pounding was getting louder. Usually it was in his brain but this time it was in his ears as well and rather than the usual throb of coursing blood, this morning his hangover sounded very strange, like shouting voices.

"Open the door! For God's sake, Eaglemeyer!"

It took Eaglemeyer a long moment to orient himself. It was with a sinking feeling that he at last realized he wasn't in his apartment. He was on a ship. He blinked at the familiar bridge of his supertanker, the *Motiv Kodiak*.

"Eaglemeyer! Eaglemeyer, turn to port! To port!"

More pounding, but this time he realized that it was external and not inside his foggy brain.

A desperate-eyed man was pounding on a window with a fire extinguisher, but the thick Plexiglas refused to break. More pounding at locked doors. Banging all around.

"Hard to port! Hard to port, now!"

Eaglemeyer dragged himself to his feet with the intention of opening the locked door and finding out just what the hell was going on. An empty Seagram's bottle rolled away as he got to his knees. As he grabbed the navigation console for support, he stumbled and finally realized that the sense of forward motion he had been feeling was not disorientation from his hangover.

The boat was moving. Confusion was seeping deep into the core of his fuzzy brain as Eaglemeyer glanced out the front windshields. For a moment he felt his heart stop.

The old sailor had spent much of the past two decades at the bottom of a bottle thanks to the accident that had cost him his captaincy. He had tried dozens of hangover cures and none of them had ever worked, but now, for the first time in his drunken life, Eaglemeyer felt the boozy cloud of a night of binge drinking burn away like a daybreak fog touched by a suddenly risen sun.

The tanker was moving fast at thirty knots through Prince William Sound. To port was Montague Island. There was no way to turn the vessel sharp at such speed without running aground. His first instinct would have been to reduce speed until the tanker had cut wide around Cape Clear and then slow to a full stop in the Gulf of Alaska. Unfortunately Eaglemeyer could not take those necessary steps toward course correction because he saw, with mounting horror, that a Carousal Cruise passenger liner was dead ahead of him.

The deck of the Alaska cruise liner was filled with tourists. Eaglemeyer could see the vast white walls of three icebergs floating to the cruise ship's port, one just off her bow. The captain of the liner was adjusting course to get out of the path of the speeding tanker, but his only choice was to nudge into the nearest and largest iceberg.

Eaglemeyer's instincts kicked in. He grabbed for the controls. They were locked. Wires hung out of open panels and were spliced into one another in a configuration that Eaglemeyer could not begin to understand. Since regaining consciousness he had been aware of a tiny electronic beeping noise, a sound new to the *Kodiak*'s bridge.

The ex-captain followed loose wires underneath the computerized navigation console to a tiny silver box with a blinking red light and a silver antenna.

It was a tiny receiver. Someone was controlling the tanker from a remote location.

Eaglemeyer kicked the box free with the heel of his shoe and tore away the wires.

"Eaglemeyer! Eaglemeyer!"

No time to unlock the door, which he saw now was melted at the edges, as if it had been welded shut.

The former captain threw his wet shoulder hard into the wheel. He could feel the ship respond. It was slow; metal groaned. Through the soles of his shoes he could feel more than fifty thousand gallons of crude oil roll lazily in the *Kodiak*'s deep belly. Eaglemeyer held fast. His shoulder ached, sweat broke out on his forehead.

For the next tense minutes Robert Standrill Eaglemeyer tuned out the shouting and the pounding. Someone had found some acetylene torches. He was vaguely aware of a spark of light cutting a glowing rim around the fused door.

The tanker and the cruise liner met. The bow of the cruise ship brushed the *Kodiak* at midship touching metal to starboard and ice to port. Chunks of iceberg exploded across the decks of both ships as the liner was squeezed between the *Motiv Kodiak* and the floating wall of ice.

The scraping seemed to go on forever, and when it finally stopped the silence was like thunder.

But the liner was clear. The cruise ship would be safe but the *Kodiak* would not be so lucky. There was no way for the tanker to steer a clear course. They were going too fast, the land was too close. Eaglemeyer saw the black rocks rise from the waves.

Eaglemeyer did not care that the rocks of Montague Island were racing toward him, did not notice that the men outside the door had abandoned their torches and were now racing for the rear of the vessel, did not care if a thousand stuffed seals dripping in oil found their way into his mailbox. At first they would say it was his fault but he knew the truth. The man at the bar that he thought was a friend might have rewired the tanker but Robert Eaglemeyer, *Newsweek*'s Public Enemy #1, had saved the day. And the world would soon know it. Redemption had come at last for Captain Robert Eaglemeyer.

Another little beep. Eaglemeyer realized there must be another remote-controlled box on the bridge. He was surprised at his calm as he went to find it.

He located it in a rear storage locker. But rather than a little steel box, this device was a plastic block the size of a brick. It was wrapped all around with tape.

The ship lurched. Eaglemeyer felt the scrape of metal deep below as the hull of the *Kodiak* was wrenched apart by a series of ever deeper gashes.

Alarm lights blinked on all around him, yet Eaglemeyer was strangely fixated on the little square of plastic fastened to the shelf of the storage locker. But when he reached for it this time, the little light that had been blinking yellow suddenly blinked red once, and Captain Robert Eaglemeyer, whose heroism in his final moments would never be known, was blown into a thousand chunks in an explosion that obliterated both the bridge of the *Motiv Kodiak* and the former captain whose mind in the last minutes of life was, for the first time in many years, blessedly free of images of oily toy seals.

On the Carousal Cruise *Alaska Serenade*, alarms blared. Seawater poured in through the gash in her side. The ship listed and deck chairs began a slow slide to port. Panicked passengers shouted even as the captain's calm voice over the speaker system assured everyone that they had passed through the worst of it and that the water from the impact was contained.

Far back in the *Alaska Serenade*'s wake, the *Motiv Kodiak* buckled at the center like a crushed soda can and cracked in two. Her bridge erupted in a ball of orange flame and a black ooze spread across the waves from her open hull, rolling onto the western shore of Montague Island.

The *Serenade*'s harried doctor noted the oil spill even as he hurried forward, black bag in hand. He had been called from attending the bumps and scrapes of the injured in the infirmary to deal with a particularly hysterical passenger.

The woman had latched onto a railing when the two ships collided and now would not budge.

She was screaming so hard the ship's doctor had to medicate her. Only when the sedative kicked in were three pursers able to pry her from the railing beneath the hanging Japanese lanterns on the *Alaska Serenade*'s Kenai Deck.

"It's all right," the doctor soothed. "Shhh."

The woman's eyes rolled back in her head. The doctor noted that she had obviously had recent work done on her eyes. "Refreshing" was the term they were using for eye lifts now. In the opinion of the ship's doctor, plastic surgeons were butchers who were transforming millions of normal-looking women into cats who could not blink.

Something hard bumped the doctor's elbow and he turned in irritation.

"Do you have to keep doing that?" he asked the nearby cameraman who was swinging his lens back and forth between the dramatic oil spill and the drugged woman.

"When I tried to get in the car with her this morning, she slammed the door on my leg and told me I was a glorified tripod and that I should take a cab," the cameraman on loan from BCN's Anchorage affiliate said. "If I drown, no way I'm letting the world miss this."

"La, la, la, just take a little off the neck, doctor," sang Kitty Coughlin as she lapsed into unconsciousness.

Her note cards, on which were hard-hitting questions about Alaska cruise tours taking advantage of global warming by ferrying passengers through fields of pretty floating ice covered in polar bears, slipped from her fingers and were carried by the cold breeze into the dark—slowly growing darker—waters of Prince William Sound.

Mark Howard locked his office door, settled in
behind his scarred oak desk and, with a sigh, popped the
tab on the can and took a sip of the vile-tasting cola.

The soda had twice the caffeine of normal cola and
was supposed to give an energy boost. Mark could use
that energy now as he pressed the hidden stud beneath
the edge of his desk and waited for his computer monitor
and keyboard to rise up from beneath the desk's surface.

Since it was no longer an active CURE mission, Dr.
Smith had left the matter of the Flight 980 hijacking
solely in Mark's hands, to be worked on in the assistant
CURE director's spare time. So in addition to his regular
duties, Mark had carved out an hour each day to devote to
Flight 980. But the trail—if there had ever even been a
trail—had long grown cold. The FBI had turned up
nothing, in large part thanks to the security blunders at
LaGuardia. The last lead had been Kitty Coughlin but

Remo had questioned her in Pennsylvania days ago and that had wound up a dead end.

There was still though the matter of iBay and Dr. Smith's assertion that the dead hijacker had been a member of the auction site. If that were the case, the parachutist's account would have gone fallow when he died. Smith had created a program to sift through expired auctions, as well as accounts that had abruptly gone inactive around the day of the hijacking. But a dormant account was not necessarily a dead account. Mark quickly found that many accounts that remained inactive for days or weeks often saw an abrupt resumption of activity. He assumed their owners lost interest in them temporarily until they discovered more junk in basement or attic to foist on a public desperate for vintage Monkees lunch pails and 1947 Singer sewing machines. There was also the matter of accounts set aside due to illness, vacation, work obligations or a thousand other reasons.

With hundreds of thousands of individuals logging in and off the iBay site every hour of every day, tracking suspected dead accounts was impossible. Mark spent yet another hour this day blindly sifting through dead and dormant accounts, with an eye on those accounts specializing in autographs, only to finally throw up his hands in surrender. With no account number, no name and no Internet address, finding the dead man's identity through iBay could not be done.

Mark took a gulp of his soda which had long gone warm and squeezed his eyes shut.

Given more time it might be possible. The Folcroft computers would be able to winnow down the numbers, but the accounts would have to be dead for weeks, not days.

Mark was leaning back in his chair, head resting against the wall, when his computer beeped.

He had stared at his monitor too long and then had pinched his eyes too tightly shut. When he opened them he had to blink several times to clear the spots of bright white light.

When Mark saw the bright blue text, his eyes and brain cleared at once. He had color-coded the alerts on his system. Bright blue meant that CURE's basement mainframes had discovered something connected to the Flight 980 case.

Mark frowned when he saw the story that the mainframes had directed to him. Apparently there had been an accident in Prince William Sound. An oil tanker had hit a pleasure cruise ship before running aground.

It was a disaster to be sure, but an oil spill was not the sort of thing that would ordinarily have drawn the ever-vigilant electronic eyes of the Folcroft mainframes.

As Mark scanned the story, which had been posted at the official Web site of BCN News, he grew more confused. Just an oil spill. A bad one to be sure, with thousands of gallons of crude lost, but an accident nonetheless.

For a moment Mark thought he had set his color code wrong and that this was a new crisis. But CURE's computers were programmed to track threats to the United States, both domestic and foreign. Short of terrorist involvement, Mark could not see how this was a CURE affair.

Only when he reached the very last sentence did he realize the Flight 980 connection. The article suggested that readers who wanted to learn more about the spill should tune in to the BCN Evening News for anchor Kitty Coughlin's eyewitness account of what the network was dubbing "Tanker Tragedy in Alaska."

The CURE computers did not know what to make of it, only that Kitty Coughlin had been linked to another news event.

Mark quickly searched BCN's travel records for Kitty Coughlin's itinerary. There were several stops in Alaska set for that day, including a few hours booked aboard the cruise ship that had been sideswiped by Motiv Petroleum's tanker. BCN's star anchor was scheduled to broadcast the evening news from Anchorage the next two evenings.

When his research was finished a moment later, Mark understood why an alarm had gone off for Folcroft's mainframes. One was ringing in his own head as well.

Mark possessed an intuitive sense that allowed him to see that which others could not. As a child Mark's siblings refused to assemble jigsaw puzzles with him due to the frustrating fact that, no matter how difficult the puzzle, Mark could put it together as if each individual piece were stamped with numbers that he alone could see. Two hundred pieces or two thousand, it didn't matter. As his older brothers and sisters searched for the duck's bill or the pony's leg, little Mark would sit at the end of the table, his legs kicking at air, lost in concentration as he click-click-clicked pieces together as if he had memorized the order in which they went. While everyone else limited themselves to houses, fences or roads, Mark simply went from the nearest section, from one color to the next, finishing off row after row until he had completed the puzzle practically by himself and, in the process, chased his angry siblings away.

Mark had carried this ability into adulthood. Whereas as a child he literally had the ability to see the whole picture while others only saw puzzle pieces, as an adult this gift extended to his work as an analyst for the CIA. Several years before, while with Dr. Smith in communist North Korea, Mark's ability to see clearly that which others could not had helped save Remo's and Chiun's lives.

So when he felt the familiar brush of his sixth sense at the back of his neck, Mark did not resist but allowed the sensation to wash over him.

An oil tanker run aground in Prince Edward Sound. Kitty Coughlin was there.

A hijacked plane nearly flying into the most famous skyscraper in New York with Kitty Coughlin on board.

The mine collapse in Pennsylvania. Not an accident

but blown up deliberately. A body had been found right where Remo had said but it carried no identification. And BCN's anchorwoman had been in Weltsburg as well.

In a flash Mark knew.

Scarcely pausing to shut down his computer, Mark raced out into the hallway. Mrs. Mikulka was at her post outside Smith's closed office door. Mark darted past her so quickly that she did not have time to cluck disapproval.

"They're all connected," Mark blurted, once he had closed Smith's office door behind him, shutting out Mrs. Mikulka's displeased expression.

Smith glanced up from his work. "What is?"

"Everything," Mark insisted. "We didn't see it with that coal mine and Flight 980 because there wasn't a pattern. It's hard to establish a pattern with two points. But we've got three now. Dr. Smith, they're reenacting disasters."

"Mark, what are you talking about?"

"The tanker in Alaska. Did you see it?"

Smith nodded. "Yes, but I fail to see—"

"Kitty Coughlin was there. She was on board the cruise ship the tanker nearly collided with."

This got a reaction from Smith. Frown lines drew deep around his thin lips as the older man pulled up the story on his computer.

"That's a replay of the *Exxon Valdez*," Mark said as Smith's gray eyes scanned the news story. "Last week was the coal mine collapse in Pennsylvania. That was a huge story when those miners were killed a few years back. They milked that on the evening news for days. And that plane that nearly hit the Empire State Building? It was 9/11 again, except they did it on the first of May. 'Mayday on May Day.' Now there's 'Tanker Tragedy in Alaska.' Dr. Smith, the originals were some of the biggest news stories the networks have ever seen. The news divisions cut into prime time programming for them, they ran updates all day, the morning shows were completely turned over to the nightly newspeople. And now it's happening again and Kitty Coughlin's been on the scene of all three."

Smith had finished reading the short article. Once he had allowed the story as well as Mark's words to sink in, he shook his head in disbelief.

"Could they be so mad?"

"I think they proved that when they paid Kitty Coughlin her first fifteen million dollars," Mark said. "Network news is cutthroat ratings game, Dr. Smith. And Kitty Coughlin was supposed to save BCN when they bought her away from that morning show she cohosted, except she's the worst anchor they've ever had and she's been in the toilet since she premiered. She had to do something to boost her ratings."

Smith glanced up at his subordinate. "No," he said firmly. "Remo questioned Ms. Coughlin. He says that she was not involved in the Flight 980 incident, and I trust that he elicited the truth from her. If it is a scheme to increase BCN's ratings, she is unaware of the plot."

"So who is it?" Mark asked.

Smith nodded thoughtfully. "Whoever else at the network would benefit from a ratings spike." he said.

Chair creaking as he leaned forward, the CURE director stretched a hand toward the blue contact phone.

14

Uriah Maddox skulked through the darkened
executive corridors of BCN Evening News headquarters
and lamented his miserable lot in life. Eight months ago
he was a rising star in BCN Sports and now, like poor
Robert Eaglemeyer up in Alaska, whose fiery death
BCN was playing wall-to-wall, Maddox was master and
commander of a doomed vessel.

As with the mine collapse and the Flight 980 near-
tragedy, BCN was experiencing another ratings spike.
But that was only due to Kitty Coughlin's eyewitness
footage. The novelty would wear out quickly, and viewers
would once more begin switching away in droves.

The Broadcast Corporation of North America had
once been known as the Diamond Network thanks to its
high standards of quality. But the news division was
sinking and taking the entire staff along with it. Including
Uriah Maddox.

It had not been this way at sports, where Maddox had

started out and where BCN killed everybody in the ratings. For the seven years Maddox had been there, his sports division job had been a dream come true. Fights, adrenaline, thrills. All those lithe young athletes in their tight uniforms.

Maddox never played sports himself. His bad knees, weak ankles, glass jaw and asthma kept him from track and field, basketball, contact sports of any kind; even figure skating, for which he had a particular affinity. Chronic earaches and a fear of diving boards kept him out of swimming pools. Once in college he had tried to catch a Frisbee but broke his glasses and had to get his eye stitched.

But although he could not play the games himself, the sports division had been a sheer delight. It was his own fault that he had been bounced from sports to news.

How was he to know that the handsome young quarterback he fancied was the nephew of the network president? The boy had never told Maddox, that was certain. It was all his bosses could do to keep that blind item out of Page Six. Maddox was forced by the higher-ups to part ways with his lovely young friend. To ensure they remained apart he had been sent over to news.

It was only out of fear of a civil rights sexual preference lawsuit that BCN had kept him on at all. Little did they know Maddox was more than eager to keep his mouth shut. Maddox was terrified of the notoriety such a scandal would bring, for if word got out that he was diddling athletes he would never get a job in the sports division of a competing network.

How on earth that dreadful man with the lemon voice from the Department of Homeland Security had found out about the hushed-up scandal was beyond Maddox.

Thinking evil thoughts about the government, Kitty Coughlin and network news in general, Maddox entered his large office suite and passed his secretary's empty desk.

He heard the television blaring in his inner sanctum. Funny, he did not remember leaving one on. Maddox pushed open the door to his private office and was shocked to find two men waiting for him inside.

The young Homeland Security agent was wearing a dark green T-shirt and tan chinos. His back was to the door as he stared out at the steel and glass canyons of Manhattan.

The old Homeland Security consultant was sitting on top of Uriah Maddox's desk. A wall of TV monitors kept track of competing network news. The tiny Asian had switched them all to a single station. On every screen a bozo-haired judge was screaming at a pair of toothless twenty-year-old litigants.

"You're both idiots," the woman shouted. "You know how many years of postgraduate work I did? You know how many years I've been a judge? And I'm reduced to sorting through the credit card bills of a couple of morons like you two."

Uriah Maddox stopped in the doorway and planted his hands firmly on his hips.

"What are you two doing here?" he demanded.

"Me, I'm working," Remo said. "He's watching TV."

"I am working too," Chiun sniffed, eyes glued to the wall of televisions. "As with Rome before it, someone must record for the Masters' scrolls details of the decline of so-called American civilization. Now hush, Remo. If you must make noise do so elsewhere and let me work in peace."

Remo crossed over to Maddox. "He calls that work but he knows I'm the one working here," he whispered. "It's all the time work, work, work. Let's go, Mary."

Maddox was certainly not going anywhere with this heathen, no matter how deep and soulful his eyes. These maniacs had broken into his office and Uriah Maddox was going to call security and have them removed. At least that's what he intended to do. That suddenly became

much more difficult a plan to act on. It was difficult
because calling security was hard to do when one has been
rolled up in the Oriental rug from in front of one's office
fireplace and hauled up to the roof of one's building.

Remo flicked Maddox out of the rug in a rolling
tumble of arms and legs.

"What on earth is wrong with you?" Maddox gasped,
getting woozily to his feet and spitting out carpet fibers.
Dusk had fallen over Manhattan. The background glow
of the city was a cold light, surrendering no warmth to the
chill air. "You people blackmail me into granting you an
interview with Kitty. God help me, I even let you know
where she was in Pennsylvania. Wasn't that enough?
Here! Stop that!"

"Here's the thing," Remo said, taking Maddox by one
ankle and flipping him upside-down. "We're going to
play a new game I just invented called 'Oopsie.' It's like
twenty questions, but with an exciting twist. If you
answer the questions to my satisfaction, I don't drop you.
If at any time I think you are being less than forthcoming,
we jump right to the splat round."

"Splat round?" Maddox demanded, the blood rushing
to his head. His necktie fell in front of his face and he
tried swatting it to one side. "What are you talking about,
splat round? Let me go, you hateful crazy man."

"Oopsie, round one," Remo said.

Remo dragged Maddox to the ledge, lifted him up and
dangled him effortlessly over the side of the building.
Maddox felt his heart shoot into his throat. He tried to
swallow it back down as he took in the terrifying upside-
down view of lighted skyscrapers and the gray dusk sky
over Manhattan. Far below, he heard the honking horns
of the evening traffic battling along Forty-third Street.

Maddox found his voice. He screeched. Remo banged
him against the side of the building.

"Sorry," Remo said, leaning over the building and
shrugging a sympathetic apology. "I should have

mentioned that. If you scream like a girl you get a penalty whap. Okay, first question. And remember, you don't want to get an 'oopsie.' Who is re-creating all these news stories?"

"What?" Maddox asked.

"Oopsie," Remo said.

Maddox felt a sudden sensation of total weightlessness as Remo released him, then he felt the sure pull of gravity and he was plummeting to the street below. He screeched, but the scream turned to a gasp when, after only falling a foot, he felt a tug at his ankle.

"Penalty whap," Remo said, banging the news executive's head against black granite. "Are you behind it?"

"Behind what? I don't even know what you're talking about. What do you mean re-creating news stories?"

"The tanker, that mine, that plane. They're all replays of past disasters. And your star reporter with the donkey gums was at the scene of all of them."

"Coincidence," Maddox insisted.

"I think someone's itching for an oopsie."

"I swear it!" Maddox pleaded. "If that's what's happening it has to be a coincidence."

"Oopsie," Remo said.

Another terrifying drop, only to be snagged at the last minute. One more penalty whap for screeching and Uriah felt himself being lifted back up to the roof line.

"Maybe it's not a coincidence but I swear it's not us doing it," he gasped. "It's not anyone at the network. I'm all alone here." He was holding back tears. "They stuck me over in news and hung me out to dry with this ratings poison shrew. If anything they want me to fail so they can fire me. They'd love the same thing for Kitty, but as much as they'd like to they can't fire her. They're stuck with her for three more years."

"Why are they so upset with her? They were the ones who paid her millions to get her."

"And she's wound up costing millions. The network

would love to unload her but she's got a pay-or-play contract so she gets her money whether she's on- air or not. For the kind of money they have to shell out they're going to run out the clock. But at this point they're done trying to help her. They tried everything to fix the ratings freefall and nothing worked. They're counting down the days till she's through."

"But these stories are helping her ratings."

"Barely. She's gotten a bounce all three times but manages to piss it away in a day or two. Anyone else could have held on for weeks, even months, after being on the scene of so many major news stories. The footage that's being collected is phenomenal. Once we edit out her panic attacks, of course. We can't let the viewers see her in full screech mode. That'd really send the brass down on me. Their million-dollar baby exposed as the wimp she is. She's never even gone to Iraq or Afghanistan. Too scared."

"Nothing wrong with being scared," Remo said. "We have a saying back in the old country. 'The mind rules the body, but fear rules the mind.'"

"Please don't drop me for saying so, but that sounds like it's saying fear is a bad thing," Maddox said.

"Does it? Yeah, maybe you're right. What's the one I want? 'Fear keeps a man always a child.' 'In fear is born a fool's courage.' No. I don't know. I'm not good at quotations. Anyway, there was one about fear being a good thing in certain circumstances."

"It's not good when you've paid millions of dollars for an anchor and she's afraid of getting monkey poop in her hair," Maddox said. He found that if he kept his eyes squinted shut he could pretend he was not being held out fifty stories over Manhattan. "The spectacular tanker footage we got today was nearly spoiled because the cameraman kept focusing on Kitty screaming her fool head off. Not that the edits ultimately matter. Nothing will help her. Please, you have to believe me that the network is definitely not behind all this. If someone's trying to help her, it's from outside BCN. Can I come up now?"

Remo knew the executive was telling the truth. Maddox was not behind the disasters, nor did he have any idea who was. "Figures," Remo grunted. "Nothing's ever easy for me."

When Maddox felt the sensation of movement he squeezed his eyes more tightly shut, assuming he was in for another oopsie, this one ending with a splat on Forty-third. Instead he felt the hard roof under his back. When he opened his eyes he saw Remo was already halfway back to the roof door.

"I need to borrow your phone," Remo called over his shoulder, muttering as he vanished through the roof door, "What did I tell you? Always more work, work, work."

Smith had spun his cracked leather chair and was watching the dark shadow of a twilight gull soar and dip in the gusting wind over Long Island Sound when the blue phone jangled to life. Spinning, he snatched it up in mid-ring.

"Report."

"It's not anyone at the network, Smitty," Remo's voice said. "They don't want to save Kitty's nipped and tucked hide. They'd be happy to be rid of her if they wouldn't have to admit they screwed up hiring her in the first place."

"Maddox did not know who it might be?"

"No clue. Which is pretty much the motto around here. I was thinking it maybe could be some psycho viewer who knows she's tanking here and thinks he's helping her out."

Smith shook his head and sighed. "It could be. Frankly at this point we have no idea the who or why. Until we have a lead perhaps BCN should pull her off the air."

"They've already done it," Remo said. "Guy here says

they've taken her off temporarily and are flying her back from Alaska while they 'evaluate the situation.'"

"How long will they keep her off?"

In Uriah Maddox's office, Remo looked up from the phone.

When *Judge Ruth* ended, Chiun had shut off all the televisions. The old Korean was standing at one of the floor-to-ceiling windows that enclosed the corner office. Hands clutched behind his back, he watched the city night.

Maddox was sitting in a comfortable chair near his unused fireplace, a crystal tumbler half-filled with Crema de Lima clutched in his shaking hands.

"Hey, Jebediah, how long you going to keep your star anchor out of commission?"

Uriah had tried several times to bring the liquor to his lips but his hands shook too much when he lifted the tumbler. He was glad for the distraction.

"We pay fifteen million a year to have her on the air," Uriah replied, "so every day she's off is costing us sixty thousand dollars. She's off for three days, tops."

"What if I hang you off the roof again?"

"Wouldn't matter. I'd quit and the next guy would put her back on right away."

"They're real humanitarians around here, Smitty," Remo said into the phone. "I can keep her off the air indefinitely if you want."

Remo could tell from the long pause that Smith was weighing alternatives. At last, the CURE director spoke. "If she's off the air, these insane acts might end. However, since we don't know the motivation, it might not stop anything. Whoever is responsible could simply move on to one of the other network anchors."

"I could take all three of them out," Remo offered. "It worked for Buddy Holly, the Big Bopper and Richie Valens."

"Remo, please," Smith said. "We are stuck between

a rock and a hard place with Kitty Coughlin. Worse, whoever is responsible for this has caused significant damage to two major industries. The airlines have not yet recovered from Flight 980. And the damage from this oil spill goes beyond one tanker. Thanks to the spill this morning, forces in the environmental movement have already begun to mobilize. They are seeking to stop all oil production in Alaska."

"I've got an idea," Remo said. "Let them stick ears of corn down the tanks of those amusement park teacups they call cars and leave the rest of us the hell alone."

"That case will be more difficult to make thanks to the *Motiv Kodiak*," Smith said. "If these groups are successful, and this spill certainly helps their cause, we will be forced to rely even more on suppliers in the Middle East at a time when, thanks to Iran, that region is becoming more unstable."

"When was the last time the Mideast was stable, Smitty?" Remo asked. " 'Cause if it was in my lifetime, I must've slept through that five minutes."

"When Sinanju found work there, Emperor Smith, there was stability," Chiun called from his post at the window. "The pharaohs of old and the Roman rule that extended through the Caesars kept stability for thousands of years. Saladin, good for us for a time, was ultimately the end for us there when his coffers ran dry. They choose now to go with cheap local help and they are reaping the consequences."

Back at Folcroft, Smith leaned back in his chair which creaked gently at his shifting weight. Nudging his glasses up, he squeezed the bridge of his nose with slender fingers.

"These maniacs are causing damage that has the potential to be far reaching," the CURE director said.

"So what do you want us to do?" Remo asked. "We can't just sit around here waiting for the next bomb to drop."

Smith had made a decision. By the sour look on his ashen

face, he was not happy with the strategy circumstances had forced upon him. He settled his glasses back on his nose and leaned forward in his chair.

"No," he said with a resigned sigh. "You won't just be sitting there."

15

When BCN did not send a limo to pick her up at LaGuardia, it was all Kitty Coughlin could do to keep from punching the cabdriver in the back of the head.

This was it. The end of the line. The network had covered up her panic attacks ever since the monkey incident. Since none had been live on-air, thank God, it was easy enough to do. But even BCN, used to cellar dwelling among the Big Three nightly newscasts, had its breaking point.

They were finally kicking her out of the center chair. She sensed it. To where she had no idea. They still owned her for another three years. They could shift her back to mornings. But after making such a big deal of her being the new face of BCN news it would be humiliating—for Kitty and the network—to stick her back in the a.m., judging pie eating contests in Alabama and interviewing dim bulb celebutards who thought all the world's problems could be solved by limiting people to one sheet of toilet paper per bowel movement.

There had already been talk of moving her full-time to BCN's popular Sunday night newsmagazine show. She had actually overheard two executives discussing this possibility months ago. But the fear at the network was that she would bring the stench of failure to that show too.

The only other option Kitty could see was that they'd make her sit out her contract off the air. And by the time she was paid off, she would be an asterisk, a Trivial Pursuit question. Worse, she could end up like Cheeta Ching, drunk and on fire on top of a piano on some dead-end cable network.

Well Kitty Coughlin would not go gentle into that good night. If she was going down, she was taking the entire news division with her. There were plenty of New York publishers who would pay a pretty penny for a tell-all screed from America's first solo female network news anchor.

When Kitty stormed through the main entrance of BCN's world headquarters, her high heels nearly drew sparks from the highly polished floor, so ferocious were her footfalls. People darted out of her way as she clomped to the elevators. The lobby security guards recognized the venomous look in her eyes and were wise enough to give her a pass without offering a good morning. On the elevator, an old woman with a visitor pass pinned to her purse made the mistake of smiling hello.

"Stick a sock in it, granny," Kitty snarled.

Word had reached the news division that Kitty was on her way up. The corridors were deserted as she stormed through to Uriah's corner office. She got the sense of many eyes watching her from just out of view. Kitty didn't care.

The only person she encountered was Uriah Maddox's prim secretary standing at a humming computer printer in the corner of her office. "Oh, Ms. Coughlin, Mr. Maddox—"

"Stow it," Kitty growled and shoved her way into the door marked URIAH MADDOX, EXECUTIVE PRODUCER, BCN NEWS."

Across the room, Maddox looked up from his desk with weariness, as if he had been alerted to her coming. Dark rims from lack of sleep shaded his eyes.

"You want me out of here?" Kitty snarled. "Fine. I'm taking you with me, you little quarterback queen. I got enough dirt on how things are run around here to ruin the marriages of half the executives upstairs, and the other half I'll have jumping out their windows from the scandals."

"Kitty, please, you don't understand," Maddox said.

"You bet I understand," Kitty snarled. "You think the guy who was anchor ahead of me has been spouting off about you people? You ain't seen nothing yet." She suddenly noticed two men standing near Maddox's fireplace. "What the hell are you two doing here?" she demanded.

Remo was clearly as thrilled to be there as Maddox. He leaned against the mantle, arms crossed. The Master of Sinanju stood at his pupil's elbow.

"Consider us new viewers," Remo said. "Which according to the most recent Nielsen's brings your grand total up to two."

"I am not watching," Chiun pointed out. Rather than at Kitty, the Master of Sinanju was staring at a potted plant.

"Make that one," Remo said, smiling sweetly.

"Uriah?" Kitty snapped.

Maddox held up a hand, begging patience. "It's all right, Kitty. You're not being benched. BCN has every intention of keeping you on the air, and you have the full support of everyone in this news division, right up through the news president and the president of the network himself."

"Okay, fine," Kitty snarled. "Not that I trust you reptiles. So what are these two doing here?"

Uriah Maddox tried to put on his most affable smile. "They're the ones who are going to see to it that you stay on the air. Meet your new bodyguards."

When she saw that her producer was serious, Kitty began to shake her head. "Oh, no," she said. "No way." When Maddox nodded, her head shaking grew more vigorous. "No, no, no," she insisted, shaking her head so sharply her bangs bopped, revealing the tiny pink lines of her latest surgery.

"Careful there, Bride of Frankenstein," Remo said. "Shake any harder and you'll rattle your neck bolts loose."

Kitty ground her capped molars so tightly Maddox's secretary could hear the squeak in her outer office. "I thought they were Homeland Security," Kitty snapped. "Since when are they bodyguards?"

"Someone recently called us thirty-thousand-a-year bureaucrats," Remo said. "It hurt my wittle feewings, so we decided a change of vocation was in order."

Kitty wheeled on her executive producer. "This is unacceptable, Uriah. Next you'll be telling me that cow Daisy O'Toole is my new publicity agent. Or that I have to start wearing long pants 'cause some old prude complained."

"I'm no prude, but that one might not be a bad idea," Remo said. "I mean, if the Rockettes were gonna call they would have done it thirty years ago."

Kitty fumed. "You're not doing this, Uriah. No way."

"Kitty, this is the deal," Maddox said. "Take it or leave it. If you take it, you get to stay on the air. If you leave it I can't give you any promises what they'll decide to do with you upstairs."

At long last, Kitty grimaced and nodded.

"They stay out of my way," she warned, her voice a low jungle predator's growl.

"I can't promise that," Maddox said.

"I don't want to hear a word out of them," Kitty said.

"Ditto right back at you," said Remo.

"Hear, hear," said Chiun.

Kitty stamped one extremely high heel. "Uriah, make them stop," she wailed.

"Make that zero viewers," Remo said.

When Kitty glanced across the room she saw that Remo had joined Chiun in staring at the potted fern.

Maddox cleared out an office next to Kitty's for Remo and Chiun. The first thing Remo asked for was all the fan mail Kitty had gotten in the past six months. The first thing Chiun asked for was a private office.

"Come on, Chiun, I could use some help here," Remo said. "If this really is someone trying to help her with her ratings, they probably wrote her some crank notes first. I don't feel like going through the mail all by myself."

"You volunteered yourself, not me. I have no interest in pawing through the demented crayon scratches of people so insane they would watch that braying simpleton of their own free will."

Before Remo could speak, a college-age intern entered the office wheeling a cart weighted down with cardboard boxes. On top of the uppermost teetering box were three thin sheets of paper clipped to envelopes.

Remo eyed the big pile of boxes warily. "Is that all of Kitty's fan mail?" he asked.

Out of breath, the intern nodded at the boxes. "This is her hate mail from the last six months. They didn't tell me if you'd want that eventually so I pulled it too." He took down the three sheets of paper. "This is her fan mail."

Remo looked at the three flimsy sheets of paper in his hand. "This is it?" he asked.

"Only two of them really count as fan mail," the intern explained. "One of them just asks where she got her porcelain veneers done, but it was neutral to her so they put it in the non-hate mail pile."

Near the door, the Master of Sinanju chuckled. "Yes, Remo, I can see how you would need help going through so many letters. That is more than you have read in ten years. I will come back in a few hours to see if you had trouble sounding out the big words. You," he said, extending an imperious finger to the intern. "Come with me."

Intern in tow, the old Korean glided from the office.

Remo sank to a lotus position in the middle of the floor and read through the three letters. The two notes that weren't about her big fake teeth gushed praise for Kitty's news anchor skills. Remo checked the return addresses to see if they had been mailed from mental institutions.

Despite their lack of taste, Remo saw nothing about the letter writers that would connect them to the three acts of terrorism. He decided to let Smith worry about them.

Remo stuffed the notes in a manila envelope he found in the big office desk and wandered into the hall. Far down the corridor, the Master of Sinanju had apparently found an office to his liking. Chiun had drafted a dozen members of the BCN Evening News staff to remove the furnishings from the office. The old Korean clapped his hands and snapped orders as men and women sweated under the weight of chairs and desks. Remo swore he recognized one of BCN's field reporters struggling to carry a heavy file cabinet into the hallway.

Leaving the Master of Sinanju to his new hobby, Remo scrounged some stamps from a secretary and brought the envelope downstairs to a mailbox. When he returned to the news offices five minutes later, Chiun was gone from the hallway and his conscripts were hustling in fear from his open office door. Remo had to hand it to his teacher. A half hour working at BCN News and people were already more afraid of the old Korean than they were of Kitty Coughlin.

When Remo reentered the office Maddox had assigned him, he found the bane of BCN News sitting at his desk. Kitty Coughlin was reading a note printed on blue stationery.

"Shouldn't you be out squatting in a tureen of stem cells?" Remo asked.

Kitty shot him a foul look. "You're my bodyguard, aren't you?" she asked.

"I only have to guard your body when you're out on assignment. What you do with it the rest of the time is between you and your plastic surgeon."

Remo noted that Kitty had taken one of the boxes of hate mail down from the wobbly cart. It was labeled MULTIPLES, with a smaller handwritten notation that explained that these letter writers had written more than once. The lid was off and a few dozen letters were piled before her.

"Can you believe this?" she asked, ignoring Remo's comment. She waved the blue stationery as if airing out a dirty sock. "This guy says he would rather have icepicks stuck in both eardrums than listen to me read the news. Who takes their time to sit down and write a letter like that?"

"Just a guess, but someone who's listened to your show?"

"Hah-hah," Kitty said. "According to the notation at the top he's written twice to say that. Twice." She pulled another note from the pile. "This one—who's written five times if this squiggle is a five and not a two—says she wants the nice man who 'hosted the show' for twenty-five years to come back. Like this is the goddamned *Price Is Right*. They say I'm 'dumbing down' and 'tarting up' the news, but the viewers can't tell the difference between a so-called serious newscaster and Bob-goddamn-Barker. And get a load of this one. This guy addressed his note to 'the dim bulldyke whore pretender.' Isn't that nice? And according to this he's written a total of twenty times so far. Twenty. This joker says that Cheeta Ching belongs in my chair. I know one thing for sure, and that's if Cheeta

Ching was back here the ratings wouldn't be half of what I'm pulling in."

Sitting at that big desk, shoulders slumped, hair frazzled, Kitty looked so small and so utterly miserable that Remo refrained from cracking wise.

"You're probably right about that. Chiun watched her every night when she used to be on but I'd usually stick my fingers in my ears and run out the front door. But that was back when he had a thing for her. Once he gave her some ancient method that got her pregnant and when she finally had the kid, Chiun dropped her. You can't imagine how happy I was when he finally lost interest in that Korean shark."

Kitty took a deep breath and exhaled loudly. "She's long gone now in TV terms, but from where I'm sitting it wasn't so long ago when she was supposed to be the next big thing; the co-anchor who was going to save the network. Of course, it didn't help her that the nutball they sat her next to as co-anchor was completely off his rocker, but if you take him out of the equation a lot of what they said about her is the same as what they said about me when I took over."

And there it was again, the same feeling he had gotten watching the BCN editor laughing at zoo footage of Kitty covered in monkey crap. Remo did not like it, but he felt it in his gut. A tiny twinge of sympathy for Kitty Coughlin.

Luckily he was saved from having to say something nice by the Master of Sinanju who chose that moment to sweep past Remo's open office door.

"Japonica rice and salmon," Chiun was demanding of the intern who was nervously trailing him. It was the same young man who had brought the mail to Remo's office. "Fish baked, rice clumpy. Repeat."

"Fish baked, rice clumpy," said the intern.

"Chiun, what are you doing?" Remo called.

Turning an irritated eye on his pupil, the old Korean paused in the doorway.

"Ordering lunch," Chiun said. "Stay, intern," he ordered the young man as if talking to a dog. Chiun pitched his voice low. "This is a remarkable thing, Remo. Something I would not have believed if I did not see it with my own eyes. It is true, is it not, that this nation fought a war to end slavery more than one hundred years ago?"

"I read that on a placemat somewhere," Remo said.

"Ah, but the practice did not end. Slaves still exist and have been renamed interns." Chiun shot a withering look at the college-age intern for no reason other than to see the young man squirm. The young man squirmed. Happy, Chiun turned his attention back to Remo.

"Interns aren't slaves, Chiun," Remo said.

"No they are better. Slavery is a terrible thing, of course, and rightly frowned upon in polite society. But that is largely because until now slaves had no say in their fates. But this one has volunteered for servitude, he does the most repellent tasks for no money and suffers in silence all manner of abuse. For no money, Remo. You tell me how that is not slavery with but a different name?"

Remo nodded. "Okay, maybe you're right," he admitted. "But what have you got him carrying that around for?"

The young man who stood behind Chiun was holding a steaming cardboard cup which he offered to the old Korean like a leper's begging bowl even as the rest of his body cowered in fear. Chiun ignored the intern and his cup.

"That is my latte," Chiun explained.

"Chiun, you can't drink latte. Coffee is like strychnine to us."

"It is free," Chiun explained. "Besides, do not lecture me about food, you who would still be drinking coffee stirred with beef jerky and washed down with squid juice had I not intervened on behalf of your stomach."

Another figure came huffing up the hallway, caught sight of Kitty sitting at Remo's desk and stopped dead.

"There you are," Uriah Maddox breathed, noting with a raised eyebrow the traffic jam in Remo's office door. "What are you doing in here?"

"Hiding from you," Kitty said, her face a glum mask.

"Really? I thought you were helping us reenact the stateroom scene from *A Night at the Opera*," Remo said.

Maddox tapped his watch. "You've got a flight to Los Angeles in two hours." He glanced at Remo and Chiun. "All three of you are booked, but you've got to shake a leg. We've been hyping your trip out there at the affiliate for a week, so we can't disappoint. Let's go."

The executive producer hustled off.

"We're going to L.A.?" Remo asked.

Sighing, Kitty got to her feet. "I was hoping Uriah wouldn't find me. I'm sick of bopping all over the country. I was scheduled to swing down there for a week after I left Alaska. L.A. is a big market, and lately we're trailing reruns of George Lopez and *The Simpsons*. Uriah hopes that by broadcasting there we'll goose our numbers in that market."

"How much goosing do you need?" Remo asked.

"We're number eighteen in our time slot," Kitty said morosely.

"Bummer," Remo said.

"Goose," Chiun said. He turned to the young college student. "Make that salmon a goose, intern," he commanded, sounding for all the world like Henry VIII demanding another rack of mutton to celebrate the dismissal of Cardinal Wolsey.

"Get it in a doggy bag, Wilberforce," Remo said.

16

The man wearing the smelly aftershave was jabbing at a map with his forefinger.

"It's simple. Some of you start here and a bunch of you start over here. You have groups of your men positioned all around here, here and here, see? You'll be positioned around a central hub which is here in East Los Angeles. You just need to coordinate right at the start and you can do that with cell phones. Once you start, it'll all pick up momentum as you move in toward the hub. It'll move like a wave toward the middle and away from the middle. He said a wave, didn't he?"

"Yeah, a wave."

"A wave. Any questions?"

Chico Ramirez looked at the maps of Los Angeles spread out on the workbenches, then glanced up at the two sweating gringos standing over the maps. They had just finished a twenty-minute explanation of their plan. Ramirez did not have a question for them but he did have a demand.

"The money," said Chico Ramirez, leader of the L.A. Casas street gang. He held out his hand.

Across the workbench, Noah Sherman elbowed Wayne Dwyer in the belly. Wayne reached into the pockets of his heavy black raincoat and pulled out six fat envelopes which he handed over to Ramirez.

"Ten thousand each," Noah said, forcing a smile. "A bargain at twice the price considering how much more you're going to make out of this deal."

"Yeah, you should be paying us," Wayne laughed.

Noah shot a horrified glance at Wayne and Wayne instantly dummied up. When Noah looked back to Chico his smile returned, more nervous now.

"You start at 3:20 Pacific Time," Noah said, clearing his throat. "That's 6:20 on the east coast. If you start right then it should hit at just the right time."

Chico was not listening. He kept one envelope for himself and passed the other five out to the five men who loomed behind him. Noah and Wayne tried not to make eye contact with the five men, who were larger than Chico and were even more intimidating than their leader, despite his gold front teeth and the spiderweb tattoos on his neck.

The other men were adorned with tattoos as well. Arms and necks were so painted with body art that one frightening image bled into another. Noah and Wayne merely saw a lot of tattooed knives, fangs, numbers and Spanish words. Noah, who at Berkeley one semester had taken a course called Understanding and Appreciating Ancient South and Central American Cultures and Their Positive Contributions to the Modern World, did recognize several Aztec symbols. In class he had understood and appreciated as much as was required to earn an A but in the real world there was something about seeing Tezcatlipoca devouring a human heart when the image was tattooed on a gigantic pectoral that made him feel less than appreciative toward the contributions of these ancient cultures to the modern world.

The men wore muscle shirts, hairnets, low slung trousers and enough chains to get a stuck bus out of a snowbank. The traditional symbol of the infamous Casas gang was a yellow bandana, which the men wore wrapped around their heads, necks or biceps.

Chico and the other gang members shook stacks of hundred-dollar bills from Noah's simple white business envelopes. As they counted the money they occasionally muttered to one another in Spanish.

"Do you understand Spanish?" Noah whispered to Wayne out of the corner of his mouth.

"I took Ancient Greek," Wayne hissed in reply. "You?"

"Latin," said Noah, worry straining his voice.

Even though Noah and Wayne had each counted the cash ten times back at the hotel, that did not rid Noah of the fear that they might have miscounted.

The air in the building was oppressive. Hot light streamed through dirty second-story windows. A large vent fan at the back of the warehouse sat dormant. Bees had built a giant hive between the blades and a wire mesh grate that was meant to block insects. The building had been home to a movie special effects house for thirty years, but the gang influence had grown too strong in the neighborhood and the company had been forced into bankruptcy. All that was left was a matte painting of the ocean which was coated with dust and leaning against a rear wall, three workbenches and a rusted toolbox filled only with three screwdrivers, a broken pair of pliers and a half-dozen tiny shattered lightbulbs.

Noah felt beads of sweat dripping cold down the entire length of his spine.

"He can't possibly make us do anything else after this," Wayne whispered in Noah's ear. "You IM'd him. Did he tell you he was finally going to stop and leave us alone?"

Noah was watching the Casas count their money. He shook his head. "I don't know," he replied quietly. "I have my doubts that he's ever going to stop."

Wayne's face fell. "But he promised," he whined. "This has to be it. After we do this for him he has to stop the Usenet flame wars. That's how it started with me. I'm sick of him claiming he's me and getting me killfiled and reported to my ISP. And what about your iBay account? He was going to leave you alone at iBay." When Noah did not reply with reassuring words, Wayne paused. "You really think he might never leave us alone?" he asked, his voice a pathetic croak.

"I don't know," Noah insisted. "Maybe."

Wayne noted that Noah did not sound convinced.

Chico and the other gang members had finished putting to good use the eleven years of first-grade bilingual math they had taken before dropping out of junior high school. Satisfied the money was all there, they stuffed their pockets with cash.

"So we're all set?" Noah said with a smile.

Chico pulled a shiny Glock from the back of his low-slung jeans and blew a hole through Noah's head. The gunshot was a thunderclap in the abandoned warehouse. A flock of startled pigeons took flight from the rafters.

"We're all set?" Chico mocked as the body collapsed to the dirty floor. The other Casas laughed uproariously at their leader's terrifically subtle joke.

A tiny, horrified yip passed Wayne's lips. Splattered blood flecked his face and clothes. As he looked down at Noah's body, surrounded by an arc of blown-away chunks of hair-mottled skull, a dark stain appeared at Wayne's crotch.

"We're all set?"

Wayne heard the phrase repeated once again, but it was a distant echo this time. He looked up at the gun barrel and grinning gold teeth of Chico Ramirez.

Ramirez held the gun sideways, the stock parallel to the floor. His hand was perfectly steady. Wayne noticed the chains hanging around his wrist tattoos. Chico's knuckles were tattooed as well. Wayne had not noticed that before. "We're all set?" Ramirez repeated.

Wayne felt himself drawn back into reality. His heart thudded. He stared at the gun, wondering if when the trigger was pulled he would have time to see the ropy forearm muscles tighten before a bullet blew apart his skull.

Why was it taking so long?

Wayne dragged his terrified eyes to the gang leader's face. Ramirez was grinning his gold teeth at Wayne. All at once, he lunged a half-step forward. "Gah!" he shouted.

To the delight of the five Casas, the pimply-faced gringo with the pants wet with pee screamed in horror and, turning on wobbly legs, stumbled as fast as his fat legs would carry him out the warehouse door.

"You so funny, Chico," insisted one of the men as he wiped tears of mirth from his bloodshot eyes. "You funny enough to be in the movies."

The five gang members were stepping over the body of Noah Sherman, a mere prop in their leader's comedy routine, when Chico called for them to stop. When they turned, they found the head of the Casas standing at the maps and notes Noah and Wayne had spread out across the workbenches.

Chico wore a pensive frown. "We going to do this thing," the Casas leader announced.

"Why? Dead gringo already give us the money."

Chico was nodding. " 'Cause, stupid, the dead gringo was right. This going to make us a lot more. And alls we gots to do is burn East L.A. to the ground."

BCN's Los Angeles affiliate sent a simple sedan to
pick up Kitty, Remo and Chiun at Los Angeles International Airport. As the driver loaded her bags in the trunk, Kitty tried to get into the backseat. She found Chiun already sitting there.

"Move it, Confucius," she commanded.

She felt Remo's hand brush her arm. "Why don't you sit up front with me," he suggested in a tone low with warning.

"What's he going to do, kill me?" She glanced at Chiun. Seated in the center of the backseat, the Master of Sinanju wore a placid expression but as she looked at the old man, he smiled faintly and Kitty realized she had never seen anything so menacing in her entire life.

"Fine, I'll sit up front," Kitty snarled, slamming the back door and accepting yet another indignity in a life that had until very recently been one of total privilege.

She squeezed in between Remo and their driver.

"There's a limo in every driveway in this town and they can't find one to pick me up," Kitty groused.

"No, there's not a limo in every driveway, Kitty," Remo said. "Take a look around."

They were crawling through a snarl of airport traffic amid cars of every model and every condition good and bad.

Kitty crossed her arms and slouched down in the seat. "There are in the neighborhoods *I've* been in," she grunted.

"Did it ever occur to you, Marie Antoinette, that maybe your problem with connecting with an audience comes from this smug superiority of yours?" Remo said. "Didn't people used to like watching you on that morning show of yours way back before you became Paris Hilton with a press pass?"

"Uriah is making me put up with you as a bodyguard," Kitty said. "But if I want opinions on connecting with the common man I'll ask the million-dollar consulting firms BCN hires, not some bum off the street."

"If that ivory tower of yours has a dictionary you might want to look up the definition of irony," Remo suggested.

"Heh-heh-heh," said Chiun from the backseat.

Since Uriah told Remo that Kitty would be broadcasting the evening news live from the West Coast, Remo assumed they would head to a studio downtown, so he was surprised when their driver took them to a small park in East Los Angeles where several high stools had been set in the grass in front of the kinds of cameras Remo had only ever seen inside television studios. There were vans and cars parked all around as well as a long bus decorated with the BCN logo and a big picture of Kitty splashed across the side.

The area was bustling with activity. The driver pulled into a reserved spot behind the bus.

"You're doing this outside?" Remo asked as he sprung the door. Kitty slid out behind him as Remo popped the

back door for the Master of Sinanju. Chiun came out the
back of the car like a puff of escaping steam.

"That's how we do it sometimes," she said. She tried to
frown but the muscles around her mouth refused to
cooperate. "We did it on my old morning show as a
ratings ploy all the time. Of course, back then I wasn't the
one having to fly all over the country, it was my cohost or
the weatherman. They'd broadcast from, say, the Grand
Canyon. So they'd stand via satellite in front of the Grand
Canyon and we'd cut to them throughout the morning. It's
the same deal here, except I'm the one on the road
grubbing for ratings. I'll do a few interviews from here as
well as the day's top stories, and an anchor back in New
York fills in the rest. And that son of a bitch better not get
too comfortable in my chair."

Kitty went to the makeup van and once she was gone
the Master of Sinanju slid up beside his pupil.

"I do not know why you are torturing me by talking to
that vainglorious female," Chiun sniffed. "By speaking to
her you are only encouraging her to talk back."

"I feel kind of bad for her, Chiun," Remo said. "I
mean, yeah, she's a nasty little twit who's rotten to
everyone who works with her. And, yeah, she dresses like
she thinks she's still got a shot at getting voted
homecoming queen. And, yeah, her face has been lifted
so many times she has to hold the Kleenex to the back of
her head to blow her nose." Remo tipped his head and
thought for a moment. "Okay, there probably should be a
'but' there by now, but just because I can't think of one
doesn't mean I don't feel bad for her."

"Misplaced pity can be a dangerous thing," Chiun
warned. "Back when I was a young man in my village of
Sinanju there was a maiden I took pity on. Everyone said
that she was a vicious, lazy thing with a wicked tongue,
but she was not that way in my presence. In my great
innocence, I assumed that the villagers were jealous of
her so in reaction to them I first took pity on her and then

I took her for my wife. After the wedding I found that the villagers were right. The moment I was bound to her she revealed herself to me as the dragon she had always been. I was stuck with her for many years until she finally slipped on a mossy rock and drown in the West Korean Bay. It took years to reach that happy ending, years that I was forced to live in misery, and all because I took pity on one undeserving of it."

"While we're out on the coast you should see about getting Hollywood to option that love story of yours. They could get Richard Gere and Julia Roberts. It'd be the feel-good date movie of the summer."

"Say what you will, but before it goes any further let it be known that I will never approve of your marrying this one. She is a worse harpy than my wife ever was. What's more she is too old to bear me grandchildren, no matter what those carvers of flesh do to make her face look like that."

"Just being nice," Remo said. "She's got as much sex appeal as a dead raccoon under the Christmas tree."

As he spoke, Remo scoped out the area. He noted that it was not the best neighborhood but a strong police presence in anticipation of Kitty's newscast had securely clamped down the streets surrounding the park.

Remo wondered how BCN had managed to get the police to send so many cops into the park. His curiosity lasted only until a long black limousine drew up beside the network bus and a familiar figure stepped from the back.

There was no way that Remo could not have recognized Governor Konrad Scheissenhauser. The man had been one of the biggest box office stars of the 1980s and '90s until a career change to politics a few years before. Now the former movie action hero was in his second term as California's governor.

Scheissenhauser was shorter than Remo imagined. Average height; nowhere near as tall as his movies led on.

He was athletic at sixty but no longer possessed the grand physique of his younger days as a world class bodybuilder. He was still powerful, with a broad chest and shoulders, but Remo noted that there was a slight paunch which was disguised very neatly by an impeccably tailored suit.

An entourage quickly gathered around California's governor, and Scheissenhauser and his people made their way to the outdoor interview set. As he walked, Scheissenhauser had to pass between sawhorses set up to keep away the curious neighborhood crowd that had gathered. Scheissenhauser shook hands with the crowd as he walked to the set.

An immigrant who spoke no English when he first came to America, Scheissenhauser spoke with a thick accent of his native Germany.

"Hello there. Yes. Fantastic. Yes. Hello."

A woman held up a toddler so that the governor could shake his little hand. It looked as if the child was not sure if the strongman with the big hands would try to eat him. Frankly, Remo wasn't so sure either.

As he watched the governor gladhand, Chiun crinkled his nose. "Is not that behemoth in films?"

"He used to be. He was in a couple of movies about a robot that couldn't be killed. I always kind of thought that it was sort of like with us and Mr. Gordons."

Chiun scowled. "Do not remind me of that wicked machine who wore the face of a man."

"I'm just saying that the robot in those movies was a lot like Gordons. Especially in the second one. He could shapeshift and impersonate people and form knives out of his hands and stuff, just like Gordons. NASA built Gordons so maybe the people at NASA helped out on the movie. I mean, it's not like the movie people were spying on our lives. But Scheissenhauser doesn't make killer robot movies anymore. He's the governor of California now."

Chiun looked at Remo as if he were spouting gibberish. "You are joking."

"Honest Hessian," Remo said.

Tufts of yellowing white hair danced in the gentle breeze as the old man shook his head in amazement.

The BCN people were already set up for an interview. Kitty, fully made up, had reappeared and was sitting on her stool. Konrad Scheissenhauser joined her on the outdoor set. The crowd was asked to quiet down and Remo watched the red lights on the various cameras switch on as the interview went live for the east coast. Kitty, her face unable to wrinkle as she smiled tightly, introduced the California governor.

"Thank you, Kitty," Scheissenhauser said. "Let me just welcome you here to California. And I want to say that I think you are doing just a fantastic job with the news."

As the governor was speaking, Chiun glanced around the area, his hazel eyes narrowing suspiciously.

"Governor Scheissenhauser," Kitty said, "we're here in East L.A. to talk about your plan for urban renewal but before we get to that let's talk global warming. Now we all know, of course, that global warming is the most pressing problem of our age. What steps are you taking here in California to ensure that the Golden State as we know it will be preserved for future generations and not be flooded under a mile of melted polar ice?"

Scheissenhauser nodded his giant head and smiled his trademark gap-toothed grin.

"Yes, Kitty, the global warming is a serious problem. I was not elected by the people of California to be the governor of this party or that party but of all Californians. These people out there want me to say I am a Democrat or a Republican, that I am this thing or that thing. That is how they do things in Washington and nothing gets done with the important problems like the global warming. The people want action not talk, because they are fed up with the talk that these other politicians all are doing in both parties. They talk about this and that while problems like the global warming get worse. That is why I am taking the lead to stop the global warming here in California."

The governor pronounced it Kell-if-or-ni-a, drawing out each precise syllable as if they were five distinct words.

Next to Remo, the Master of Sinanju looked over each shoulder, then up and down, and finally shook his head.

"What's wrong, Little Father?"

"There used to be a television show where a camera would be hidden so that cruel tricks could be played on the unwitting. After these poor souls embarrassed themselves, a bald man would come out and laugh at them and tell them he had tricked them into acting like fools for his camera. I assume, Remo, that someone is trying to trick me into believing that the people of this province are stupid enough to have appointed this musclebound lummox to govern them."

Remo nodded sympathetic understanding. "Sorry, Chiun, but Allen Funt's not waiting to spring out at us. The people of Kell-if-or-ni-a really elected him. In their defense I think it was either him, Gary Coleman or some porn merchant."

Remo was distracted by something unseen rising up from the city just beyond the surrounding buildings. By the way the Master of Sinanju's neck craned ever-so-slightly from the collar of his kimono, chin up and head tipped, Remo could see that his teacher had sensed it too.

The normal sound of human activity was constant background noise in a major city like Los Angeles. The thrum of vehicles on streets and freeway combined with the symphony of bustling everyday activity—from construction noise to radios blaring music to cell phone chatter to the whine of lawnmowers. Normal human brains would be unable to cope with the overload were they not instinctively able to filter down into an innocuous hum most of the audio distractions that bombarded them every minute of every day. But Masters of Sinanju, more attuned to their surroundings than other men, had filters of a different sort. Remo and Chiun were aware of all the sounds that came to their ears, but their brains instinctively prioritized the information so that a threat to life would not be drowned out by a nearby lawnmower.

It was the sound that first tripped the trouble trigger in Remo's brain. The noises Remo had begun to hear were not sounds of normal city life. They were dissonant, introducing a sense of disharmony into the natural flow of the city.

People shouting, glass shattering. Gunshots. It was the sound of a riot and it was closing in around them.

"Looks like we've got trouble," Remo said.

Chiun nodded seriously. "If Smith wants you to protect that woman, you should get her now," he said, his sharp ears focused on the approaching commotion. It was louder now.

People at the fringes of the gathered crowd had picked up on the leading edge of the disturbance. A few curious heads turned to the roads leading into the square.

Remo glanced over at the outdoor news set. Kitty and Scheissenhauser continued to chat, oblivious to any mounting danger. Sawhorses kept at bay the several hundred people who had turned out to watch the live show.

"We weren't here for Kitty," Remo said. "We were here to get whoever's behind all the stuff that's been happening around her. Looks like we've got our chance. This sure doesn't feel spontaneous to me."

"It is not," Chiun said with certainty.

"Then we might be able to follow this back to a source. Let's go, Little Father."

But a hand touched his arm, stopping him. "There is no need to go anywhere, my son," Chiun said. "It is here."

The distant sounds of whooping car alarms began to filter down to the area around the park. The sharper tones of commercial alarms shrieked, intermixed with human shouts.

Remo glanced at the surrounding buildings. "Closing in on all sides."

"Thus, planned," Chiun said.

Radios in squad cars around the park started squawking. Scheissenhauser was yammering on about how blowing the roof off state spending would somehow bring back businesses that had already fled California's choking high taxes. Kitty nodded appreciation at the bold fiscal strategy that was making California unlivable for anyone but the extraordinarily wealthy and the extremely poor, oblivious to any danger even as police officers hustled to their cruisers.

Most of the cops had not reached their cars when the first rioters began pouring into the streets around the park, bringing chaos in their wake. Dozens of parked cars seemed to spontaneously erupt yellow fire as the crowd flooded through. A Molotov cocktail was tossed onto the hood of a squad car and exploded in a ball of wicked flame.

Remo noted that dozens of the rioters wore yellow bandanas, probably a street gang symbol. Everybody had them nowadays.

The crowd that had gathered to watch the live BCN News broadcast seemed shot through with an electric charge. When the rioters appeared, led by the Casas gang members, some primal instinct seemed to kick in.

The flooding wall of rioters met the waiting crowd, and the crowd immediately flowed to join in. Shouting full-throated war whoops, the throng overran the barricades.

Remo was ready to snag the first yellow bandana that raced past when a single scream rose above the other noise, brushing Remo's sensitive ears. It was the same terrified shriek he had heard for the first time in New

York, but this time it was not coming through tinny computer speakers.

Remo glanced over at the news set.

Only when the barricades were breached did Kitty Coughlin realize that she was in the middle of a full-scale urban riot. Shrieking, she threw down her microphone and, flapping her hands like a frightened hairdresser, hid behind the nearest, largest object she could find. That object happened to have starred in *Pre-School Policeman, I Married a Nerd*, and *Killbot 4: Kill or Be Bot*.

"Get your fingernails out of mein shoulder," Konrad Scheissenhauser demanded of BCN's screeching anchor-woman.

The governor's security detail was taken by surprise by the sudden appearance of the mob. The three armed men attempted to reach their boss but instead found themselves battling for survival amid the savage crowd. They finally gave up altogether. Guns drawn and firing warning shots into the air, they dove into the governor's limousine and slammed the bulletproof doors on the surging mob.

Windows were smashed in buildings all around. Bricks and chunks of cement were hurled through car windshields. Car stereos and speakers were wrenched free, trailing wires. Streams of vandals poured into apartment buildings and small businesses. Almost as quickly as they entered, the crowds streamed back out again bearing televisions, microwaves, clothing and anything else they could carry, save books and soap.

A liquor store on one corner was particularly hard hit. Locusts swarmed with less focus than the thick crowd that attacked the small store. Men and women raced out carrying bottles and cases. One looter had his pockets stuffed with lottery tickets. When another man spied the roll of quick pick tickets sticking from the man's pocket, he smashed a bottle of Chivas Regal over the first man's head and, as the original thief lay bleeding on the ground, stole the instant winner tickets from his pocket.

One young gang member was delighted to find what he imagined would be an easy target, an old man in a weird-looking costume that looked like a dress. But the dress looked expensive and all these old folks had *mucho dinero*. The Casas raced up to the old man before anyone else claimed him.

"Gimme your money or you die," the Casas member menaced.

Chiun appeared baffled. "Remo, is this cretin addressing the Master of Sinanju?"

"Think so, Little Father," Remo said. "Ask him if there's a third option while I get Kitty."

"I thought you were leaving her," Chiun said.

"I can't," Remo sighed. "Get a load of her."

The rioters had flooded the park. Some were making off with cameras and microphones. Governor Scheissenhauser had grabbed his stool and was using it to swat anyone who came near even as he tried to battle his way toward his limousine. Clinging to the back of California's governor like a remora in a too-short skirt was Kitty Coughlin. BCN's uber-expensive anchorwoman was screaming and bawling.

"I've gotta help her out of there," Remo said. "Just make sure you keep this one alive, Little Father," he added, nodding to the gang member. "It looks like these guys are the ones running the show here. We can use this one to track back up the line."

"Shut up," the Casas snapped at Remo, but when he glanced around he discovered that the old Asian's companion was gone. The gang member swore and turned full attention on Chiun. "You not gonna get away so easy," he snarled. "Gimme your wallet or your belly gets slit like a pig. Don't think I won't. I cut up two old tour bus ladies good last week." The Casas flicked a switchblade.

A cold stillness settled about the old Korean. "You assaulted the elderly?" Chiun asked.

"You know it, old man." The gang member flashed his

blade menacingly. The crowd was surging around them
and he was afraid that at any moment a stronger member
of the pack would step in and steal this easy kill.

"Foolish whelp," the Master of Sinanju intoned. "A
blade is only a weapon in the hands of one who knows how
to wield it. My son has recently dealt with one who would
prey upon the aged. And now it is the Master's turn."
Chiun's hands appeared from the folds of his kimono,
fingers opening to reveal ten razor-sharp talons. "See you
now what it means to have one's weapons always at hand."

Remo heard the shrieks of pain rising behind him.

"That can't be good," he said even as he drove forward.

The rioters were black and Latino. Remo's light skin
was as good as a bull's-eye to the most aggressive
members of the mob. On his way to rescue Kitty, he was
assaulted seventeen times; five times with fists, six times
with knives, twice with guns, and once each with a stolen
toaster oven, a barbecue skewer, a baseball bat and a
cinder block.

Those who used their hands got a reprieve, suffering
only broken arm and leg bones. They dropped to the
ground in Remo's wake, cradling in agony their various
injuries.

The knives and guns he shattered, along with large
portions of the frontal and parietal bones of their owners'
skulls. The barbecue skewer landed like Cupid's arrow in
its wielder's heart, the toaster oven wound up fused with
its owner's chest cavity and the baseball bat man, seeing
the carnage wrought by Remo, dropped his bat and ran
directly in front of a busload of fleeing BCN employees.

The man with the cinder block did a little premature
victory dance after hurling his makeshift weapon at
Remo.

Remo caught the cinder block lightly in one hand and
sent it rocketing back at the thrower. When cinder block
met head, cinder block won. The dancing stopped abruptly

and the headless body collapsed like a marionette with cut strings.

The head bounced between the legs of Governor Scheissenhauser who did not even notice, so busy was he swatting back would-be attackers. Kitty, however, still latched onto the governor's mighty back, did notice the rolling head.

"Aaaahh!" BCN's anchorwoman shrieked.

"Oh, stop it mit the girly screaming," the governor snapped.

Sweat poured down Scheissenhauser's face. Another man charged. The governor hauled back and rang the attacker in the side of the head with his stool. The man fell but the stool finally surrendered to the stress it had not been designed to endure and cracked into two neat halves.

"Aaaargh!" Scheissenhauser howled and buried two stool legs deep in the chest of another charging gang member.

"Why is this happening to me?" Kitty cried.

The last stationary camera fell on her mournful wail. Kitty watched the red light wink out as the neighborhood scavengers set upon it, pulling out wires and dragging it away amid cries of triumph like Stone Age hunters dragging a felled antelope back to the communal cave.

A trio of men swarmed Scheissenhauser and Kitty. The governor was ready to bash them with the remaining two legs of his shattered stool, but as he swung back he felt the pieces of stool leg plucked from his hands. For one unarmed instant he thought that he was staring in the face of certain death from which, unlike his celluloid adventures, there would be no last-minute reprieve. And then he felt a sudden, strange feeling of weightlessness and bodies began to drop to the ground around him like fluttering autumn leaves.

"The stool was a nice touch," a voice said. "Gray Davis would've just bored them to death."

Scheissenhauser could not see the face of his savior. He did not see that Remo had bundled Kitty up under one arm and tossed the governor over the opposite shoulder as he raced for Scheissenhauser's limo.

The security men were still hiding inside the safety of the limo. They flung a rear door open when they saw the governor being carted to them. Remo dumped Scheissenhauser and Kitty in the backseat.

"Get them out of here," he ordered. "And then you guys go find a new line of work."

The limo took off in a peel of smoking tires. Rioters darted from in front of the sleek, speeding car.

Running back to the Master of Sinanju, Remo noticed a cluster of Los Angeles police officers cowering behind a parked SWAT van. Remo had forgotten the police were even there, so silent had they been throughout the crisis.

"What the hell are you doing?" Remo demanded. "Get out there and stop this thing. Shoot some of these bastards."

"We can't discharge our weapons," whined one officer, a powerfully built black sergeant. "If the looters were white, maybe. But these are people of color. Discharge a weapon at a person of color in L.A. and we'll be trading in our blues for prison gray by tonight."

"You're black," Remo pointed out. He noted that more than half the officers in hiding were not white.

"Doesn't matter," the officer insisted. "A black man puts on this uniform, he turns white as far as the community and the news are concerned."

"Well if you won't shoot them, use your nightsticks. Beat the hell out of them and disperse them," Remo suggested.

The cop bit the inside of his cheek. "What if someone's videotaping?" he asked. "*Inside Edition* would have a field day. Not to mention the ACLU and the Justice Department."

Remo glanced around the SWAT van. The entire block was at risk of going up in flames. Fires erupted from dozens of buildings. Remo heard no sirens so he assumed the fire department was afraid to drive into the war zone to put them out. He looked back at the cowering cops.

"Maybe—just maybe—you and Los Angeles deserve each other," he said. Shaking his head in disgust, he raced off to locate the Master of Sinanju.

Chiun was standing on the sidewalk where Remo had left him. At the old Korean's feet was a pile of bloody meat which, with a little imagination, one could tell had once been a human being.

"I told you to save him," Remo groused. "Didn't you hear me say to save him? Do you ever hear me? Why do I even bother if you're not going to listen to a word I say?"

Chiun's hands were folded back inside the voluminous sleeves of his kimono. "It lives," he said.

The pile of damp meat moaned.

"Fat lot of good it does me," Remo growled. He dropped a heel on the forehead of the shredded gang member, mercifully ending his torment. "Let's go find a live one. And I would very much appreciate it if just this once you'd actually listen to one thing I say and not kill him. Hmm? All right? Okay? Is that so hard to do? Sheesh."

"What did you say?" said the Master of Sinanju.

18

Orville Wilbur Feldon sat bathed in the dull blue
glow of two dozen television and computer monitor
screens and watched the riot footage caught live by the
BCN Evening News cameras. When it came up to the
part just an instant before Kitty Coughlin realized what
was happening, Feldon quickly hit the slow motion
button on the nearest VCR.

There was the usual empty-headed perky expression as
Kitty was interviewing California's governor. Then there
was a sudden moment where her tightly pulled eyes
glanced off-camera. And slowly, like melting ice cream,
the face of BCN's fifteen-million-dollar-a-year prize
anchorwoman turned from stunned surprise to sheer
terror.

Feldon hit play once more and the tape jumped back to
normal speed. Kitty screamed just as she had screeched
that day back in the monkeyhouse. She screamed like
Chet Huntley and David Brinkley never would have

screamed. She screamed like the panicked lightweight she was and then dove for protection behind Governor Konrad Scheissenhauser.

Very little in life made Orville Wilbur Feldon happy but when he saw Kitty Coughlin finally having a panic attack on live television he clapped his hands in delight.

Scheissenhauser became briefly the action hero he had been on the silver screen, hampered the entire time by a clinging, screaming, sniveling excuse for a real reporter.

The footage became a funhouse ride when the camera toppled over. There were a few stomping feet of looters, and Feldon swore he saw a decapitated head in the background. Then the screen went to black and Orville Wilbur Feldon was certain beyond doubt that Kitty Coughlin was dead.

Feldon rewound the tape and played it for the tenth time, and for the tenth time he found himself clapping with joy as the expression of horror tried desperately to form on the taut flesh of Kitty Coughlin's unwrinkled face.

This time when he clapped, he heard a kitchen chair skid across the floor upstairs.

"What are you doing down there, Orville?" shouted a female voice, hoarse from years of cigarettes.

"Cementing my future, Mother!" Feldon called back.

This brought a rasping laugh from the unseen woman.

"Hah! What future? You're a bum, Orville. To think of the money it cost me to send you to that Columbus Journalism school. Fired from every job you ever had. Couldn't even hold the job at the post office, could you? You know how many strings I pulled to get you that job? All these years hiding down in that basement while I'm out providing for us. Planning your future. Hah. When are you getting a job?"

"Sooner than that rodent Postal Service brain of yours could possibly imagine, you old battle-axe," Feldon muttered.

"What was that?"

"I said soon, Mother."

This elicited more cackling from on high followed by a racking cough that ended with the grinding hum of the garbage disposal. Feldon's mother often hacked up globs of phlegm in the kitchen sink and ran it down the disposal.

After thirty seconds of grinding, the disposal clicked off. Although Feldon could not make out all the words, he could hear muttered maledictions directed his way.

Feldon tuned his mother out. Nothing was going to ruin his great, magical moment.

All the months of planning had finally paid off. He had known all along that he could do it, of course. Ever since he had seen the footage of Kitty Coughlin covered in monkey manure online, crying and screaming, Feldon knew that she was a woman completely out of her element in the rough and tumble world of news reporting. It would be an easy matter to create the circumstances that would nudge her over the edge.

But the trick was how to get the world to see it?

That monkey incident had amazed Feldon. When he first saw it on MyTube he was certain it would be Kitty's undoing. Anchors were supposed to face down the worst tragedies with icy cold dispassion. America would not trust an anchor who came apart in the heat of battle. Who could possibly put faith in an anchor who went to pieces at the zoo?

For nearly a week he sat in front of the television with a bowl of cheese doodles in his lap waiting for someone—a competing evening news broadcast, a newsmagazine on a rival network, one of the nightly scandal shows, even Leno or Letterman—to air the monkeyhouse footage. But no one did. The Internet and the old-fashioned broadcast networks truly did exist in two completely distinct universes. Maybe someday MyTube might be like the

Drudge Report and everyone would turn to it but for now, for all the impact it had upon the networks, it might just as well have been broadcasting on Mars.

Feldon had read a million articles online about how the network newscasts were skewing older and older with each passing year. People who watched the Big Three's evening news these days generally did so over an evening meal of oatmeal and banana mush in the common room of their nursing homes.

Feldon knew there were demographic differences between those who got their information from television and those who got their news via the Internet but until the monkeyhouse incident even he did not realize how great was the divide.

The video of Kitty covered in ape-poop had been an underground sensation on MyTube, but it had not made so much as a blip in the old dinosaur medium of television. Then the scheme came to him. Beautiful, full-blown and startling in its simplicity. The trick would be to deliver an all-new Kitty Coughlin breakdown directly to the wheezing codgers who still got their news the old-fashioned way.

Feldon had first tried to arrange footage so perfect that BCN would not dream of editing out Kitty's certain meltdown. The hijacking of Flight 980 was sure to make her snap. And according to Noah Sherman, she had popped off precisely as Feldon had expected. Unfortunately Feldon had not anticipated BCN's total lack of journalistic ethics.

In retrospect, Feldon should have known they would restage some of the footage. After all, Kitty had cost them a fortune and no one would want to admit to such a monumental blunder. Besides, network news was not above a little creative juggling of facts in order to present a story in a certain way. One of the most famous cases Feldon had studied in the Columbus School of Journalism in New York was of the network that had rigged a certain model of car to explode in order to prove the alleged danger of that type of automobile.

At first he had thought some of the other passengers would come forward to point out that the footage of Kitty was obviously fraudulent. But so many people must have been panicking on Flight 980 that no one noticed Kitty Coughlin.

Feldon had to rethink his plan.

The problem as he saw it was he had thought too grand right out of the gate. The coal mine was his next choice. A more intimate environment with only a few people around during the actual event to corroborate Kitty's breakdown. Unfortunately, Feldon had not counted on a happy ending. When those miners were saved, the focus shifted entirely to them. And the duplicity of BCN News and the complicity of the Weltsburg Coal and Mining Company had not helped. The coal company was only too happy to put the story behind them, so no one there was breathing a word about Kitty's panic attack. Once more BCN staged heroic footage of their celebrity anchorwoman, imperturbable in the face of adversity.

The fact that the genuine footage showed up once more on MyTube was Feldon's only proof that Kitty Coughlin had reacted precisely as he had expected she would.

Knowing from experience what to expect from BCN, Feldon's hopes with the tanker in Alaska lay with a random passenger on the cruise ship. It was possible that someone with a camera would videotape Kitty's hysterical fit at the moment the two ships went nose-to-nose. But truth be told, by that point he didn't have much hope of success. The big score would have to come, Feldon knew, in Los Angeles.

The mistake he had made in his previous attempts was allowing BCN the opportunity to edit the raw footage. What he needed was for the world to see Kitty go bonkers as it happened. It needed to be on the air. A full-scale crackup live on the air during a crisis would prove to everyone that this dimwitted, bobbleheaded tramp was unsuited for what had once been the prestigious post of nightly news anchor.

Then Orville Wilbur Feldon would step in as BCN's new executive producer to restore credibility to network news.

The arrangements were all made. Feldon had the promise of someone he trusted and Orville Wilbur Feldon did not find it easy to trust. He would have the job as soon as he took care of all the pesky details, the first being the public humiliation of BCN's current anchor. And finally today things had worked out on the air with Kitty Coughlin.

Now would come part two. The bread crumbs had been carefully dropped along the path by Orville Wilbur Feldon. The hijacked plane in New York, the coal mine disaster, the oil spill and now the L.A. riots. Kitty Coughlin at the scene of all of them. Soon someone in the news media, someone with credibility, would step forward and point out that these were all re-creations of big ratings-grabbing news stories. Fingers would point at BCN, the last-place evening newscast. It would be the story of the car wired to explode all over again but this time on a monumental scale.

Kitty Coughlin was already dead, murdered by the rampaging mob. The network would fire everyone else, from Uriah Maddox right on down to the lowliest segment producer.

A thing of beauty. A brilliant plan.

Feldon's mother was watching television in the kitchen. From his basement lair, Feldon heard the low tones of somber voices. His mother was tuned to the riots.

"Terrible," Mrs. Feldon's hoarse voice said. "Just terrible what people can do."

The kitchen chair creaked above his head and he heard his mother lumbering across the room. The television shut off and the heavy squeaks on the floor moved toward the back door. When the screen door slammed Feldon stood on his tiptoes to peek out the small basement window. He saw the back of his mother's big blue USPS uniform as she climbed into her beat-up old Dodge. Only when she had backed out of the driveway did Feldon go upstairs.

The first floor reeked of Cheyenne Light cigarettes. The ceiling, curtains and walls were stained yellow from smoke. The window panes were a translucent gray haze.

In the two hours between her part-time job at the grocery store and her full-time job at the post office, Feldon's mother had made a halfhearted attempt to clean some of the dirty pots in the kitchen sink. Still encrusted with burned-on food, the rusted old pots sat drying in the moldy plastic rack on the side of the sink.

"June Cleaver you are not, Mother," Feldon said. He shifted a pot in the rack. Kraft Macaroni & Cheese residue gunked up the rim and smeared the outside. "It's a wonder I don't catch typhoid fever or some other exotic affliction given the appalling conditions in which I'm forced to live."

He remembered a time when his mother had not been such a poor housekeeper. Feldon sometimes thought that she had deliberately become more slovenly over the years in the vain hope that her son would pitch in with the housework.

Feldon carefully put the macaroni pot back in the precise spot he had found it, lest its movement cause his mother to believe he held any interest in the dirty dishes.

He pulled a loaf of bread and a plastic container of margarine from the grimy old fridge. Feldon smeared a wad of margarine a half-inch thick on a slice of cold bread, slapped another slice on top and licked the excess margarine from the butter knife. He examined the knife when he was done and, finding that it was no worse than most of the silverware his mother had allegedly cleaned, slipped it back in the drawer.

He snapped on the countertop television and, butter sandwich in hand, sat down at the kitchen table next to the overflowing ashtray, hoping that the reporting had finally caught up to the events in L.A. and that the networks were reporting the demise of that vacuous tart Kitty Coughlin.

Feldon flipped from channel to channel but found it was still more of the same.

So engrossed was he in the little screen that he ignored the sound of the mail truck out front.

Ordinarily the Feldon mailman was not allowed to pass the front gate without receiving a good tongue-lashing. The pervert civil servant was a knuckle-dragging troglodyte who regularly mauled the covers of Feldon's magazines. Orville suspected his mother had abused her post office contacts and was involved in a grand conspiracy to shred her only son's *Entertainment Weekly*, but so far she had refused to confess to her complicity under even the most intense questioning.

Feldon had gone against his nature and suppressed the urge to lodge a formal complaint for this postal casus belli. A tart-tongued complaint to the postmaster might cost his chain-smoking crone of a mother her job, thus leaving the Feldons' refrigerator bare and Orville's stomach empty. Left without his normal avenue of addressing one of the many slights that constantly crossed his path, Feldon had taken to personally berating the lecher mailman on a daily basis.

The fact that he was spared the full wrath of Orville Wilbur Feldon's poison pen was a unique boon that would no doubt be lost on the Feldons' ungrateful dimwit mailman.

Bullying was in Orville Wilbur Feldon's blood. He had come to manhood in the pre-Internet age, so in his salad days most of his browbeating was on the local level.

Feldon had filed a dozen complaints with his local

bank for a five-dollar service charge after he had allowed his savings account to drop below the hundred-dollar minimum. So brutal was his prose that the faceless usurious brutes could finally take no more and relented, refunding the cash.

The ushers and concession operators at the local multiplex were regularly stung by sharp letters of complaint about the sticky floors and cold popcorn, and woe betide the waitress who did not bring another basket of breadsticks when the time came to fill out the little "How's our service?" card on the table of the little mom-and-pop diner downtown.

Daily letters to the editor of the local paper on important issues of the day went unpublished, so Feldon began a direct and personal letter-writing campaign aimed at the editor himself. Eventually the slack-jawed local police were involved in the matter and a bloated imbecilic judge had issued a restraining order against Feldon.

What the dunderpated thickwits did not realize was that Orville Wilbur Feldon was particularly suited to newspaper criticism. His degree from the most prestigious journalism school in the world placed him head and shoulders above the gaggle of hopheaded community college dropouts the paper employed. Truth be told, Feldon would be running the local editorial fishwrap if the prospect of so debasing himself did not make his delicate skin break out in an itchy rash. Besides, the application he had submitted to the paper after he graduated from Columbus had been ignored, no doubt thrown in the trash by a jealous rival fearful of suffering the wrath of Editor-in-Chief Orville Wilbur Feldon.

Fortunately for Feldon, his failure to find employment at the local free newspaper came right around the time a new medium began to filter into the national consciousness.

The rise of the Internet was a gift to Orville Wilbur Feldon. Suddenly a great vista was spread out before him.

Gone were the niceties that polite society forced upon him. Feldon had anonymity to spew his venom without fear of either restraining orders or punches to the face.

In no time Feldon became adept at the art of the "flame war," an Internet term for written provocations posted by individuals whose sole desire was to foster animosity. He became the bane of message boards the world over. He was despised on alt.tv.dr-who for repeatedly bashing Tom Baker's portrayal of the Doctor. Feldon's treatise on the superiority of the 1970s silver Cylons over the updated android versions had gotten him banned from three separate *Battlestar Galactica* boards. And his nasty Amazon.com and iBay customer reviews as well as his sarcastic Wikipedia update commentaries were the stuff of legend.

Orville Wilbur Feldon had not even heard of the term "cyberbully" until the first time it was applied to him on a *Buffy the Vampire Slayer* message board. He liked to think he was the inspiration for the term, which had since passed into such common usage that cyberbullying had been featured on programs ranging from *Dr. Phil* to *Maury Povich*.

The World Wide Web was the great leveler. The puniest weakling in the real world was an untouchable god online. Those who eschewed the Internet would never understand it but for a small percentage of people who lived their lives online, the greatest terror did not exist in the physical world. The thing that caused the worst nightmares was a biting comment added to an Amazon.com review, a negative rating on iBay, and endless torment on a Usenet newsgroup.

Even Orville Wilbur Feldon was surprised at how easy it was to recruit his minions online and it all started by insinuating himself into his victims' lives. He would start off with minor criticisms, small complaints, and when they rose to the bait, he would be in their lives and instantly raise the stakes. Masquerading as someone with access to powerful forces at all levels, he would roll out complaints, protests and build to threats of arrest, indictment, tax evasion charges, even having people listed in sex offender rolls. Constantly increasing the pressure, Feldon had found it easy to shanghai Noah Sherman and the rest to assist in his cause.

And now it was all coming together.

". . . reporting that Governor Scheissenhauser and BCN anchor Kitty Coughlin are safe and in good health . . ."

Feldon choked on his last bite of sandwich. At first he thought he had heard wrong. He pushed the crusts of his butter sandwich to one side and leaned toward the TV.

"You'll recall," said a male reporter's voice over helicopter images of mayhem in the streets of Los Angeles, "how we reported earlier that the governor and Ms. Coughlin were in the center of the riots, the eye of the storm, as it were. You'll also recall the spectacular footage of California's governor fighting off rioters just before BCN's live feed died. Well, we now have confirmation that both have survived and are safe and sound, Charlie."

When the footage cut to a BCN rival news anchor in New York, Feldon noted the smirk of delight on the man's face.

"That is definitely good news," the anchorman said. "And I understand the riots are coming under control?"

"Partly, Charlie. Unfortunately it's not all good news. There are reports of dozens of deaths in the area of the riots. Most seem to be members of the Casas street gang, one of the more notorious gangs to plague Los Angeles. Some civic groups are already complaining of police brutality although the Los Angeles police claim they have not involved themselves in the civil unrest and indeed have not taken an official position on the New L.A. Riots."

The phrase "The New L.A. Riots" appeared on the bottom of the screen. For some reason Feldon could not fathom, a cartoon sword sliced through the tops of the letters. Feldon assumed someone at the network had decided that the sword would make an eye-catching addition to the graphic even though it had nothing whatsoever to do with the riots.

Feldon reached out a shaking hand and snapped off the TV. "Impossible," he hissed. "This cannot be happening."

According to his calculations the riots should have gone on for two days. And there was no way the police could have been involved in the Casas deaths. Feldon had read online at The Smoking Gun months ago the infamous internal LAPD memo that issued strict guidelines governing the use of force against crowds that lacked proper permits. Rubber bullets and tear gas were permitted to disperse ROTC recruiters, rallies in support of U.S. troops, armed citizens defending their own businesses in the face of civil unrest, and college Republicans, but the use of any and all force against rioters, gang bangers, illegal immigrant protests and gatherings of more than four individuals of any racial minority darker than Halle Berry was strictly off-limits.

How could such a police department have stopped anybody from doing anything? Feldon wondered. And, most shocking, Kitty Coughlin had survived. To succeed, his plans did not require her death, only her public humiliation. But dead was good too. Dead she represented no threat to his ascension to the bully pulpit of BCN executive producer.

She should have been dead. She had been at the center of the storm. He had seen what should have been Kitty Coughlin's last seconds alive. Why was she still around?

Feldon's head swam. The police were definitely not involved, nor had the national guard been called in. That meant that another force was on the scene, something that existed below the radar. This force, whatever it might be, must have saved Kitty Coughlin.

Feldon's mind drifted to the mine in Pennsylvania and suddenly something that had nagged at him ever since the happy resolution of that story popped into his head. Those miners should definitely have died. There was no way they should have gotten out alive. For a week, until the *Motiv Kodiak* oil spill had supplanted it as America's major news story, TV reporters had called the miners' escape a miracle.

No miracle. Something had saved them. Or someone.

Feldon's chair toppled over as he shot to his feet. His slippers slapped against his heels as he hustled downstairs.

Searching along his wall of videotapes, he pulled the tape that Noah Sherman had mailed him from Pennsylvania and popped it into one of the empty VCRs.

Feldon fast-forwarded to the stranger with the blurred face who had killed SamEyeAm with a piece of hurled coal.

The man's clothes registered bright on the special infrared camera, which meant that they were actually dark. Just a T-shirt and trousers. Average height and build. While everything killer in the video was as clear as the camera allowed, the face was impossible to see. The only distinguishing characteristic was the man's wrists. Feldon was so quick to dismiss the tape when he first viewed it that he had not noticed them before. The wrists of the man who had killed SamEyeAm were freakishly thick with almost no discernible narrowing from forearms to hands.

Feldon paused the tape. All around him came the clicking sounds of his computer e-mail boxes filling with answers to complaints as well as irate notes from victims of his online bullying. Feldon ignored the noise.

Feldon knew that he was looking at the big news story that would inaugurate his auspicious reign as executive producer of the All-New BCN Evening News. And although she did not know it, Kitty Coughlin, that nitwitted, Mary Kay-slathered, plastic surgery-addicted lightweight, was going to help Orville Wilbur Feldon bag the story of a lifetime.

19

Chico Ramirez sat like Croesus on a pile of swag pillaged from the homes and businesses of East L.A.

His loyal subjects had been bringing tribute to the Casas gang leader all day. Many were utilizing his services as a fence for stolen goods; others just wanted to exchange looted twelve-hundred-dollar refrigerators and six-hundred-dollar camcorders for eighty bucks' worth of smack; while still more came on bended knee offering their stolen merchandise to wipe out or at least barter down debts owed to the Casas.

There was so much loot that Ramirez had been forced to move temporarily into the abandoned special effects company warehouse where he had met with the two gringos who had delivered this brilliant scheme to him.

From the grimy window of his catwalk office, Chico looked down at the astonishing amount of merchandise piled in what had been an empty warehouse just a few hours before. Two dozen sweating men in yellow bandanas worked like bees in a hive as they carted stolen goods along narrow corridors carved in piles of boxes.

There were stacks of televisions, microwaves, washing machines, dryers, dishwashers, and a hundred other appliances still in factory-sealed boxes piled to the second-story windows of the dusty warehouse. Clothes still on the rack were lined up a dozen racks deep. Armloads of expensive leather jackets, vests and pants were tossed in bundles over clothes racks which were bending from the strain.

There were cases of pet supplies, children's toys and boxes of junk food and liquor as far as the eye could see.

Some enterprising individuals had looted an above-ground swimming pool which a few of the Casas had tried to assemble in the middle of the warehouse earlier in the day. But Chico's men had had a hard time with the English instructions and an impossible time with the Spanish instructions and when they tried to fill the pool with a stolen Home Depot hose the pool's seams burst and flooded the main floor.

Chico had nearly blown their heads off for being so *muy estupido*. But the damage had mostly been limited to the looted inventory of a vintage record store and the garden tools and terra-cotta pots from a hardware store which could be dried off easily enough, so Chico was lenient and only pistol-whipped one man as a warning to the rest.

As it was he needed all the men he could get. Chico had just started hearing reports that some of his people had been turning up dead on the streets of L.A. This had shocked the gang leader. Chico had thought that decades of riots, urban unrest and lawsuits had finally broken the back of the LAPD. He never imagined they would come out in force. Chico wondered how soon the TV people would venture back into the war zone to ask the residents of the community if they intended to march on city hall to protest the horrible rapacious brutality of the LAPD against the poor Casas members.

Probably the news crews would wait until the shooting that was not being done by members of the LAPD had slowed down a bit and all of the fires, none of which had been set by members of the LAPD, were out.

Chico had turned his attention to a stolen television which sat on a stolen desk in the abandoned office when he heard a commotion down on the warehouse floor.

At first he was afraid that his men were trying to piece together one of the looted Adventure Center Outdoor Children's PlaySets that would, like the pool, inevitably collapse. But then Chico heard a shout of fear and a sudden burst of gunfire.

Chico shot up from his stolen seat and ran to the office window.

From high above, the Casas leader could see the entire warehouse floor and was shocked to see three of his men lying on the cracked cement floor near the loading dock door, their spines bent at impossible angles. Racing from the bodies and into the main warehouse were two men. One was a young white, the other was very old and looked Chinese.

Chico quickly determined that these men were not LAPD. The Los Angeles Police Department had been trained away from employing violence as a method to control the criminals who preyed upon the helpless citizens of the City of Angels, and these two were obviously not averse to using violence. Chico realized this when he saw one of his gang members attack the young intruder with a stolen golf club, only to wind up airborne and flying backward into a looted Nova Craft Kevlar canoe. The canoe became a stepped-on beer can, crumpling at the center and bending into a boomerang shape.

As the crumpled Casas settled into the crumpled canoe, the young intruder shouted something so innocuous so calmly that it turned Chico Ramirez's spine to ice.

"First floor! Cosmetics, canoes, humidors, Slip 'n'

Slides, ladies' intimate apparel, and dead punk gang members. Everybody off the car, no shoving, please."

On the warehouse floor, the Master of Sinanju shook his head at his pupil. "It is bad enough you have dragged me all around this benighted area eradicating vermin, the least you can do is keep your asinine comments to yourself," he said, clucking his tongue in annoyance.

Two Casas members charged the old Korean. A single fluid swipe of one heel and four Casas patellae were skipping across the floor. With their kneebones detached, the legs of the men buckled like folding chairs. Before they hit the floor, the gang members greeted eternity with a pair of fingernails buried deep in their brains.

"Hey, we had to work our way up el chaino de commando," Remo said as the dead men slipped from his teacher's extended hands. "Besides, Smith would want us to pitch in. God knows the police are useless the way they're wetting their pants over how to deal with the riots."

From behind a stack of boxes filled with DVDs jumped a Casas thug who buried the business end of a brand-new double-barrel shotgun deep in Remo's belly. Screaming triumph, he pulled both triggers.

The blast rattled the tin roof and should have blown out Remo's belly and severed his spine. But somehow in the infinitesimally small moment between the time the impulse to pull the trigger registered in the man's brain and the actual moment he pulled the trigger, the barrel of his gun had been redirected. When the smoke cleared, the largest chunk of the gang member's body fell where it stood. The rest was scattered amid shotgun pellets against a box of DVDs labelled *The Loopy Instructor 3*.

Remo and Chiun split up and as soon as he rounded a corner, the Master of Sinanju met two more gang members. "You dead, old man," shouted one of the Casas. He smiled a set of perfect white teeth in a face covered from forehead to chin in tattoos.

Both men held pistols in each hand. The two men opened fire. Four guns exploded in the hot warehouse.

Chiun did not break stride even as he twisted and spiraled around the incoming volleys of screaming lead. Upon the gunmen, his hands were invisible blurs, cutting an X in air as he passed between them.

Arms separated at the elbows. Four forearms dropped to the floor still clutching triggers, involuntary twitches blasting a dozen more rounds.

The last gunshots were still firing as Chiun collapsed two foreheads with the heels of his hands. The shock of losing their arms so horribly was eclipsed by the dull look of sudden death. The men joined their severed arms on the warehouse floor.

"Let that be a lesson. Pick on someone your own age," the Master of Sinanju lectured the corpses.

In a self-satisfied swirl of kimono hems, the old Asian darted deeper into the warehouse.

In the office high above, Chico Ramirez peered over the windowsill and watched the carnage below. He had seen the two intruders split up. They had bisected the warehouse and were now moving toward the center, clearing out Casas as they went. Chico could see a dozen yellow scarves stained red with blood.

There was no rear exit from the offices. The only way out for Chico was to take the steps down to the killing floor. As he watched his men fall one by one he began to lose hope that he would escape with his life.

Suddenly Chico spotted something large moving in from the back of the building. His heart soared.

"Jorge," Chico hissed, nearly singing the name.

Jorge Alvaro had been a massive brute even before he had discovered weightlifting during his first stint in San Quentin at the tender age of eighteen. Jorge weighed north of three hundred pounds and could bench-press twice his own weight. He had no neck, just a fat bulge of shoulder muscle atop which his head squatted like an egg in a nest.

Chico watched Jorge sneak up behind the young one. This was it. There was no way the young one would survive. Jorge would take care of the skinny gringo and then squash the old one like a bug. Two big hands reached out for the young one and Chico began to stand up at the window, so confident was he that Jorge was about to eliminate the two intruders.

Then something happened that Chico Ramirez would not have believed had he not seen it with his own shocked eyes.

Just before Jorge's hands wrapped around the young one's throat, the young one did a little pirouette. It looked as simple as that, just a little dance move, and all of a sudden he had the two ends of Jorge's yellow bandana in his hands and had the cloth wrapped around the fat roll of muscle that would have constituted a neck on a less mighty man.

As the hulking mass that was Jorge Alvaro swatted helplessly at hands that were somehow more powerful than even his own massive mitts, far above, Chico Ramirez felt a damp warmth spread across the crotch of his newly-liberated, six-hundred-dollar black leather trousers.

"Who's the boss here?" Remo asked the pile of meat with the barrel chest and pig-like eyes.

Big, powerful Jorge Alvaro was like a helpless baby as Remo tightened his yellow bandana around his throat. Arms flailing, he managed to point up to the office window where Chico Ramirez was peering over the sill like a wide-eyed Latino Kilroy.

There was a terrible crack as Remo tugged the bandana tight, Jorge's head lolled on what was a neck after all, and Remo was vaulting off the warehouse floor.

Ten feet up, one toe barely brushed the top of a Whirlpool range still in its box and, with a push and a flip, he was on the catwalk and strolling over to a shocked Chico.

Chico ran out the office door and darted along the catwalk in the opposite direction. The jump to the floor could cripple or kill him, but he knew he stood a better chance leaping from the catwalk than he did at the hands of a man who could strangle Jorge Alvaro in a brutally hot L.A. warehouse without so much as breaking a sweat.

Chico took but a single step when he found the path in the other direction blocked.

The terrifying old wraith in the golden kimono was on the catwalk and closing in from the opposite end.

Chico decided that here was as good a place as any to take the plunge, and hopped onto the railing. His toe scarcely brushed the lower rail before he felt a sharp tug at the back of his neck.

The many gold chains that adorned his narrow neck cut deep into his Adam's apple, his shoes slipped off the rail and he fell back hard onto the catwalk.

"This is the boss-man, Little Father," the young one said when the old one padded up.

Chico found himself being dragged to his feet, half-strangled by his own chains.

Remo held tight to the fistful of chains and gave a sharp twirl. Chico's face turned red. Through the window, Remo spied something hanging on the wall of the office. He brought the gang leader back inside the small room and held him up to a stolen antique mirror. Chico's toes dangled two inches off the dirty floor.

"See the pretty color?" Remo said, pointing out the mirror image of Chico to the real-life, strangling Chico. "The color is red. The next color is blue, then white. It's all very patriotic. You do not want me to get to white. We have spoken to enough of your men on our way here to confirm that someone told you how to run these riots. You're going to tell me who that is. Okay, go."

Remo eased up on his grip. Chico took in a mighty, ragged breath.

"He paid us to do it," Chico gasped on the exhale. "Ten thousand each for me and five of my men. He said if I followed the plan I could make a lot more from the free stuff people would take. There. The plans he gave us are right there."

Remo noted the maps stacked up on a shiny mahogany table that still had a store label attached to the leg.

"What's his name?" Remo demanded.

"It was like the Bible," Chico wheezed. "Like Adam or Eve or one of those stories like that."

"The Bible's a big book," Remo said. "Let's see if we can narrow that down a smidge."

Remo squeezed. Chico's eyes bulged.

"The ark one," the gang leader choked desperately when the pressure on his windpipe was once more relaxed. "With the giraffes and the other two-by-two animals. Moses."

"Moses was the Red Sea, dope," Remo said. "Burning bush, plague of locusts, 'Let my people go,' Charlton Heston in a big, fake beard."

"Indeed," Chiun said from the doorway. "That man caused all manner of trouble for good Pharaoh Ramses. And his plagues made a complete mess of Egypt. Do you know how many years it took to clear all the toads out of the royal bath? Ramses, who had employed us in the past, made the mistake of not keeping Sinanju on retainer or we would have dealt appropriately with that nuisance Moses. Of course, you would not have approved, Remo. Moses lived to be one hundred and twenty so you would no doubt have run off to carry in his groceries for him while leaving me, your elderly father who has given you everything in life, home to starve."

"Let it go, Chiun," Remo said. He turned his attention back to Chico. "Okay, so Moses was the Red Sea. Noah was the ark. Was it Moses or Noah?"

"Noah," Chico gasped.

"You sure?"

"That was it. His name was Noah. I don't know his last name, but that's what the other one call him. The other one was called Wayne. I do not know his last either. There were only two of them. They told me what to do but they were not in charge. Someone else gave them instructions, someone they never met and were afraid of. They said that he contacted them only through the Internet."

Remo's face soured. "That thing again?" He gave Chico a little extra strangling just for mentioning the Internet.

"Gccchhhkkkk!" Chico said, tongue bulging.

"That's blue," Remo said. He loosened up on the gold chains. "Is that everything?"

Even with the chains loosened, Remo still held Chico off the floor. The jewelry cut deep into the back of his neck.

Chico thought desperately. "I shot him. Noah's body is in a van out behind the building." It was clear the gang leader had surrendered all he knew.

"I thought his body was on Mount Arafat," Remo said, giving one extra hard twirl. Chico's neck snapped and his face went pale in death. "That's white," Remo added. He let the body slip from his fingers.

Remo went over to the table and gathered up the maps and written instructions Chico's contact had given him.

"Ararat, not Arafat," Chiun said. "But he is not buried there," Chiun said as his pupil folded the papers and stuffed them in a leather valise that still bore a nine-hundred-dollar price tag.

"What?" Remo said.

"Noah. The Noah you people have latched onto became a vintner and lived three hundred and fifty more years after the Flood. You would have liked him, Remo. Another old man who is not me for you to worship."

"I don't worship you, Little Father, I like you."

"Talk is cheap," Chiun sniffed.

Remo was satisfied that he had collected everything. Turning from the table, he nodded. "Let's swing by dead Noah's van and see what he has to say before we call Smith."

Mark Howard stood behind Smith's office chair as the two men studied the computer monitor.

Mark had just completed his analysis of the riots. On the computer screen, the section of Los Angeles that was under siege was laid out in a simple grid with the parallel lines of streets around a central square of green.

"Here's the park where Kitty Coughlin was interviewing Scheissenhauser," the assistant CURE director said. "It's basically ground zero. According to reports, the first incidents took place in these spots." Mark pointed out a dozen locations on the map that were arranged around the central park. "That was all it took to strike the match."

As he studied his assistant's analysis, Smith was forced to keep reminding himself of the chaos that had occurred as a result of the rioting in Los Angeles not to mention the nearly seventy deaths that had been reported so far, lest he find himself becoming too impressed with the twisted brilliance that had engineered the scripted riots.

"Whoever managed them knew precisely what to do," the CURE director admitted.

According to the accounts that had thus far been pieced together, the unrest started when gang members descended en masse on a few stores in strategic areas. The first retail outlets were near densely populated public housing. When the people there witnessed what was happening in the streets below, they swept out to join the marauding hordes. Looting and rioting had spread like wildfire after that, moving inward and outward from the original circle. At the center of the storm, Kitty Coughlin and crew had been surrounded.

"On the plus side, it looks like things are coming under

control," Mark said. "Are you sure Remo and Chiun are responsible?"

Smith nodded curtly. "The police are in full retreat. Spokesmen for the LAPD have tripped over one another to get out and claim they are not responsible for the Casas deaths. Even as the riots continue, the mayor and police chief have scheduled a joint news conference an hour from now to deny any involvement of civil authorities in quelling the riots. Yet in the face of this insanity, pockets of disorder have begun to come under control. If you have another explanation, Mark, I would be glad to hear it."

The assistant CURE director nodded. "Remo and Chiun," he agreed. As if his words were a summoning spell, the blue phone on Smith's desk rang sharply. Smith snatched it up.

"Report," he said.

"The Left Coast's got a Bavarian bodybuilder as a governor, the media's got the cops afraid to look cross-eyed at the bad guys, and somewhere Rodney King is lamenting they just don't make riots like the good old days," Remo said. "Just another day of fun in the sun in batshit L.A. On the plus side we maybe found something."

Remo quickly recounted his and Chiun's trip up the Casas hierarchy to Chico Ramirez.

"I assumed you were responsible for suppressing some of the civil unrest," Smith said.

"Responsibility and L.A. are mutually exclusive terms, Smitty," Remo said. "Anyway, this gang clown gave up the guy who cooked up the riots. He was dead but even stinking up a hot van parked all day in the California sun couldn't squelch the man-perfume he was wearing. It was the same stink I smelled in that mine in Pennsylvania."

Smith placed a flat palm on the cool surface of his desk. "The ringleader is dead?"

"No, just a run-of-the-mill circus clown. No ID, just like the one on the roof in Weehawken. But I've got two first names. Noah and Wayne. Noah's the dead one. I guess Wayne got away. I forgot to ask. Anyway, the gang guy said they talked to their boss through that Interwhatsit."

Smith pressed the phone to his chest. "Mark, do an iBay search again, this time limited to first names Noah and Wayne. Hold on." He brought the phone to his ear once more. "Remo, how long has this Noah been dead?"

"Maybe nine hours," Remo said.

"For Noah, check on iBay accounts that have gone fallow in the past few weeks, but particularly in the past day," Smith said to his assistant. "Check purchases and sales as well as links to individuals named Wayne."

"I'm on it," Mark said and hustled from the office.

"We've got some maps and stuff too, Smitty," Remo said. "This Noah jerk gave the gang guys step-by-step instructions to start things off. I'll ship them along."

"Very good," Smith said. "Although that Kitty Coughlin fan mail you sent along was of no use. We did a thorough search. If someone is doing all this to help her ratings, it was not one of the three individuals who wrote those notes."

"Her secret admirer could have gotten buried in her hate mail by mistake, but you'd need a forklift to move the boxes," Remo said.

"That is assuming it's an admirer behind all this," the CURE director pointed out.

"I thought that was the plan," Remo said. "Did someone switch the playbook without giving me a copy?"

"Mark brought something to my attention," Smith said. "A video-sharing Web site called MyTube. I am used to the Internet as an information gathering tool, and am not as aware of these—" The CURE director paused, searching for the word "—these younger uses for the

Web. There is raw, unaired video of Kitty Coughlin posted there."

"I've seen it," Remo said. "Kitty and a bunch of monkeys getting into a snowball fight with crap. It's the heartwarming holiday movie of the year. I give it five opposable thumbs up."

"There is more than just that video posted," Smith said. "The raw video from Flight 980, as well as footage of Ms. Coughlin in the mine in Pennsylvania and on the cruise ship during the *Motiv Kodiak* accident have been posted too, each time by a different BCN employee. However, this is not some subversive attempt to oust her by low-level employees. Only one had contact with her prior to the incident in which he was involved, and that was the Flight 980 cameraman. These are apparently just employees blowing off steam."

"Kitty does have a way of making friends and influencing people," Remo said.

"My point exactly," Smith said. "The video you mentioned was posted months ago. Coughlin's reaction was, to put it mildly, less than professional. Perhaps someone with an ax to grind against her, someone who possibly wants her fired from her anchor position, saw that footage and was inspired to create circumstances that would drive her into another fit. We had thought until now that it was a friend attempting to help, but this could be an elaborate attempt by a foe to humiliate her and possibly drive her from the air."

"Well, today might have done it," Remo said. "I've been bonking heads of gang members all afternoon and on at least five looted big screen TVs in five different barrio dives I saw Scheissenhauser wearing Kitty like a knapsack while she screamed sweet nothings in his ear."

"So you're saying BCN has pulled her from the air?"

"Beats me. I haven't seen her since I got her and Governor Steroids out of the riots."

"Remo, you had better stick with the woman," Smith said. Even as he spoke, the CURE director slid his chair up to his desk.

"I've got a better idea," Remo said. "How about I stick my head in a blender and hit puree?"

"Remo, Kitty Coughlin still remains the focal point of all these events," Smith said as he typed. "All I have right now is a theory so we have no way of knowing if whoever is behind this thinks he has succeeded. If I'm right, much depends on how BCN reacts to her performance today." He finished typing with a flourish. "She's at a hotel in downtown Los Angeles. They've got her scheduled for a flight back to New York at seven o'clock your time. You and Chiun are now scheduled to come back on the same flight. And as long as you are coming back to the East Coast, it would be quicker for you to bring back with you the materials you found rather than mail them from out there."

"Cheaper too," Remo grumbled. "We're on our way home. But I won't promise not to toss Kitty out over Kansas."

The phone went dead in Smith's ear. The CURE director stretched his hand across the desk and replaced the blue receiver in the cradle with a soft click.

Ordinarily Smith detested guesswork. He liked to deal in cold, hard fact which was why he felt a kindred connection to the emotionless CURE computers. But on those rare occasions that Smith felt the stirring of instinct in his gut he knew enough to trust it, for it was instinct guided by decades of experience. And right now he did not need Folcroft's four basement mainframes to tell him that he was finally on the right track.

Whoever was behind these events was not someone out to boost Kitty Coughlin's ratings but someone determined to force her from the air. Although he did not express his certainty to Remo, Smith was confident this was the case.

It was now a matter of determining who would benefit most from Kitty Coughlin's professional demise.

With the renewed vigor of a young hunter hot on the scent of his prey, Dr. Harold W. Smith attacked his computer keyboard.

20

This was really it. The day she had been dreading
ever since those wretched little apes had forced her to
break down on tape. Her ratings had already been bad
before that disastrous trip to the zoo but it was at that
moment that she understood her own weakness, that
moment she realized she was a pretender, a fraud.
Although she had never shared her insecurities with
another living soul, it was the instant after the first glob
of feces hit and she realized what had happened, the
moment when the chimpanzees started laughing and
pointing at her, the moment she felt her emotions slipping
away from her, that she knew she was doomed to fail.

She had always been emotional, even in her morning
show days. Didn't her eyes always get moist when
discussing terrible diseases? Didn't she bubble with
enthusiasm when she pinned on a campaign button for the
first lady who had gone on to become a senator? Didn't
she look appropriately disgusted when discussing other

newsmen who wore American flag lapel pins, almost as if they were proud to be Americans? She had been good but what had worked on an informal morning show did not translate to hard evening news.

BCN should have known. They knew what they were getting when they hired her. She didn't just read the news, she emoted on the air. She made people want to feel.

But now they were going to pull her off the air for displaying a teensy little emotion, a possibility she had secretly feared ever since those monkeys had gotten the better of her. And now that it was finally here it was more horrible than Kitty Coughlin had ever imagined it would be.

At least the local affiliate had sprung for a ride to the airport. But the rude little intern spoke to her only once all the way to LAX. Kitty was sobbing uncontrollably in the backseat and the young man offered a sympathetic smile.

"Would you like a tissue, ma'am?" he asked.

The sobbing snapped off like a spigot. "Shut your goddamn face and speak when spoken to," Kitty snarled. And in the next moment the waterworks started anew, more ferociously than ever. "Why doesn't anyone like me?" she wailed out the car window at uncaring Los Angeles.

At LAX, the intern dumped her luggage onto the sidewalk and when Kitty demanded that he carry it inside he responded with a hand gesture that Kitty took as a "no" before hopping back in the car and leaving her in a cloud of burning rubber.

BCN's fifteen-million-dollar-a-year anchorwoman gathered up her own bags and struggled through the terminal door.

She bawled openly as she walked, stopping only to growl at every kindly soul who offered to help.

Uriah was going to fire her when she got back to New York, and it was all the fault of those damn monkeys. They had revealed to her the truth about herself.

Kitty wished she'd had a machine gun that day. She would have blown their little monkey brains all over their cages. She wondered how much it would cost to buy them all. BCN would still have to pay out her contract even if she wasn't on the air. She could buy the chimps and donate them to medical research. The little crap-flingers could contribute to something useful, like cosmetic ear reduction or foot liposuction. Stuff that would benefit all mankind.

Kitty was halfway to the counter when she became aware of a presence beside her. Someone had slipped in next to her as she walked. Kitty glanced to her right and when she found Remo keeping pace with her her tears dried instantly.

"What are you doing here?" Kitty demanded, sniffling.

"Wishing we were anywhere else," Remo said.

"We?" Kitty said. She glanced to her left where the Master of Sinanju was padding silently alongside.

The old Korean was once more looking anywhere other than in Kitty's direction, his disdain palpable.

"You know I score high among old people," Kitty told him. "It's the one group I still do okay with."

"Advanced age must make them too weak to operate their remote control devices," Chiun suggested, hazel eyes studying a light fixture that was clearly more interesting than Kitty.

Kitty turned her attention to Remo. "Some bodyguards you are. You abandoned me pretty quick when I needed you."

"My mistake," Remo said. "In all the excitement we followed the wrong facelift. Joan Rivers says hi. But we're here now. Reluctantly—"

"Very reluctantly," Chiun interjected.

"—and we're going to get you back home safe and sound."

Remo offered a reassuring smile.

Kitty gave a little scoffing snort. "You're delivering

me to my own execution," she said. "I'm like that high school girl who helped the British beat France in World War One and got burned like a steak. Joan Van Ark."

So twisted in knots was Remo's brain over Kitty's historical inaccuracies, he scarcely noticed the fat man who nearly plowed into him. He did a little sidestep without breaking stride and allowed the man to pass. The passerby bumped Kitty's big cosmetics case from the crook of her elbow and it fell to the floor with a rattling thud.

"Blind asshole!" she screeched at the man's retreating back. "What the hell was his problem?"

"Probably distracted," Remo suggested. "Maybe he can't figure out where he knows you from without Governor Bratwurst glued to your torso."

"Perhaps he would recognize you if you were covered in chimpanzee offal," Chiun suggested.

"Hah-hah," Kitty said. "Pick up my bag," she ordered Remo.

"Sorry. No can do. Bodyguard union rules. I'll go see if I can find a skycap who won't mind getting kicked in the teeth and undertipped for his trouble."

Leaving Kitty to struggle with her own bags, Remo and Chiun wandered off to the ticket counter.

Orville Wilbur Feldon waddled rapidly away from Kitty Coughlin and her two companions.

Feldon had not intended to get so close. He was only at the airport to reconnoiter. He was certain that BCN would recall Kitty to New York City after her disastrous on-air performance that day. Thanks to BCN's Web site, he had known long before Flight 980 that BCN had an exclusive contract with TransAmerican Air, so all he had to do was wait for Kitty to arrive for one of the evening Los Angeles to New York flights. And when she showed up and those two men joined her, Feldon knew he was right.

They were the ones who had saved Kitty Coughlin and stopped his riots. He knew it with an instinct for the great news story, the story of the century, of the millennium— a news instinct that would have surprised his professors at Columbus University School of Journalism, all of whom had regarded Feldon as a second-rate student headed for a second-rate career. At best.

The younger man with Kitty Coughlin Feldon recognized from the video Noah Sherman had taped in the mine in Pennsylvania. He had not seen the man's face, but he had the same build, thick wrists and wore similar dark T-shirt and chinos. The clincher was that effortless gait. The young man drifted easily along the floor as if his legs could not be bothered with the enterprise of movement. It was as if he was gliding over an invisible conveyer belt.

The old one walked with the same easy glide although it was less obvious in his long kimono. There was a perfect stillness to him even while in motion that was at once fascinating and frightening.

Feldon had inched close but not so close that he would attract their attention. But at the last minute a very tan middle-aged man in a sports coat so hideously orange he could only be a movie producer had shoved past and nearly pushed Feldon directly into the younger of Kitty's companions.

Feldon was so stunned by what happened next that he failed completely to snap an insult at the film producer.

The younger man in the T-shirt had missed Feldon completely. It was impossible. They should have bumped one another but it was as if the man had disappeared just before the point of impact and reappeared on the far side of Feldon without breaking stride. The phenomenon had thrown Feldon off his clumsy gait and he wound up knocking a bag out of the hated strumpet Kitty Coughlin's hands.

Feldon felt a thrill of excitement deep in the jiggling,

flabby mass that was his belly. As he walked away, he glanced back only once, trying to find something, anything that would help him discover who these two were.

The young one surrendered nothing. Even a logo on the back of his T-shirt might have offered some clue, but it was a plain black cotton T. Nothing out of the ordinary there.

But the old one. . . .

Feldon pulled a bus schedule and a pencil stub from his sweaty pocket and made a quick doodle. Turning from Kitty and her two companions, he hustled from the terminal.

His mother had recently refused to continue paying for insurance and gas for his 1984 Ford Escort. Feldon could scarcely contain his excitement as he waited for the bus.

On the ride back into the city, he did not even sit in the seat behind the driver and complain about his driving. Instead he sat in the back and smiled out the dirty window. Orville Wilbur Feldon rarely smiled for life rarely gave him anything to smile about. Still this was a special occasion.

He had been right. This would be the first big news story of his career as executive producer at BCN News. He could almost hear his anchor, his great benefactor, reading the text off the teleprompter, text Feldon would personally write.

These men were special. They could toss a piece of coal in pitch-black from twenty yards down a cramped mine tunnel while being shot at and manage to kill an attacker. Feldon had rewatched the tape over and over that afternoon and could now see why Noah Sherman had thought it might buy him his freedom. In fact, for a little while Feldon had very briefly considered removing the negative iBay ratings and comments he had posted on Noah's account, the ratings that he had first used to bamboozle Noah into working for him. But Noah had yet to e-mail after his meeting with the Casas gang and besides the riots had not played out as they should have so Feldon had changed his mind about letting Noah off the hook.

Feldon was certain that these two men with Kitty Coughlin were responsible for all the Casas deaths. Dead gang members showing up all over East L.A. was enough to put the fear of God into the rest of the rioters. The civil unrest in Los Angeles was over, and those two men were responsible.

If his knees weren't so prone to sharp pains from carting around an extra hundred pounds for the past twenty years, Feldon would have skipped down the bus steps. As it was he waddled as fast as he could down the street.

Two blocks over he turned into a door over which hung an old sign on rusted brackets: ALL THINGS READ.

A bell over the door tinkled and an old man in a tattered sweater looked up from the counter near the door. His glasses were thick and his white hair was long and hung in strings down to his bony shoulders.

"Oh, you," he said, irritated, and stuck his nose back into the fat volume of Greek lore that held down the counter.

A ratty old cat either slept or had recently died next to the cash register. Either way, the tabby did not move as Feldon waddled up to the counter.

"I'm sorry," Feldon said, breathless, his cheeks flushed. "You were right, I was wrong."

The old man looked up. Surprise filled the creases around his mouth along with, Feldon calculated, two-day-old encrusted ketchup.

"Asimov's prose more than equaled his ideas," Feldon continued rapidly, hoping speed would mitigate the pain of a sham apology. "Arthur Clarke was not fit to change his typewriter ribbon."

The old man weighed Feldon's words, grunted, nodded

and turned his attention back to his book. "You haven't been around much lately," he said.

"My Nazi mother confiscated my car keys," Feldon explained. "Here." He pulled the bus schedule from his pocket and shoved it into the old man's hands. "Have you seen this symbol before?"

The old man glanced at the doodle on the damp bus schedule. Tipping his head back, he held it to his bifocals.

"Hmm. Looks familiar. Where did it come from?"

"Some old Chinese guy was wearing it on his kimono. It was that sort of raised embroidery stuff. It was on the back with a bunch of flowers and a couple of dragons. It seemed to be significant since it was the central bit. Everything else was arranged around it. And no one knows more about old symbols and the lore connected to them than you. So what is it? Is it Chinese?"

The old man nodded. "Chinese? Could be. But, I think I've seen this before. Yes. Yes, I know this." He crumpled the bus schedule in his hand and got up from his counter.

Muttering to himself, he shuffled off into the stacks of dusty books. Feldon followed through the labyrinthine path that cut through overflowing shelves and tables piled high with battered old volumes.

In the back of the shop, the old man wheeled a three-step ladder to a tall shelf and took a fat book down from the second shelf from the top. He had to swipe away cobwebs and dust with the cuff of his dirty, threadbare sweater.

There was no title on the cover. *Myths of Ancient Asia* was printed in gold letters on the spine.

The old man futilely licked his thumb with his dry tongue and began leafing through the crinkling pages. Feldon noticed the copyright was 1897 and that only one other copy of the book sat up on the shelf.

"Know it was in here. We got two volumes of this back in '76. Estate sale in Oxnard. Don't think they've been touched since I put 'em up here back then. Yes, here it is. That trapezoid is their symbol. Knew I saw it before."

He handed the book to Feldon.

Feldon's face was a thrill of triumph when he saw the picture of the symbol he had sketched back at the airport. It was a simple trapezoid bisected by a vertical line.

" 'The House of Sinanju?' " Feldon read.

"A house of ancient Korean mercenaries," the old man said, without glancing at the article. As he spoke, he sent the exploratory tip of his tongue out to chip away at the encrusted ketchup. "Only one master and one pupil per generation. Hired out to the highest bidder. Capable of superhuman feats. 'Where the Master of Sinanju walks, men weep and gods tremble,' or something like that. Worked for kings and pharaohs. Anyone who could afford their very expensive services. Would accept other methods of payment, but preferred gold. Died out hundreds, possibly thousands of years ago, if they ever existed at all."

Feldon scanned the article as the old man talked. There were a few more details, but the entry was short. It finished up on the next page with a simple black-and-white etching of a Korean in a kimono. He was younger and much taller than the man Feldon had seen at the airport, but there seemed to be some ghostly resemblance to Kitty Coughlin's companion. Feldon slammed the book shut.

"How much?" he asked.

Feldon had to haggle the man down to twenty-eight dollars which, not counting bus fare, was all that remained of the money he had filched from the secret hatbox hiding place in the back of his mother's closet that morning.

He studied the article at home that evening while irate e-mails racked up unattended and his mother shouted abuse from upstairs, and by the morning bus ride into the city he had committed the most important passages to memory.

After a short discussion with a bank manager, Feldon withdrew a little over twenty thousand dollars from his special account and was off to a gold broker down the street. The bank manager had phoned ahead and in half an hour Feldon was lugging a 32.15-ounce gold bar into the nearest OverNite Express Office. Ten minutes later he was back on the sidewalk, two pounds lighter and with a promise that his package would be in New York by late afternoon.

Feldon whistled merrily to himself.

Only one master and pupil per generation. Feldon knew now that these were Kitty Coughlin's two companions. Much more than a legend. This Sinanju could not possibly have lasted as long as it apparently had without being the best at what it did. And the best would certainly be paid well and would absolutely entertain all offers.

Feldon had just paid for Kitty Coughlin's demise, the extinction of an ancient house of assassins and the premier story of his all-new executive produced BCN news, and he had done so entirely on someone else's dime. Not a bad day's work for his first day's work in almost a decade. And all before ten a.m.

Feldon celebrated by stopping off for three Big Macs, two large orders of fries, two Egg McMuffins, a strawberry shake and a large Coke. When the countergirl told him that he did not have enough for everything, he sent one McMuffin back, cursed his mother for not hiding enough in her hatbox vault, and made a mental note to write McDonald's through its Web site to complain about a fascist, bean-counter employee named Callie who had placed underneath the heat lamps an Egg McMuffin sandwich that had been handled by a customer whose hands had been God only knew where.

21

Uriah Maddox rested his elbows on the big conference table and pressed his fingers to his temples. The late afternoon sun shone through the tall windows to his right.

"This is a disaster," he moaned.

A large high definition television screen decorated one wall of the long boardroom. On the screen, Governor Konrad Scheissenhauser battled rioters as if he were back in his 1980s silver screen glory days. There was already talk of million-dollar offers wooing California's governor back to the movie business even though his actions during the riots had already prompted more than a dozen civil lawsuits.

Scheissenhauser had come out of this with his image burnished. There was even renewed talk of amending the Constitution to allow foreign-born citizens the right to become president of the United States.

And what did BCN have to show for it?

"Freeze," Uriah ordered.

Down the table, someone punched the remote control.

The image paused. There was Kitty Coughlin, BCN's answer to the tough-as-nails reporters of yesteryear, clinging to Governor Scheissenhauser, Botoxed face frozen in terror, mouth open wide as she screeched for her life.

"A disaster," Uriah repeated, closing his eyes on the TV, as if the image of Kitty screaming caused him physical pain. "Shut it off." The TV winked off and Uriah moaned. "Fifteen million dollars. We're bleeding here. We're a hair from dead. What can we do for damage control? I want ideas, no matter how far-fetched. We've got to fix this."

An eager young executive suggested they hire back BCN's most recent full-time anchor, the man who had anchored their newscast for twenty-five years.

"You've got to be kidding me. He's nuts."

"It doesn't have to be permanent. Just temporarily, as a stopgap until we can find a replacement for Kitty."

"We can't bring him back," Uriah argued. "Not only has he been bad-mouthing us ever since we fired him, he's been in and out of nuthouses the past two years. They found him just last week in the men's room of a Bed, Bath & Beyond in El Paso. He'd shaved his head in the sink and kept asking employees 'What's the frequency?' "

"How about Grandfather Clarence?" the young executive said. "We got him to do that voiceover for Kitty's newscast. He was up for that, he might be up for this."

Clarence Wenthall was the dean of American television journalism. In his early career he had been a radio broadcaster who had moved into TV in the medium's infancy. Because of his grumpy, jowly face and somber delivery he had been dubbed "Grandfather Clarence."

He was also a petty, bitter tyrant who terrorized the staff at BCN for twenty years. Far from his benign grandfatherly image, he was the man most responsible for transforming the evening news from a simple accounting of daily events to a nightly half-hour of poisonous bias. The old-timers at BCN knew Wenthall well.

Uriah nodded as he considered the suggestion. "Do you think he'd do it?" he asked. "Just for a few months even?"

"No way you can bring him back," a white-haired executive said, shaking his head firmly. "He's nearly a hundred. We've got a youth problem as it is, that'd kill us demographically. Besides, I was on his boat up at Martha's Vineyard last summer. The galley was stocked with nothing but Pepto, Viagra, Seagrams and Depends."

"He'd be sitting," Uriah said. "No one would see him from the waist down. This would just be temporary."

"I think he's gone senile," the old executive said. "He was calling his captain Rosalinda all day and kept trying to stuff dollar bills down the poor guy's pants."

"We can work around that," Uriah insisted.

"At one point he burst into tears, shouted 'That's the way it was,' stripped off his clothes and jumped naked into the ocean. When they fished him out of some lobster nets he was yelling about how Vietnam was a lost cause."

Uriah considered for a long moment. "Okay, let's put him in the maybe pile. Anybody else? Anybody at all?"

"I hate to mention her," a female executive said, "because I worked with her when she was coanchoring here but there's always Cheeta Ching."

There were more than a few groans around the table.

"Cheeta," Uriah said, nodding even as he raised a questioning eyebrow at the naysayers. "I was over in sports when she was here. Was she really as bad as her rep?"

"Even nastier than Kitty," insisted one man.

"Yes, but if we're talking a temporary fix while we look for a permanent replacement, Cheeta might work," the woman said. "She knows the job, she can read from the teleprompter and she'd kill to get back on network. The first ratings dip of Kitty's in her first week on the air,

Cheeta smelled the blood in the water and faxed me over her résumé. She's sent it a few times since then."

"Cheeta's credibility is too damaged after that disaster on the piano," the white-haired executive insisted. "If she hadn't set fire to herself, maybe. But we can't go from a catastrophe like Kitty clinging to Scheissenhauser to an embarrassment like Cheeta in that burning gown of hers. We're still the Diamond Network, for God's sake."

Uriah nodded reluctantly. "You're right, Bill. Of course, you're right." He took a deep breath and exhaled loudly. "Anybody else, people? Anyone at all?"

"What about you-know-who?" someone suggested.

There was a collective gasp around the room.

Everyone knew who you-know-who was. The man had been a high profile reporter at BCN for years until the bias of the Diamond Network's news reporting became too much for him to bear. He'd had the temerity to suggest that maybe their newscast could be improved by introducing a smidgeon of fairness and a scintilla of balance to the lopsided single-party dogma that BCN nightly gussied up and paraded across America's screens as impartial news. For sounding a wakeup call at the network, you-know-who had first been marginalized and finally fired, and employees of the Evening News were forbidden to speak his name within the hallowed halls of BCN ever again. This became an even greater imperative once you-know-who began to spin himself a very successful post-BCN career penning best-selling books detailing just how corrupt and politically motivated the BCN Evening News had become.

"Hire back you-know-who? Are you out of your mind?" Uriah demanded of the middle-aged executive whose suggestion had paled faces around the gleaming table and had caused one female executive at the far end to faint outright.

"Um, it'd shake things up," the executive said.

"We shook things up when we hired the first solo

female anchor and look where that's gotten us." Uriah groaned and buried his face in his hands. "That's it. We're sunk. We're stuck with Kitty for now."

"What do you mean 'stuck with Kitty'?" a furious voice screeched from the doorway.

Uriah, his face in his hands, had not seen the door burst open. Kitty stormed into the boardroom, accompanied by Remo and Chiun. The appearance of Kitty Coughlin was the equivalent of shouting "fire" in a crowded movie theater. There were a dozen rapidly muttered excuses as the other executives abandoned ship and raced for the two exits. In a flash they were gone, the doors slammed shut and Uriah was forced to face down BCN's irate star anchorwoman alone.

"Kitty, welcome back," Uriah said, his lips pulling back into the best facsimile of a smile he could manage under the circumstances. He made a mental note to chew out his secretary for not warning him that Kitty was in the building.

"What's all this?" Kitty snapped.

Uriah suddenly noticed all the papers and publicity head shots that were scattered on the table before him. He made a mad grab to gather them up but was too slow for Kitty.

"Cheeta Ching? Clarence Wenthall?" she said, spying the photos even as Uriah clutched the files to his chest. "Clarence Wenthall! You're actually thinking of replacing me with that old fart? The day we had him here to do the voice intro for my first newscast, he felt me up, crapped his pants and fell asleep all within a span of two minutes. You think people will tune in for that?"

"Actually, I'd probably watch that," Remo said.

"That is because you have no respect for the elderly," Chiun said. "At least not those who matter."

Remo had had enough. "Dammit, Chiun, I have respect for you," he snapped. "More respect than I guess you'll ever know."

The old Korean took in his pupil's words and, finding only deep sincerity, turned his attention to Uriah and Kitty. "Please, Remo," Chiun admonished, unable to keep the brush of a smile from his thin lips, "stop jabbering. This is an important meeting." He nodded to Kitty. "Carry on, most beautiful lady."

"Uriah—" Kitty began.

"Listen, Kitty," Uriah pleaded. "You've got to understand the position we're in. They're laughing at BCN news. Have you seen the *Wall Street Journal* editorial today? 'What's Happened to the Diamond Network?' It's brutal. I hear *Newsweek* is giving you the cover next week. They've dredged up everything, all the way back to the monkey-shit incident. Now don't worry. As you heard, we're not pulling you off the air for good. But it's probably a good idea to take you off for a week while we retool. If you feel threatened, we can pull up someone from one of the affiliates to anchor. Hell, a weatherman or a sports guy if that makes you happy. No competition in-house. How's that sound?"

Kitty pulled the files from Uriah's hands and, with an angry grunt, heaved them at the wall. Headshots and papers fluttered to the floor as Kitty stormed silently between Remo and Chiun and out of the conference room.

Uriah groaned. "That went better than I thought it would," he said.

"How hard can it be to get someone to read the news?" Remo asked. "You've got a good voice. You do it."

Uriah shook his head. "You've got to be able to connect with the audience. There's a bond of trust between anchor and viewer. Kitty had a hard time with that even before this. We tried to back her up in every conceivable way, but it just wasn't there. Now this." He glanced at Chiun. "What did you suggest when we first met? Doing the whole news in Korean? That might pull in bigger numbers than Kitty. Hell, the Spanish channels do their own news."

"As spokesman for my community, there is no self-respecting Korean who would deign to host your news program now nor would any watch," Chiun said. "Not after that woman has befouled your airwaves."

"What about her?" Remo asked. He stabbed a toe at a publicity photo that had fallen face-up on the floor near Uriah. Cheeta Ching was like a grinning barracuda.

Uriah had squatted down and was gathering up his fallen paperwork. He paused to gaze wistfully at the picture. "I watched her demo this morning. It wasn't bad. She's matured into the role. Problem is that damned piano. If she hadn't made a fool of herself on that piano—or maybe if she just hadn't set fire to herself— we'd probably have hired her back by now. Put Kitty back on mornings maybe. As it is, if we hire anyone new it's probably going to have to be a man."

A knock on the door and Uriah glanced up.

"Excuse me, sirs," said a timid voice. Chiun's intern stepped hesitantly into the room carrying an OverNite Express package. "It's addressed to the Master of Sinanju?" the young man asked, wincing when Chiun and Remo turned his way.

Remo reached for the package but Chiun was quicker. The old man plucked the box from the intern.

"You know, I'm technically the Master of Sinanju," Remo pointed out as the old man sliced open one end of the box with the edge of a fingernail.

"You have entrusted the business affairs of the House to the Reigning Master Emeritus," Chiun said. "Which is why I must spend my retirement years traipsing around the world with you when I should be watching the children play in the waves of the West Korean Bay while I sit on the shore of my beloved Sinanju and mend fishing nets. Or, Remo, if you are suddenly interested in business, do you now want to sit in that cheerless office and stare down Smith's gray face when the next contract negotiations come around?"

"Good point," Remo said. "So what did we get?"

A solid gold bar slipped into Chiun's palm. Eyes widening, he shook the empty box looking for more. No more gold fell out, but a scrap of paper did. Remo picked it up off the floor but Chiun snatched it from him before he could read it. It was a short note. All Remo had seen was that it was signed "A Friend" in a tiny, painful scrawl.

"Who is that from?" Remo asked.

"Can't you read? It is from my friend."

"You don't have any friends, least of all friends who would send you gold out of the blue."

"I have you," Chiun said. The gold bar vanished up the sleeve of his kimono. The note he read again, turning the paper front and back to see if there was any more writing.

"Since when do you consider me a friend?"

"That is not what I meant. I meant that if I have no friends it is because of you always hanging around chasing nice people away. But in point of fact I have many friends including my very good friend who sent me this gift. When I find out who he is I will have to do something nice for him."

"Yeah, you do that," Remo grumbled. "Send your good buddy a fruit basket."

Chiun stroked his thread of beard. "Oranges are always nice," he said, nodding.

"Could you two please excuse me?" Uriah begged morosely. He was seated at the conference table once more, the publicity photos of several impossible-to-hire news anchor candidates spread out before him. "Aren't you here to bodyguard Kitty? Can't you go off and do that and leave me and my ruined career in peace?"

Chiun's intern was hovering near the door. "Ms. Coughlin?" he said. "She's gone. She had the desk call her a cab." When he saw the look on Remo's face, the young man darted from the room.

"Crap," Remo said. "We were supposed to make sure nothing bad happened around her."

"You were worried about her going on the air, weren't you?" Uriah asked. "Well, that's not a problem now. Forget what I told her just now about one week. After her performance at the riots we've pulled her for at least two weeks, maybe three. We have to try to get the memory of her glued to Scheissenhauser's back out of viewers' minds. All ten of them that are still watching."

"A week is more than enough time," Chiun announced. The OverNite Express note disappeared up the same voluminous kimono sleeve as had the gold. "Come, Remo, we have business to conduct." He turned for the door.

"Wait. Whoa. Hold your horses. What business?"

"If you are now truly interested in the business end of our business, I will tell you in the air," Chiun said, breezing past his pupil and out of the room.

Remo exhaled loudly. "Why is it always such a freaking mystery all the time?" he demanded of Uriah. "Why is it I'm always kept in the dark? Why can't anything with him ever be simple and straightforward?"

"And bring your credit card," Chiun's disembodied voice called from the hallway.

Kitty waited inside the Forty-third Street entrance
of BCN's world headquarters and watched the security
guard standing out on the sidewalk.

"Uriah, you son-of-a-bitch fruit," Kitty snarled to
herself. A middle-aged couple spotted her loitering as
they entered the building and smiled in her direction.
"What the hell are you looking at?" Kitty yelled, sending
the pair running.

A yellow cab pulled up to the curb outside and the desk
guard leaned into the passenger window. When he
ducked back out, he waved and nodded at Kitty.

"Pull me off the air, will he?" she said as she hustled
out the gleaming doors. "Maybe I'll just take a vacation.
Maybe if they want me back on in a week the whole
damn board will have to fly down to Barbados on bended
knee begging me to come back. They'll have to pay me
on the air or on the beach. The hell with Uriah, the hell
with all of them."

The guard opened the back door and Kitty hustled past him without so much as a nod of thanks. She was picturing BCN's board of directors in their French suits standing in the tropical surf begging her to fulfill her contract. She wondered if Uriah liked spearfishing and what that spineless queen would look like with a spear sticking out of his neck.

So distracted was Kitty that she did not notice the man in the backseat until she was already in the cab.

"No-the-hell way," Kitty said. "I'm not sharing any goddamn cab with any goddamn plebe."

She suddenly felt a pair of very strong hands on her shoulders. The lobby guard had leaned far into the cab and was pinning her to her seat.

"Are you nuts?" Kitty snarled. "Get your hands off—"

The man in the backseat reached over and slapped a cloth over her mouth and nose. The cloth was damp and smelled vaguely medicinal, like a hospital ward hallway.

And then the veil of night drew down over Kitty Coughlin and she slumped into the seat of the cab.

"Is she out?" the guard asked.

The man in the backseat nodded. Sweat ran down his pale face between the avenues crafted by ravaging acne.

The guard slammed the door and leaned in the window.

"So does this mean he'll leave me and my wife alone?" the guard begged, glancing from the man in the rear to the nervous driver. "He's practically destroyed our credit."

In the backseat of the taxi, Wayne Dwyer shook his sweaty head. "He never leaves you alone," he said.

The window slowly powered up. Leaving the BCN guard on the sidewalk, the yellow cab pulled into the thick late-afternoon Manhattan traffic.

23

As the boy ran through the living room, a dollop of dripped chocolate slipped from the tip of the sugar cone and dotted the white shag carpet between his bare feet.

Daisy O'Toole leaned forward and with one mighty paw slapped the melting ice cream cone out of the little boy's tiny hand.

"Whaddaya gettin' crap all over the goddamn carpet for?" Daisy raged. Tears welled in the child's big eyes.

As messes went, the drop on the carpet was nothing compared to the shattered cone and splattered chocolate ice cream which, thanks to Daisy's outburst, now decorated two walls and a piece of erotic lesbian artwork on velvet.

"I'll get it," said Daisy's live-in girlfriend, a thin attractive woman of thirty who had followed the boy into the room.

"No!" Daisy snapped. Stamping one huge hoof, she aimed an imperious fat finger at the six-year-old boy. "No, no, no, no, no! Him. He's gonna do it. You do it, Slobbo! Mr. Slobbo Wobbo! Get down there and lick it up."

Although the boy was often on the receiving end of verbal abuse from his tyrant adoptive mother, his little lip still quivered as he got down on his hands and knees to lick up the spot of chocolate. Daisy's young stablemate stood helpless, tears welling in her eyes, as she watched the boy smear more chocolate on the carpet than he managed to clean. Daisy roosted far back on the sofa in a white T-shirt with the word PEACE stretched nearly to tearing across her enormous torso. She wore a pair of too-short pants that revealed every cellulite bump and varicose vein. She had long ago given up trying to cross her legs.

Daisy kept one eye on the boy and another on the television which was tuned to a cable station that was playing an ancient rerun of the old *Merv Griffin Show*. Two pastry boxes sat on the cushion beside her and as she watched the TV she lifted a thick wedge of brownie from the nearer box and slipped it far back on her thick, darting tongue.

Her adopted son's sobbing distracted her from something Dick Cavett had just said to Merv.

"Keep your crying down, Mr. Crybaby Baby," Daisy commanded over a mouthful of brownie as she nudged up the volume with the remote control. She chased a few loose crumbs around her T-shirt with chubby fingers and tossed them back into the gooey brown mess that stained teeth and gums.

There was a time that a glimpse of this private Daisy would have shocked the public but her carefully controlled media image was a thing of the past. It was two decades since Daisy O'Toole had managed against the odds to gain celebrity and in recent years the world had gotten far more than a peek at the bully behind the curtain.

A C-level actress, Daisy had minor roles in a few moderately successful films and a decade ago parlayed her small-time Hollywood success into a daytime talk show gig. At the time her TV show debuted, Daisy repeatedly complained about the coarse nature of modern television and vowed that her show would be different. Dubbing herself the "Princess of Polite," Daisy insisted quite vocally that only niceness would reign on her show and for a few weeks she delivered on her promise. But Daisy, who couldn't stop telling everyone how she hated guns, broke her pledge when Rich Statler, National Rifle Association member and star of the long-running BCN drama *Colt, Private Eye*, was booked on her show.

Politeness was tossed overboard in favor of politics. Daisy went for Statler's left jugular.

Statler had been polite and firm in his convictions, with facts to back up his opinions. Daisy was rude, dismissive and hostile. Statler pointed out that he had noticed backstage that Daisy's bodyguards carried sidearms. Daisy said that was because she was famous. Statler pointed out that the Constitutional right to bear arms had not been written just for celebrities. This received applause even from Daisy's New York audience. When it was clear the debate was not going her way, Daisy had called Statler "Mr. Bangy-Wangy Gun Nut" and ordered her director to cut to a commercial.

For anyone wanting to pinpoint the precise moment that Daisy O'Toole's career began its steep decline, the on-air debacle with Rich Statler was the moment.

Daisy's talk show sputtered along for a few more years but was eventually cancelled. A magazine in which she voiced opinions on a wide array of subjects she knew nothing about went bankrupt. The movie roles stopped coming.

For years Daisy had pretended to have a crush on Cal Tracy, the Hollywood superstar and high-profile member of the controversial Poweressence cult. In a desperate grab for attention, Daisy called a press conference to tell the world that the crush was a sham and that she was

really a lesbian. This turned out to not be as much of a
surprise to the world as Daisy had expected since, she
quickly discovered, the world had always found her about
as feminine as a tractor-trailer filled with doorknobs.

It was alleged that Daisy was a comedienne, but a pack
of bloodhounds specially trained to sniff out humor could
have watched every tape of the old *Daisy O'Toole Show*
and not tracked down a single laugh in any of Daisy's
monologue jokes, scripted comments or ad-libs. So as
much as her agent tried, it became impossible for Daisy to
land even one night at one of her old comedy club haunts.

In her forties now, with no job opportunities in sight,
Daisy soon slipped into the most dreaded twilight
nightmare of all celebrities, that of fame without income.
She began to fear that her young girlfriend would leave
her and that the state would take away the three adoptive
children she had collected like China dolls and which had
become hers only due to her fame.

At her lowest point, covered in powdered sugar and
jelly doughnut ooze in her basement Long Island rec
room, salvation came to Daisy in a phone call from Gail
Meadows, the legendary octogenarian newswoman.

Gail was creator and executive producer of *The
Scenery*, a women's affairs program that aired weekday
mornings. On the show, Gail and her three female cohosts
sat around a table sipping coffee and discussing events of
the day for a live studio audience. One of the other
women had left the show recently and Gail was looking
for a replacement.

"I was hoping tewwibwy dat you would be innawested,"
Gail had said.

Between Gail's bizarre speech impediment and the
jelly doughnut that Daisy was eviscerating, Daisy was
lucky to have heard the offer. As it was, Daisy jumped on
the opportunity as if it were a bag of Double-Stuf Oreos.

The Daisy that lumbered onto the set of *The Scenery*
that first day was not the Daisy that most of her fans

remembered. Since her talk show had gone off the air, the self-proclaimed Princess of Polite had freed her heretofore caged id. For this latest version of Daisy O'Toole, there would be no imprisoning her true personality.

Daisy was the worst instincts of Man set loose without conscience and without script. Her nasty disposition, only glimpsed in her ambush debate years before with Rich Statler, was on full display every weekday at eleven a.m. EST.

The world soon learned that Daisy was a conspiracy theorist who believed 9/11 was an inside job perpetrated by the president on orders from the vice president.

"Big Oil," she proclaimed bombastically to one cohost, a polite young blond woman who dared question the insanity of her fringe ideas. "You want to know who did it, that's who. It's on the Internet. Look it up."

More often than not this was Daisy's ace-in-the-hole argument. When questioned, a fat paw would raise, dull eyes would turn away as if the questioner was not worthy of a glance and Daisy would announce that all the answers one needed were available online. To Daisy, the Internet was the modern Oracle of Delphi, a great mystical source of arcane knowledge. It did not occur to her that the Internet did not limit content to fact and that any crackpot with a modem could deliver half-baked theories into the waiting arms of an international audience of crazies.

Soon, reading conspiracy theories was not enough. While cohosting *The Scenery*, Daisy created her own Web page where she wove theories of her own.

According to DaisyOToolesBrain.com, there was no plane that hit the Pentagon on 9/11 since there was no visible aircraft wreckage at the site.

The United States had been given several warnings about the 9/11 hijackings but had allowed them to take place anyway to provide a pretext for the eventual invasion of Iraq.

Fire does not melt steel.

The planes that hit the Twin Towers were piloted remotely and the passengers had never gotten aboard but had been held for a time at Guantanamo Bay before being executed by order of the president.

For a year Daisy repeated her unlikely online hypotheses on the stage of *The Scenery* until one day her blond cohost—fed up with Daisy's rantings—called her on her lunacy.

"Daisy, you're one hundred percent wrong about that."

Daisy had just claimed that the vice president had traveled in secret to meet with the British prime minister and the pope to make final terrorist arrangements the day before both the London transportation system and the Madrid train bombings.

"I'm wrong? I'm wrong, Missy Wissy? Why don't you spend less time bleaching your roots and more time online?" Daisy had said. "You know, learning's not the Big Bad Wolf, gonna huff and puff and blow your pretty Missy house down. Missy Wissy might just learn something if she reads something other than *Cosmo* at the beauty parlor."

Until that day a rude comment or a dismissive put-down had been enough to silence the younger woman. But that day had been the end for the blond cohost.

"What is with the baby talk, Daisy?" the girl asked. "You're forty-eight years old. You sound ridiculous. Why don't you try growing up? And why don't you—get your hand out of my face, Daisy. That's another thing, you have no manners. You're a bully. And if you think saying 'It's online, look it up' ends an argument you're, frankly, stupid. I hate to say that, because it's not in my nature to be impolite, Daisy, but I've put up with your obnoxious, rude, condescending garbage for over a year now and I've had it. If you're going to—get that damn mitt of yours out of my face, Daisy—if you're going to keep being this rude and this ignorant, I'm going to start calling you on it every day. I'm through being nice to you because you haven't been nice to me for so much as two seconds. You have a right to your ridiculous opinions just as I have a right to tear them and you to shreds on a daily basis. You ready to deal with someone who's going to fight back? What do you say?"

Daisy quit *The Scenery* that day. On her way out of her dressing room, she drew mustaches all over the young woman's publicity photos before storming out of the building.

Work had been sporadic since then. She had recently been fired from another TV job and paying gigs were once more getting harder and harder to come by.

The downside to this extended unpaid vacation was that Daisy was spending more time at home. And the downside to that was that sometimes she could not hear her beloved Merv Griffin reruns over all the carpet slurping.

"I said lick it up, Slobbo Wobbo," Daisy snapped from the groaning sofa. She shoveled another brownie into her gaping maw as she supervised her adopted son.

The sobbing boy had smeared an area on the carpet six inches around with ice cream and saliva.

Daisy pried a walnut loose from her molars and spit it at the back of the boy's head.

"Slobbo Wobbo makes a bigger mess, Slobbo Wobbo doesn't get dinner tonight," she said.

Fortunately for the boy, a low electronic tune suddenly chirped from the next room. With difficulty, Daisy pushed herself to the edge of the sofa cushions, then with a last-minute shove and groan, managed to haul herself to her feet.

"Make sure Mr. Slobbo Wobbo McDobbo cleans it all up," Daisy commanded her girlfriend.

"Yes, Daisy," the woman agreed timidly. But when Daisy lumbered into the adjacent room, her girlfriend hustled off to get a damp, soapy sponge and another ice cream cone for the sobbing child.

In the next room, Daisy dropped into a chair before her computer and checked her e-mail box. She had been waiting to hear from her agent about a job but the box was empty. Instead, a window signalled an incoming Instant Message.

When she saw who the message was from, Daisy sat forward excitedly. The chair creaked beneath her ample bottom. The box read, WINGERDINGER: U there?

Daisy's thick fingers hunted and pecked her keyboard.

DAISYDUKE69: i m hair wats up

As she waited for a reply, Daisy absently sucked moist brownie goo from the tips of her fingers.

Daisy did not know much about the man with whom she regularly communicated. She only knew her online friend as "WingerDinger." They had met on a chat board three years before and the two of them had joined nasty forces in a series of flame wars that had driven every other participant away. For Daisy, WingerDinger was her online soul mate, the great unrequited heterosexual love of her Internet life.

WINGERDINGER: Flite 980, Alska oilspil, LA riots all conected.

Daisy could not believe what she was reading. She attacked her keyboard with chocolate-smeared fingers.

DAISYDUKE69: vise presedent?????

WINGERDINGER: no. Kitty Coughlin an BCN news key to all. can ruin her career but need u to film. Inerested?

Daisy's disappointment that the vice president was not implicated in any of the events WingerDinger had listed was mitigated by her online friend's mention of Kitty Coughlin.

Back on her old *Daisy O'Toole Show*, Daisy had once made a pass at Kitty in the green room and Kitty who at the time had still been a network morning show cohost had been so repulsed that she had fled the studio.

Her pudgy fingers shaking, Daisy tapped her keyboard.

DAISYDUKE69: wood luv 2 nale pretty kitty what due i due

Daisy found a pencil and jotted down WingerDinger's instructions. When he gave her a time, she checked the Felix the Cat wall clock and realized that she would have to move fast if she was going to get the big scoop. Before grabbing her tinfoil hat and marching from the room, Daisy leaned over the keyboard and stabbed out a last message.

DAISYDUKE69: wish u werenot man. we culd make buetyful music togeter ;-)

She sighed wistfully at WingerDinger's reply.

WINGERDINGER: :-)

Shutting off her computer, Daisy struggled back to her feet and thudded from the room.

In the basement of his Los Angeles suburb home, Orville Wilbur Feldon finished typing the little :-) smile face emoticon and closed the instant message box.

"Retard bovine lesbo," he said with a chuckle.

As a rule, Feldon liked to bully, but manipulating a bully like Daisy O'Toole was almost as enjoyable. When he stumbled upon her on a chat forum a few years before, he had made certain to keep the contact in his pocket for future use, figuring that the nasty cow might someday come in handy.

How easy it was to manipulate her. Shaking his head at the microbrains he was forced to live among, Feldon climbed up out of his chair. His knees creaked in protest.

From his favorite VCR, Orville ejected the tape Noah Sherman had collected from the Pennsylvania mine, the tape of the young Master of Sinanju in action. That footage would make a great intro to the story of the century. He could see the news teaser now, with that blurred face played a hundred times for a revamped and resurgent BCN Evening News, Orville Wilbur Feldon, Executive Producer.

And there would soon be more footage, this time of both men in action, just before their deaths.

Kitty Coughlin was still alive which Feldon had not expected so late in the game. But now she would serve double duty, as sham reporter and bait. Soon Feldon would have more footage of Kitty breaking down in the face of adversity which would add to all the monkey-house and other footage that had finally made it onto the air. A final, fat nail in the coffin of her career. And Daisy O'Toole would make sure that he had great footage of the two Masters of Sinanju for the premier story of his first major evening newscast.

Yes, everything would be perfect if not for the sound like a wounded hippopotamus coming from above his head.

As he went around the room shutting off TVs, Feldon tried to block out the screams from upstairs.

"Six hundred thousand dollars?" Mrs. Feldon shouted from the first floor.

Mother Feldon had been fixated on that particular sum of money ever since her son came back from mailing the bar of gold to the Master of Sinanju and had failed to properly hide his checkbook. She'd found it five minutes after he came home, sticking out of the secret hiding place under a mound of moldy laundry in the corner of his bedroom.

"What's this bankbook?" Mrs. Feldon had screamed, waving the book under her son's nose. "Six hundred thousand dollars deposited three months ago? Where did you get that kind of money? Are you doing something illegal, Orville? Is it drugs? Is that why you can't hold down a job even with the post office? You're a junkie pusher?"

Feldon had snatched the checkbook back, accused his mother of being a stormtrooper for searching his room and scurried downstairs to write to Daisy O'Toole. It was now twenty minutes later and his mother was waiting for him when he tried to sneak back upstairs.

"Six hundred thousand dollars!" Mrs. Feldon yelled when her son waddled up into the kitchen. "How did you spend almost six hundred thousand in three months, boy? That book of yours says you've only got a few thousand left."

She was shorter than Feldon but weighed fifty pounds more. Her big perm was arranged above her wide face like a bleached haystack. The kitchen chair strained under the elephantine shift of weight as she got to her feet.

"Please, Mother," Feldon said.

"Don't you 'please Mother' me. Six hundred thousand you got and here I am paying for everything around here!" she yelled as she followed him into the dining room and around to the second-story stairs.

The staircase was too much for her to negotiate a second time in under an hour so when her son ascended she stood at the bottom shouting up at his retreating back.

"No rent, nothing for that car of yours you had me paying for all those years, not even a dime for food. You have any idea how much you eat, boy?"

Feldon and most of the neighborhood heard her continued screams as he hurried around his room stuffing clothes into his late salesman father's old American Tourister suitcase. His mother had not done his laundry in a few weeks and so he gave everything he grabbed a quick smell test as he gathered it up from closet, drawer and floor. He carefully wrapped the invaluable videotape in a pair of yellowed underwear and stuffed it into the heart of the bag. The copy of *Myths of Ancient Asia* he'd bought at All Things Read was placed reverently in the side pocket of the suitcase. He tucked a laptop computer deep into the bag.

Feldon waddled into his mother's bedroom and made a telephone call from her nightstand phone. He waited

seven minutes at the window until the taxicab pulled up
outside the rusted chain-link fence before risking descent
into his mother's den of accusations.

Mrs. Feldon was out of breath and leaning on the back
of the tattered sofa when her son came back downstairs.

"Where did you get that kind of money?" she yelled.

"From my benefactor, Mother," Feldon replied. "It was
not salary so you needn't get your penny-pinching brain
all aflutter. It was cash to help me get things moving in the
right direction, which I've done resoundingly so. In fact,
I've gone above and beyond. As a reward for housing me
all this time, I will share a secret with you."

When he lowered his voice his conspiratorial whisper
reeked of stale Big Macs. "There is an ancient order of
assassins operating in this country, Mother. Men with
skills the likes of which the world cannot possibly
imagine. And they have been hired to do the dirty work of
a news department of a major television network. More
than that I cannot say. You will have to tune in to BCN
news to learn the whole remarkable truth. Suffice it to say,
my benefactor will reward me even more greatly. Perhaps
I won't just be news producer, perhaps I'll be news
president. Thanks to this business arrangement, I am
finally going to achieve the station I so richly deserve."

"Station? What are you talking about, Orville? What
benefactor? Is that drug talk?"

But Feldon hustled past her, avoiding one swipe of
a meaty paw, and headed out the door.

"A taxi!" he heard his mother shout when she spied the
cab at the end of the short walk. "Here I'm clipping
coupons every day and you're out gallivanting around in
taxis?"

"Is there something wrong?" the driver asked. He was
standing at the rear door but looking up the walk at the
huge woman waving flabby arms in the doorway.

"Yes, lamentably," Feldon said. "Her progeny was
born far above her menial station and it is more than her

porcine brain can comprehend. Good-bye, Mother! The son you tried so desperately to cage as a frog forever is, despite your best efforts to the contrary, about to become a prince."

Feldon would not risk parting with his luggage and its valuable videotape and book cargo, so he kept it on the backseat with him. Once he was settled, he gave the driver the address of a storage facility in Pasadena.

"And make it snappy, my good man," he said to the mouth-breathing vagrant driver. "My destiny awaits."

As his carriage whisked him off to his extraordinary future, a curling smile stretched across the toad-like face of Orville Wilbur Feldon.

24

On his hidden monitor, Smith watched the skeletal frame of the plot beginning to come together.

Noah Sherman was the individual who had enlisted the L.A. Casas into rioting. Sherman had been an active trader on iBay until two months before. The body in the L.A. warehouse was confirmed as his and Smith had tracked Sherman via credit card and plane records to Weltsburg, Pennsylvania.

Remo was right. Sherman had been involved in both the riots and the mine explosion. What's more, Smith had placed him in Alaska just before the *Motiv Kodiak* ran aground, and also in New York prior to Flight 980. Smith assumed that Sherman was one of the men who had used false ID to get aboard that flight and ultimately hijack the plane.

Thanks to flight records, the man named Wayne that Remo had found now had a full name: Wayne Dwyer of

Schenectady, who had been reported missing by his family a month before.

Except for his four years at the Massachusetts University of Technology, Dwyer had never left home for such a long period of time and even when he was at school a decade before he had come home every weekend. His elderly grandparents, with whom he lived, were frantic with worry.

Harold Smith was not worried for Dwyer but for his victims, past and future.

The latest report from Alaska found evidence in the ruined cabin of the *Motiv Kodiak* that the oil tanker might have been rigged to run remotely. Dwyer worked in robotics, Sherman was a model helicopter and plane enthusiast. Between them they had the skills to rig the tanker.

Yes, it was starting to take shape. Smith could feel it. But there was still one missing piece to the puzzle.

"Why Kitty Coughlin?" the CURE director asked. A rare moment of frustration colored his ashen cheeks. "There is nothing to connect these men to her before now."

Across Smith's desk, Mark Howard shook his head. "Still could be the simplest of two explanations. Either they're crazy fans trying to help Kitty or they're crazy enemies trying to help the other network anchors by hurting her."

"No," Smith said. "Kitty Coughlin certainly poses no threat to the competing networks, so the latter cannot be the case. As for the former, these men lived their entire lives online. There were no secrets that we could find and there is simply no evidence that they were interested in the news. In fact, they seem totally uninterested in current events."

In their research, Smith and his assistant had pored over page after page of material on the two men in question. In addition to their iBay auctions, Sherman and Dwyer each maintained personal Web sites, each had online accounts to handle iBay and other bills, both participated in online forums, and each man posted to dozens of message boards and Web sites. Besides robotics for Dwyer and model planes for Sherman, their interests appeared to extend no further than science fiction television programs, books and movies.

"Well, those maps and stuff Remo sent along seemed to indicate there are others involved here," Mark pointed out.

Indeed, it was Smith who had determined that, unless Sherman and Dwyer had hidden talents, the level of planning involved in staging the riots was beyond their abilities. "I have surreptitiously forwarded the riot instructions to the FBI for analysis," Smith said. "Perhaps they will find something in them that I missed. In the meantime, what about your research into what these madmen might have planned for future events? Perhaps we can get out ahead of them."

Howard pulled some papers from the briefcase at his ankle. "I based these on the big news story pattern," Smith's assistant said, "but that doesn't mean they won't deviate from that pattern in the future." He checked his list. "There's Callie Mae Angus, the *Playboy* model who OD'd and choked to death on her own vomit. That was the worst media circus I've ever seen. Not far behind that is London Forsythe, the hotel heiress who got sent to jail for a week for drunk driving on a suspended license. There's B.O. Anson, footballer and wife murderer, but Remo took care of him a few years back. I guess with imagination they could come up with a scenario similar to any of these."

"Those seem too small," Smith said.

"There was that little girl who got stuck down a well but I guess that's too small too. The Collablaster was big while he was mailing bombs to universities all over the country but Remo took him out too. There was Lady Di. They didn't come bigger than that at the time. And there's a whole new generation of British royalty to go after now."

"No," Smith said. "Those seem too small as well."

Mark rattled off the last items on his list. "There's the Branch Davidians, Ruby Ridge, the Northridge earthquake, Columbine, Virginia Tech, New Orleans, the 2000 election recount in Florida. Aside from the school shootings it'd be pretty hard to stage most of the rest of them. I mean, it's not like anybody's got an earthquake machine." Mark laughed but when he looked up and saw that his employer's face was deadly serious, he hesitated. "There isn't, is there?"

Smith shook his head. "Not now, Mark. There is the problem at hand to deal with." He forged ahead. "You're right about the school shootings. We should have the FBI send out warnings to state and local police to be on high alert as far as high schools and universities are concerned. The election would be attractive to him; assuming, of course, it is a 'he' we are dealing with. But while it does seem to be the kind of chaos he enjoys, it's too far away." The CURE director nodded. "New Orleans," he said. "Each of the events has gotten bigger than the last, with only the coal mine deviating from that pattern. And that would have had a far higher human cost than Flight 980 had Remo not intervened."

"Well, if the goal was to get Kitty Coughlin off the air, we may have seen the last of these staged events."

Smith shook his head. "Remo said that BCN has not fired her. They are only taking her off the air for a few weeks. No, if there is to be another event, it will be in New Orleans."

Mark lifted his eyebrows quizzically.

Smith nodded and said simply, "Instinct." He snaked a hand for the blue phone.

But when Smith called BCN he found that Remo and Chiun had left the building.

"Would you like to leave a message for Mr. Chiun?" a worried young voice in Chiun's office asked.

"No, thank you," Smith said.

The young man sighed relief. "Thank God. He'd kill me if I got it wrong. With other bosses that'd be an exaggeration, but with Mr. Chiun you never know. Please, please, don't tell him I said that, will you?"

"I won't. Thank you," Smith said, and hung up the phone. Nimble fingers sought his desktop keyboard. A quick search, and the CURE director nodded satisfaction. "Good. Flight records indicate they are on the right track. It's odd Remo did not tell me when he called to check in."

"So we're all set then?" Mark said.

Smith tapped a contemplative finger on the edge of his desk. "Perhaps and perhaps not," he said, reaching for his keyboard.

Remo watched the southern shore of Lake Pontchartrain grow large out the tiny airplane window as the ground raced up to meet the belly of the 747. When the tires squealed and the pilot announced they had landed safely in New Orleans, Remo turned to the Master of Sinanju.

"Now will you tell me why we're here?" he asked.

"I told you already," Chiun replied. "I am here to meet my wonderful new friend." He flashed the note that had accompanied his bar of gold. "Did you see this, Remo?"

"You've showed it to me only about fifty times since we left New York," Remo said. "Why not let me read it?"

Chiun continued as if he had not heard. "It says 'I hope to retain your services, but if not please accept this small token.' A bar of solid gold is but a small token to my delightful new friend and potential employer. When has Smith ever been that generous?"

"Setting aside for a minute that 'potential employer'

crap, Smith is plenty generous with both of us. Or are you forgetting that submarine filled with gold he ships to Sinanju every November?"

Chiun's hand swept Remo's words from the air. "Pah. That is because he is bound by contract to send that pittance. This, Remo, was a gift, sent without strings attached, given freely whether or not we perform a single service. Such generosity is the mark of a true emperor."

"Sounds like a true loon to me," Remo grunted. "Who gives away gold bars to total strangers?"

Chiun could scarcely contain his joy. "Someone who can afford to," he sang.

"You want me to get a napkin from the stewardess to mop up that drool?" Remo asked.

Apparently the note had given street directions, for the Master of Sinanju seemed to know where they needed to go. Remo sulked in the backseat of their taxi while the old Korean barked out orders to the driver.

The area around the airport was identical to any modern major American city, seemingly unscathed by recent history. But before long they were heading into landscape still scarred by the aftermath of Hurricane Katrina. Abandoned ramshackle houses that had not been in good shape to begin with were buckled and collapsing from flood damage. Some of the ruined homes had been torn down and were piles of rubble awaiting a bulldozer. But there was new construction too. Hope rose in humble, single-story dwellings and in the faces of laborers—black and white—carting shingles, nails and lumber. If not for the circumstances, the sight of optimism in the midst of tragedy might have done Remo's heart good.

"I still don't know why we're here," Remo said. "You can meet till the cows come home but we're not leaving Smith. This is a wasted trip as far as I'm concerned."

"You could have stayed behind," Chiun said.

"My credit card and I had to keep an eye on you or we might end up working for Iran again. Besides I didn't have anything to do in New York anymore. We were supposed to be bodyguards but the body we were supposed to be guarding went missing." Remo sighed. "I guess Kitty had enough. She's probably out in a cabin in the Rockies hoping like hell the *Hindenburg* doesn't blow up over her roof."

"The *Hindenburg* did not just blow up," Chiun said. He was craning his neck to make sure the driver took the right turn. "We were paid handsomely for that. Remind me to tell you the story one day. It has to do with the family of a Prussian countess. There were Gypsies too. And a horse."

"See, there's my problem," Remo said. "You make me babysit you all the way down here because I'm afraid I'll wake up tomorrow morning working for goddamn Prussians."

Chiun shot his pupil a scowl. "Are you going to ruin this ride with your constant complaining just as you did the flight?"

"I think I have a right to complain when we're schlepping off to New Orleans just because some anonymous wacko sends you a chunk of gold. And I don't know why you didn't let me tell Smith we were coming down here."

"Emperors do not need to know every little thing we do."

"Especially when we're out scoping out a new boss."

"Precisely," said Chiun, allowing himself a small glimmer of hope that the boy was not so lost a cause as he sometimes seemed to be.

"I'm not quitting Smith," Remo said, immediately extinguishing said glimmer of hope.

They entered an abandoned industrial area that had been hit hard by flooding and drove into the shadow of a levee. The road was mostly flat, but when they passed over a bridge that spanned a wide culvert Remo saw the ominous expanse of the Mississippi lurking high on the other side. At the shore was a maritime graveyard. Two derelict barges, a burned-out casino boat with a shattered paddle wheel and a dozen houseboats tethered to crooked pylons rose on the waves only to slouch back down into a huddle of scarred hulls.

Then the cab was off the bridge and back on flat road and a minute later they were turning into what appeared to be an auto junkyard built adjacent to the levee.

"You sure this the place you want?" the cabdriver said. "This not 'zactly the best neighborhood, you know, chief?"

"I'm with him, Little Father," Remo said. "If your newest bestest buddy told you to come here, I think he's full of it. This doesn't look like the sort of business that generates two-pound bricks of solid gold."

"Business?" the cabdriver hooted. "Whatchoo talkin' business, boy? This ain't no business, it's a boneyard for cars. Them cars what got flooded that the city can't get rid of, they all get towed here. No gold here. Not so much's a dime. Nothing come in here ever go out. S'abandoned."

The Master of Sinanju considered the man's words for all of one second. "Pay the man, Remo," Chiun commanded.

Remo peeled off the fare, added an extra twenty and as the cab drove off joined Chiun for a stroll amid the piles of abandoned cars. Near the levee they came across several acres of water-damaged school buses.

"So this is where they ended up," Remo said.

"Where what ended up? What are you babbling?" Chiun was looking intently around the area for a sign of his mysterious benefactor. Remo could see that the look on his teacher's leathery face was slowly turning into one of suspicion.

"Before New Orleans flooded, the mayor had time to send out this fleet of school buses to get people out of town. Instead he left the buses to get washed out and abandoned the people to fend for themselves. When the hurricane came and the levees breached, he blamed everyone under the sun for the problems here except himself, even after pictures of all these waterlogged buses started showing up all over the place. I'd say he was the biggest dope in town except the people here reelected him even after they knew all that. Personally, I'd've nailed him to the roof of the Superdome and stuffed buzzard feed down his Fruit of the Looms but maybe I'm not nuanced enough to be a New Orleans voter."

The two Masters of Sinanju sensed a heartbeat up ahead.

Chiun's face grew hopeful once more and he quickened his pace. Remo reluctantly trudged behind his teacher. When the old Korean rounded a block of eight buses stacked two high, his parchment face fell. Hazel eyes narrowed to thin slits.

"Who toys with the Master of Sinanju?" he demanded.

Remo followed the old man's gaze. "What the hell?"

A construction crane that was used to move the vehicles around the junkyard rose from the ground like some prehistoric metal beast. Lashed to the very end of the cable that extended from the crane's arm was Kitty Coughlin, long, artificially tan legs hanging from her too-short skirt. The crane had been positioned so that Kitty was hanging directly in front of the levee. On the other side of the artificial shore, millions of gallons of water rolled relentlessly past.

Kitty's head hung over her chest. When she heard voices, BCN's anchorwoman looked up. Her face lit up hopefully when she spied Remo and Chiun staring up at her.

"Remo, thank God," Kitty gasped, breathless. "These people are insane. They kidnapped me. A guard from BCN was in on it. You've got to get me down from here."

"Only if you say please."

"Remo, I'm serious."

"So am I."

"Get me down," Kitty insisted. She wiggled like a worm on a hook. "They're up to something bad here. I heard one of them say this was going to be bigger than the L.A. riots and the *Motiv Kodiak* put together."

"I don't think she's going to say please, Chiun."

"Why waste time awaiting the impossible?" the Master of Sinanju sniffed. "This impolite wench will never develop manners. I expect it is far more likely that the rest of her butchered face will snap and roll up like a too-tight window shade before the word please passes her altered lips."

"Please!" Kitty begged.

"What do you know?" Remo said. "Maybe she's educable after all."

Remo made a move toward the crane when he heard the sound of an engine racing through the gates of the junkyard. Chiun's last glimmer of hope that this might be his late-arriving benefactor faded when a local New Orleans news van emblazoned with the BCN logo came racing around the pile of buses and squealed on the brakes.

A news crew came pouring from the back of the van armed with cameras and microphones. For a moment Remo wondered if the ASPCA had learned that the run-of-the-mill depravity of New Orleans had apparently not been sufficiently stimulating and that the locals had now sunk so low they were dressing hippopotami in cream-colored pantsuits. But then the hippo spoke and Remo realized who they were dealing with.

"I told you!" Daisy O'Toole's Klaxon voice shouted. A finger like an Italian sausage stabbed the air. "There she is! Miss Pretty Kitty! Get that camera on her."

"Thank you for the tip, Ms. O'Toole," said an attractive young newswoman. "We'll take it from here."

"Like hell, Little Miss Susie Q," Daisy snapped. "I

didn't lead you here and give you the scoop about her and all these disasters so you'd be the one to hog the glory."

"About those disasters you claimed she was responsible for," the newswoman said, squinting up at Kitty dangling from the crane. "She looks kind of like a victim here."

"Take your opinions and go squat on a microphone with them, Little Missie," Daisy snarled. "Gimme that camera."

The two women advanced on each other slowly. Momentarily forgotten, Kitty begged, "Would someone please get me down?"

The new arrivals had not spotted Remo and Chiun. Fading back between the pile of buses, Remo was content to let the news crew film Kitty to their heart's content, assuming they would eventually get bored and cut her down. Either way Kitty Coughlin was no longer his problem.

"You know what concerns me, Little Father?" Remo said.

"That someone apparently finds it the height of hilarity to trick an innocent old man into coming to this depressing swamp city?" Chiun replied.

"That too," Remo said. A dark cloud of concern had settled on his face. "You said that gold bar was worth twenty thousand? Whoever this guy is, he thought it was worth paying twenty grand to get us down here, right to this spot, right where someone has dangled Kitty out in front of the mighty Mississip. And now a news crew has shown up to film it, just like they were at every other disaster Kitty was at. And Kitty says they said what they had planned here would be bigger than Alaska and L.A. combined and we know what big story happened in New Orleans recently."

"Yes," Chiun agreed, pleased that his pupil clearly understood the enormity of the pernicious fiend with whom they were dealing. "Some swine with too much time on his hands played an unfunny prank on the Master of Sinanju."

Remo looked up at the levee. The flat top was an access road which he followed with his eye. A quarter mile along it he spotted a man crouched down holding a small square object in his hands. Wires ran from one end of the box and disappeared on the water side of the levee.

The man's hand reached for the face of the box.

He was too far away to stop.

Helpless horror swelling in his belly, Remo looked off for an instant toward a city that was still in the midst of rebuilding, an effort that would take many more years and which would this day see all its efforts thus far erased at a madman's whim; a city that this time would not have days of a gathering Atlantic storm to warn it of impending disaster.

Without thought for the countless lives he was about to take, the cold-blooded man on the levee turned a plunger, then ran for a waiting boat.

Remo felt a soft foom-foom of muffled explosions through the damp packed earth beneath the soles of his shoes.

And then there was a terrible tearing sound and the only line of defense that New Orleans had against the muddy waters of America's mightiest river split open, vomiting a great rush of churning foam around Kitty, Daisy, and the horrified New Orleans news crew.

A split second before the Mississippi burst into the
auto junkyard, Remo and Chiun were already running
toward the levee. Shock waves from the hidden underwater
explosions rolled off through damp earth beneath their
racing feet.

Either by accident or design, the bombs were not as
powerful as they could have been. The blasts had served
to weaken the levee, but the pressure of the water behind
would soon exploit the vulnerability and collapse this
section of the wall. When it went down, the rush of water
would carry more of the levee down with it until there
would be no way to stop the redirected Mississippi River
from flooding the bowl of swampy delta on which New
Orleans had been built, killing tens of thousands of
unsuspecting victims.

"Not this time, Little Father," Remo yelled.

A yellow school bus covered in moss sat in the shade
of the levee. Communicating with a nod, Remo ran to the

front, Chiun to the back. Leaping simultaneously, the soles of their feet struck the side of the abandoned bus.

Yellow metal crumpled beneath their powerful blows and the bus groaned and tipped to one side. Windows shattered as the far side collapsed against the levee wall.

The small shaft that had yawned open directly before Kitty shot water as if from a fire hose, slamming Kitty's legs and sending her dancing helplessly on the end of the cable. The pressurized blast of water launched beyond Kitty and sprayed the ground to swirling mud around the feet of Daisy O'Toole and the New Orleans camera crew.

Kitty's screams were drowned out by the screams of the local BCN reporter. "We have to get out of here!"

"Pipe down, Susie Q!" Daisy commanded. All business in her pantsuit, she screamed and waved at the camera crew like a general commanding troops in the field even as water started to rise around her ankles. "Up there!" she yelled. Daisy pointed at Kitty but the angle at which they were filming made it appear as if she was directing the crew to film the dramatic split in the levee.

Missed in all the excitement were the two men who were laboring to save New Orleans from catastrophe.

Remo knew that one bus would not be enough to stop the flood. The water would sweep it aside like a child's toy.

He darted aboard another bus, threw it in neutral and raced to the back. Chiun was already there. Together the two men rolled it in beside the first, bracing it hard against the levee. They were rolling in a third when a tow truck carting an abandoned Chevy pulled in behind them and two burly New Orleans city workers jumped down from the cab.

The heavy supports Remo and Chiun had shoved against the levee wall were holding. The problem was not below, but high above where water continued to pump into the yard and where Remo and Chiun could not reach. Water swirled around their ankles as the two black men waded up beside the two Masters of Sinanju. The levee buses flooded and when the internal pressure burst the windows an instant later, the city workers covered their faces to protect themselves from the blasted glass.

"Holy mackerel," one man gasped over the roar of water.

"Can you operate that thing?" Remo yelled, pointing up at the crane from which Kitty dangled. The man nodded. "You need to start stacking them up like here." Remo pointed at the two-high pile of derelict school buses. "Pile them as high as you can against the wall, then pile more rows out to brace them."

"We can't do it with her on there," the man yelled, stabbing a finger toward Kitty. BCN's anchorwoman was beyond hysterics now and was holding on for dear life as the steady stream of water pummelled her rag-doll body.

"I'll take care of her. You get going," Remo shouted. "You guys are going to be heroes before this day's over."

The workmen waded to the crane.

Across the yard, Daisy's panicked crew was in the process of abandoning the biggest story of their careers. Most of them, including the hysterical blond reporter, were already back in their van. Only one cameraman remained.

"Hold your ground, Mister Sissypanties!" Daisy screamed at the frightened young man.

The man lost his footing and fell on his backside in the desperately churning froth of muddy water. "To hell with this," he yelled as he climbed to his feet.

"Dammit, I'll do it myself," Daisy bellowed. Grabbing the camera from him, she waded into the flood. But when she hefted the camera onto her shoulder and swung the lens back to the crane, Kitty was no longer there.

A pair of workmen were inside the crane's cab. As they swung the arm to a nearby bus, Daisy swept the cable from top to bottom. She found that the end now dangled loose.

"Dammit, where did you go, Pretty Kitty?" Daisy groused.

Assuming BCN's anchorwoman had been swept away in the miniflood, Daisy turned the camera to the ground and splashed off like a waterlogged sow to search for Kitty's floating corpse.

Behind a pile of abandoned cars, Remo massaged a knot of muscles in Kitty Coughlin's shoulders. The feeling quickly came back and she was able to lower her arms.

"How—" Kitty panted. Her clothes were sopping wet and strings of hair hung over her face. "How'd you get me down?"

"If you don't remember, let's just say you fell and I caught you," Remo said. "It'll make the paperwork easier."

There was shouting out in the yard.

The men operating the crane had just stacked a bus atop the first that Remo and Chiun had tipped against the levee. The crane arm swung as they went to collect another. They were working slowly but surely to prop up the levee wall. Water still flooded through, but only in a single spot and even that slowed to a trickle when the next bus slammed into the wall and settled on the growing pile.

Remo could see that the momentum had turned against the river. There would be time to repair the damage.

"We've got to warn them about this," Kitty said. "New Orleans is going to be flooded again."

"Absolutely," Remo agreed. "But not today it isn't. Anyway, don't sweat it. I know a guy who gets off on taking care of catastrophes just like this."

As if on cue the sound of helicopters rose up over the rumble of the crane's engine.

Remo realized that only Harold W. Smith could have mustered such awesome governmental forces so quickly. As it was, the CURE director must have pulled every string he could access. They came from air, land and water. In a matter of minutes the area was swarming with construction and disaster crews hauling pumps and heavy equipment. Remo saw scuba divers falling off the backs of boats. Men raced from trucks, cars and aircraft to assess the damage and to begin the work of repairing the weakened levee.

"See? I told you," Remo said. He ushered Kitty and the Master of Sinanju to a waiting truck with a running engine. So busy were the work crews that no one noticed Remo as he opened the truck door. "Come on, get in."

Kitty noted the FEMA insignia on the door. "Is this yours?" she asked.

"Sure it is," Remo said. "I pay taxes."

"No, you don't," Chiun pointed out as he climbed in.

"Details, details," Remo said.

27

They pulled over to the side of the road a mile away. Remo borrowed Kitty's cell phone, which she did everything but dial for him. He still accidentally hung up four times; twice before Smith answered and two times after.

"Why is everything always so complicated?" Remo complained. He was about to smash the phone on the dashboard when his rhetorical plea was answered by a lemony voice.

"Remo, is everything all right?" Smith asked.

Remo brought the phone to his ear. "Smitty? Yeah, we're hunky-dory here. Good job sending in the cavalry. Have your sack of beads ready for Fat Tuesday, Sodom and Gomorrah should be safe for another Mardi Gras."

"So there truly was an attempt on New Orleans?" Smith said. "I wasn't certain but I put the local authorities on alert when I learned you were there. When your cabdriver reported your destination, I took a gamble and sent help."

"Gamble paid off. Problem is we're still right where we were. They tried to blow the levee but they got away. I still don't know who the hell they are."

"I may have something," Kitty said.

"Hold on a sec, Smitty," Remo said.

Sitting between Remo and the Master of Sinanju, Kitty looked like a drowned rat. Most of her makeup had washed off and the faint scars from her various fruitless attempts to hold onto her rapidly fading youth were visible around jaw, behind ears and high on her forehead at her hairline.

"There were three men," Kitty began. "One was a guard at BCN like I told you. He didn't come here. I didn't wake up until the other two were tying me up down here. They were complaining about the guy who was behind all this, the one who was blackmailing them into doing all this horrible stuff. Someone named Wing Ding or something. No offense," she said, nodding an apology to the Master of Sinanju.

Chiun merely shook his head in disgust and turned to look out at the forlorn junkyard landscape.

"Wing Ding?" Smith's voice asked excitedly. "Remo, she means WingerDinger."

"If you say so," Remo said. He heard the soft taps of Smith's fingers on his special capacitor keyboard.

"We tracked down those two men you learned about in Los Angeles," Smith explained as he worked. "They were active on many Internet message boards. There was overlap of many other individuals with the same interests. One of the names was an AIC user who called himself WingerDinger. Wait, here he is. Orville Wilbur Feldon."

"His parents must have really hated him," Remo said.

"Graduate of Columbus University School of Journalism," Smith said, his voice growing more excited at the journalism connection. "No gainful employment yet he's spent hundreds of thousands of dollars from his bank account in the past several months. Where did he get so much money?"

"While you're looking that up, tell me: Did he withdraw twenty thousand in gold recently?"

"By the looks of it, he had just over that amount converted to gold yesterday morning," Smith said.

"We found your prankster, Little Father," Remo said.

This brought Chiun's attention back to the matter at hand. "Tell me where is this jokester," the old Korean demanded. "It is time for a manners lesson."

"Wait," Smith said. "It appears as if he has used this money to fund all of this madness. Yes. It will take time to track through the dispersal of funds but someone must have supplied him with the cash. Let me check back to the initial deposit and . . ." Smith's voice got very small. "Oh."

Remo knew when to be worried. He sat up straight behind the wheel of his stolen FEMA truck.

"What 'oh'?" Remo asked. "What's wrong, Smitty? Who cut the check? Who's this nutbar's crackpot sponsor?"

Smith's reply brought a look of shock to the faces of both Masters of Sinanju. As the truth settled in, Remo whistled and Chiun scowled. Between them, Kitty shrugged.

"What?" BCN's number one reporter asked. "I didn't catch that. Who's the mastermind?"

28

"That's my parking space!" yelled Cheeta Ching.

"Sorry, no assigned parking," the English teacher called out the open window of his rusted Nissan as he nudged past Cheeta's BMW and into the space beneath the big beech tree in front of the Sackwood Building of Career Training.

When Cheeta came trudging up from the distant student parking area five minutes later, the English teacher was hauling from his trunk a cloth bag filled with books and papers and emblazoned on both sides with the faded logo of a local bank.

"My, my, my. How the mighty have fallen," he sneered as Cheeta walked past.

Cheeta did not even glance at the man. They'd had a confrontation at a staff meeting the previous week. Cheeta could not even remember what it was about. Frankly, she couldn't be bothered to recall. But apparently this balding, aging windbag with his pilly white dress shirt with the yellowed collar and too-wide tie remembered.

Cheeta knew it was not the argument she'd had about how community college was a joke and that the teachers there could not call themselves professors and probably should be sued by the truth-in-advertising people for even calling themselves teachers. She had mentioned this to a group of teachers in the quad one day. She remembered distinctly, because it was the same day she'd found all four tires on her Beemer flat, the front and back windshields shattered and various curse words written in shaving cream all over the paint. When she had pointed out to the staff the next day that two words and one phrase had been misspelled and the possessive had been misapplied and that even professors at a state college would probably have gotten all that right, the same thing happened to her precious BMW once more, this time with everything spelled and punctuated correctly.

That had been months ago, and the balding English teacher hadn't been there that day anyway. No, it was at the staff meeting. She had upset him in some other way.

"So nice when bad things happen to bad people," the English teacher said.

"Just you wait," Cheeta panted. She wore a sweater too big and bulky for a hot spring day and was sweating in the heat. "I'm going to be the Phonics that rises from the ashes."

"Phoenix, Cheeta," the teacher corrected, shaking his head as if talking to an idiot child. "It's Phoenix."

"No, it's not, it's Highwater, New York," Cheeta said. "No wonder a real school wouldn't have you, you don't even know where the hell in the country you are."

Cheeta left the moron who was too dumb to be a professor at a real school and hustled into the Sackwood Building. She realized she was walking faster than usual and made a conscious effort to slow to a more normal pace. It was difficult to do. After all, today was a big day for her.

It had been a long time coming.

Cheeta Ching had once been a rising star in network news. For a brief time in the early 1990s she had even coanchored the BCN Evening News in the real New York. New York, New York. But her coanchor had been crazy, mean and deeply devious, while all Cheeta had going for her was mean with a touch of devious. She was out on her ear before she even knew she'd been aced out of the biggest job of her career.

The TV newsmagazine jobs had dried up not long after. If it was not for the income of her husband, who hosted a daytime TV talk show, she would have been foraging for cans at the local garbage dump. She and her husband had briefly co-hosted a cable TV show two years before but the ratings were lousy even for cable and the show had been mercifully and quietly cancelled. If not for the drunken stunt on a piano on the last episode, the show would have been forgotten completely.

Her husband was in New York City now, more than likely taping an episode of his popular show. Right now she thought he would be in a cushy studio talking about makeovers or fat babies or husbands impregnating their daughter's lesbian girlfriends while his poor wife was off teaching a course in journalism at some godawful community college in Highwater, New York.

Well, not for much longer.

Cheeta found her classroom but this day she did not sigh in defeat as she pushed open the door.

As she did every morning she arranged on her desk an apple, two pens and a picture of her daughter. At least she thought it was her daughter. She had not seen the girl in quite some time. Cheeta's daughter was fifteen now and off at some boarding school, probably in New England. It was her husband who handled the details of all the boring, everyday stuff. Cheeta could not be bothered with every little detail of someone else's life and anyway the picture, pens and apple were all just props. Just as everything else in this minor career detour was all part of setting the stage for Cheeta's triumphant return to glory.

Cheeta was settling in behind her desk and drumming her fingers anxiously when she heard a gentle tap at her open door. When she looked up, her eyes grew wide.

She hustled over, yanked the man at the door into the room by one arm and shut the door, careful not to slam it.

"What the hell are you doing here?" she spat.

"You think I was going to miss our big day?" Orville Wilbur Feldon answered.

"What if somebody sees us together?"

"Can't an old student visit one of his old teachers?" A grin creased his fat face.

"I was never your teacher, Orville," Cheeta said. "I was a guest lecturer at your school. And the day they'd have me lecture at Columbus University was a long time ago."

"Still it made an impact on me," Feldon said. "And it put the two of us in touch with each other. If it wasn't for that, we wouldn't be poised to stage the coup of the century at BCN News. They won't know what hit them."

Cheeta dropped her voice low. "Is everything ready?"

"Keep your eye on the clock. Nine o'clock sharp we go Columbine. Oh, and have I got a story for our first show. Did you hear how New Orleans got flooded again yesterday?"

Cheeta's face puckered. "It did?"

"No," Feldon said triumphantly. "Exactly my point. I'd hoped it would finish them but this will work out fine, too. I've just got to hear back from our ace reporter in the field on some footage and we should be good to go. Trust me. Not only will this put the last nail in the coffin of the old BCN regime, it'll blow your socks off."

"Fine," Cheeta said. "Tell me all about it. Later. For now, get out of here. Class is starting any minute."

Cheeta pushed Feldon from the room. She peeked

around the corner and saw the big man's massive back lumbering down the hallway. Blowing a lock of black hair from over her eye, she ducked back into the room.

Cheeta found something attractive about Feldon, even back when she had guest lectured at Columbus U. Not a male-female thing, for Feldon was repulsive in every conceivable physical way, but there was something about his nastiness, about his bullying that reminded her of a young Cheeta Ching.

Orville Wilbur Feldon was foolish to come here today, but Cheeta was not surprised. Feldon had a right to be excited. He had cooked up this brilliant scheme to rocket them both to the top. Cheeta had signed on, even bankrolling it with her husband's money but she had never really thought that it would actually work. But now the foundation had been firmly laid. It was time for her to do her part.

Her students began to trickle in twenty minutes later.

Most had signed up out of curiosity but when they had found Cheeta's class worthless even by community college standards they had switched over to more worthwhile classes such as Interpretive Dance, The Healing Power of Crystals and The Art of Native American Basket Weaving in the Twenty-First Century and Beyond. There were only nine students left in Cheeta's class and just seven of them showed up this day. A better turnout than normal.

One of the boys set up a video camera and angled it toward the front of the room. Since her first class all of Cheeta's lectures had been videotaped. When the camera was running and everyone else was settled in their seats, Cheeta brought out some videotapes and dragged out the TV trolley.

"Grace under pressure is the most important quality a TV reporter has," Cheeta instructed. "Yes, good hair and teeth matter, but if you can't keep a cool head under difficult and dangerous circumstances then you might as well be bald with an Englishman's teeth. Lights."

The first tape Cheeta popped into the VCR was of Kitty Coughlin screaming and crying on Flight 980.

"Can anyone tell me what Ms. Kitty Coughlin, light-weight celebrity interviewer, did wrong here?" Cheeta was not surprised when no hands went up. Not one student had raised a hand all semester. She answered her own question. "She accepted the job of serious news anchor when she should have stuck to interviewing dog groomers during tick season."

The next tape was of Kitty screeching on the elevator in the Weltsburg, Pennsylvania, coal mine.

"How about this one?" Cheeta asked. "What did Ms. Coughlin who, if there was a God in heaven would still be on mornings asking Uma Thurman's personal trainer how Uma gets those rock-hard abs, do wrong here? Anyone? Anyone at all? No? She should never have taken a job that might require her to get down and dirty like a real reporter."

Cheeta played the footage of Kitty on the Alaskan cruise ship and at the Los Angeles riots, offering similar commentary. The last tape Cheeta played was of Kitty at the zoo covered from head to toe in monkey dung.

"The conclusion we can draw from all this is that a reporter's life is not a glamorous one," Cheeta said once the tape was finished and the lights were back on. She eyed the clock and saw that it was just a few seconds before nine. "What makes an individual good at, for example, testing barbecues in an outdoor setting outside a morning show studio, does not necessarily a great reporter or anchor make. If you want to get the big story you have to have nerves of steel in circumstances that would make a lesser woman break down and cry like a sniveling little baby."

A loud pop suddenly sounded somewhere down the hall. The students glanced at one another.

"Why, what on earth was that?" Cheeta asked loudly.

She struggled to keep the flicker of a serpent-like smile from her lips even as she glanced to make certain the camera at the back of the room was still running.

Another pop, followed quickly by several more. Screams erupted in nearby classrooms.

"Stay in your seats, children," Cheeta announced. "I'll check to see what's going on."

She was halfway to the door when it suddenly burst open and a mountain of fat waddled desperately into the room.

"Watch out, Miss Ching!" Orville Wilbur Feldon cried.

Cheeta battled to keep the rage from her face. "What the hell do you think you're doing?" Cheeta demanded in a furious stage whisper. "You're not supposed to be here. You're screwing everything up."

"Just making certain there's no double-cross," Feldon said out of the corner of his mouth. "We're in this together. To the end." Feldon waved a warning finger in the air. "There are armed students on campus!" he announced over a fresh series of pops, now clearly gunshots, that rolled up from the corridor outside Cheeta Ching's classroom. "Hey, wait. Hey, what are you . . . ? Stop that!" he screamed.

At his announcement, rather than wait for the slaughter, the seven students in the room ran immediately for the windows. The last student, a girl with a wide bottom, ankle tattoo and too-short shorts was yanked outside by two boys. Cheeta's class joined an exodus of students and teachers that was running across the front lawn toward the parking lot.

"You couldn't get a classroom on the second floor?" Feldon whispered to Cheeta.

"Shut up," Cheeta hissed from the corner of her mouth. "We can still make this work."

So preoccupied were they with watching the closed classroom door, neither of them seemed to notice that the sounds of gunfire were petering out. When the door burst open a moment later and an armed man raced in, Cheeta jumped protectively in front of Feldon.

"Stand back!" she shouted.

Wayne Dwyer was dressed in a long, black trenchcoat and carried a pistol in each hand. His broad acned face was pale and covered with a sheen of glistening sweat.

"Something's wrong!" Dwyer shouted. "Ledding is already dead. They got Bullings. They're coming!"

"Let them come," Cheeta Ching announced, with another glance at the still-running videocamera. "You picked the wrong news reporter to mess with, sonny."

Reaching under her bulky sweater, Cheeta pulled out a pistol and squeezed the trigger.

Dwyer was tossed back by the force of the blow to his chest. The guns fell from his hands and he slammed back against the side wall under a large corkboard speckled with pushpins and a faded map of the United States.

"You weren't supposed to . . ." Wayne panted as a dark stain seeped across the chest of his black jersey. "WingerDinger. WingerDinger said I wouldn't . . . wouldn't . . ."

Cheeta walked over to the dying man, pointed the barrel at his forehead and blew Wayne Dwyer's brains all over the cheap, multicolored vinyl floor tiles.

"Grace under pressure," Cheeta announced.

She wondered if she got the line right. It had sounded good in her head. Maybe she should do a retake. This was, after all, going to be shipped immediately to BCN in New York. Her sources told her the brass were looking to replace Kitty Coughlin, and that they were considering going back to their stable of old talent. After this performance, juxtaposed with Kitty's abysmal performance these past few weeks, there was no way they would not hire Cheeta back. But she wanted to make certain everything was perfect.

"I think I should probably do a retake on that line," Cheeta said. "Orville, wind the tape back."

"It worked fine for me," a voice that was not Orville Wilbur Feldon's said from the back of the room.

When Cheeta looked up, she saw two men standing near the tripod videocamera. She blinked in shocked recognition.

"Grandfather Chiun?" she asked.

Chiun's face soured. "Do not call me that. It is to my eternal shame that I helped you conceive when Western doctors failed you. Woe the child born to one such as you, one who would murder innocents and wreak havoc for personal gain."

"What are you talking about, Chiun?" She shrugged helpless confusion. "Reno?" she asked the man standing next to the Master of Sinanju. "Reno, what is he talking about?"

"It's Remo, not Reno, you nit," Remo said. "And we know the whole deal. You Feldon?"

"Orville here just happened to stop by today to visit," Cheeta interjected quickly. "We met years ago when I guest lectured at his school. I haven't seen him since."

"Bulldookey. I know how you financed Blubberpot here to do all that stuff so you could get back in the anchor chair. Somehow, babe, I always knew it would end like this for us."

Feldon looked from Cheeta to the two intruders. "I know you," he said. "It's you. From the mine. And you were the meddlesome dastards who stopped my beautiful Los Angeles riots, weren't you?"

"Dastards?" Remo said. "Is this suddenly 1872?"

"Shut up, Orville," Cheeta hissed.

"Ah, but I've got you," Feldon continued, as if he had not heard Cheeta speak. He aimed a fat finger at Remo. "I know all about the vaunted Masters of Sinanju, BCN's hired killers. Well, Daisy O'Toole got you on tape in action down in New Orleans. Not one move or you'll be on coast to coast in prime time on my new bully pulpit, the BCN Evening News with Cheeta Ching, Orville Wilbur

Feldon, News President. No more lurking in shadows for you, no more secret assassins to the stars. Hah! Got you!" he said triumphantly.

"Breath mints are your friend," Remo advised.

Feldon's moment of triumph collapsed into confusion. "What?" he asked.

But Remo had turned to the Master of Sinanju. "Roll 'em, Little Father."

Cheeta had not realized the two men had paused the video recorder until the old Korean reached out a tapered finger and pressed a button and the camera whirred to life.

Remo advanced from the right, careful to remain out of the camera's range. Feldon stood between the two of them.

"Stay back," Cheeta warned, raising her pistol once more. "You're sexy but that doesn't mean I won't kill you. I've got to have this, don't you see? I can't stay out here in the vast wasteland forever. I earned that anchor chair. It's my destiny. It's mine and I'm taking it back by any means necessary."

Remo continued slowly walking toward her. Cheeta had no choice. "Sorry, Reno." She pulled the trigger.

The tape made in Cheeta Ching's final moments of life would be investigated more carefully than Abraham Zapruder's film of the Kennedy assassination. On conspiracy theory sites all over the World Wide Web, some would insist that there was a blur of movement in the instant before the barrel flashed. The Internet site DyingCheetaConspiracy.com would introduce the most popular theories on its main page thusly:

> It makes no sence that Cheeta wuld shoot Feldon in
> the face like that. Feldon had got her almost back to
> hosting BCN newz. Some thing (blur on tape!)
> intrvened at last minute and made Cheeta shoot
> Feldon. Someone else was in room!!!! And it is not

possible that some one Feldons size culd do that to Cheeta. Sure he wuz big but when he fell on her he wuld not have crushed every bone in her body. Some thing made Cheeta shoot Feldon unintentionaly and then crushed her under Feldon's body. At DyingCheetaConspiracy.com we have all the theories. Click one to take you to proper page.

   —Aliens

   —CIA

   —Venezuela

   —Kim Jong Il

   —Vice President

   —Big Oil/Vice President

Once Chiun had shut off the video recorder, Remo stepped over to the bodies. All that was visible of Cheeta jutting out from under the mass of dead blubber that was Orville Wilbur Feldon was one arm and both legs.

"I'm sorry, Little Father," Remo said.

"Do not be sorry for me," Chiun sniffed in reply. "Be sorry for the poor soul who was married to her all these years. Although the pair of ingrates never thanked me for helping them conceive so he will probably not send me a thank-you for this even bigger favor." Turning on his heel, the old Korean marched from the room.

Remo gazed down at the visible portions of Cheeta's body and smiled sadly. "That's the biz, sweetheart."

29

Two days later Remo was on the kitchen phone of the Connecticut condominium he shared with the Master of Sinanju. "Air travel is bouncing back," Smith was saying. "It has nearly reached the same level as before Flight 980."

"Yeah, I noticed the cabins seemed to be filling up more with each flight while I was bouncing around the country," Remo replied. The living room TV played softly in the background. Through the open door Remo could see the back of the Master of Sinanju's age-speckled head, his wizened form suffused in the flickering glow cast by the screen.

Remo was happy that the TV wasn't blasting the rafters off the roof, for Chiun frequently played it loud enough to irritate the neighbors a block away.

"In many ways I can't understand the modern age," Smith said, "yet at times like this the resilience of the American people amazes me. Unfortunately I fear the damage in Alaska will be more long-lasting than that to the airline industry."

"I heard the oil spill was cleaning up fast."

"The cleanup is not the problem," Smith said seriously. "The environmental groups are not letting it go. The oil industry will be made to suffer, so ultimately will the American consumer at the gas pump. A lasting legacy of the madness of Orville Feldon and Cheeta Ching."

"Speaking of Feldon, thanks for the book," Remo said.

Feldon's copy of *Myths of Ancient Asia* sat on the counter next to the fridge. As he spoke, Remo flipped to the House of Sinanju entry. Chiun had told him when the book arrived by courier that the Master in the sketch was his father. Remo was surprised that Chiun knew nothing about the old book or his father's apparent involvement with it.

"We found the book at a storage unit that Feldon kept in Pasadena," Smith said. "He was apparently piecing together information for a story about you and Master Chiun for Cheeta to present on the news once the two of them took over. Mark destroyed some notes as well as a tape he found of you that was taken in the mine in Pennsylvania. My first instinct was to destroy the book as well but when he described it to me I did not see the harm in letting you have it."

"So you've got everything of Feldon's?"

"Yes," Smith said. "It was a simple matter to track down his online contacts. Noah Sherman and Wayne Dwyer seemed to be involved more heavily than the rest. I guess Feldon knew how to push their buttons harder. But the BCN employee who aided in the kidnapping of Kitty Coughlin has been arrested. And it turns out that a security officer at LaGuardia was another online victim of Feldon as well. One Edward Nole passed along to Feldon information about the security upgrade that blinded the airport to the hijackers, as well as distracted the other screener on duty. That was how the weapons and explosives were brought onto Flight 980 during the scheduled security maintenance period. There were a few more individuals as well, beyond Dwyer and the ones you, er, took care of at Cheeta's school. All have been arrested."

"Good," Remo said. "I guess Kitty can go back to her sinking BCN Evening News ship."

There was a pause on the line. "You haven't heard?" Smith asked.

"Heard what?"

Smith sighed wearily. "It is nearly six-thirty. Why don't you go put on BCN News? And brace yourself, Remo."

The line clicked in his ear. Frowning, Remo left the copy of *Myths of Ancient Asia* on the low taboret in the middle of the floor and wandered into the living room. On the mantle were Chiun's autographed photos of Judge Ruth and Rad Rex. Remo noted that Chiun's once-prized Cheeta Ching picture was nowhere to be seen. The Mexican soap opera that the Master of Sinanju had been watching was just ending and the old Korean was about to shut the television off.

"Smitty says we should put on BCN News," Remo said.

"Why?" Chiun asked. "Are we finally going to get credit for repeatedly saving this nation from disaster?"

"Beats me," Remo said, sinking cross-legged to the floor next to his teacher.

When the BCN Evening News logo came up without Kitty Coughlin's name, Remo was surprised. When he saw whose name had replaced Kitty's, he was stunned. When the enormous head appeared on the screen, Remo pinched his own forearm a dozen times to make sure he wasn't having a nightmare. Unfortunately he was wide awake.

"Hello, America. A bomb went off in Baghdad today, killing twenty. A White House spokesman claims that the vice president, who should be impeached for high crimes against humanity and funneling war profits to his buddies in Big Oil, was not directly involved in the bombing. Hah! Who believes that?"

Remo turned from the giant head on the screen. "What the hell is Daisy O'Toole doing hosting the evening news?" he asked the Master of Sinanju.

"Do not ask me. I recommended a Korean for the job. It figures it would go to just another fat white."

They watched the news for several more minutes, Remo in stunned silence until Daisy introduced some video footage.

"Some of you might be wondering how I got this job," Daisy said. "It was this footage of the recent rupture in the levees in New Orleans, taken by yours truly, that caught the eye of the honcho-wonchos here at BCN."

Remo had to admit, Daisy was tougher in the field than Kitty Coughlin. After water began gushing from the levee breach, she screamed at the real reporters to hold their ground even as the local New Orleans news crew scattered. Even abandoned, Daisy did not surrender. After the news crew was gone, Daisy grabbed the camera and marched off on her own, filming the aftermath as she walked. No one but Remo and Chiun watching at home knew that she had really been searching hopefully for Kitty's floating corpse.

"So that's why I'm here, America. And Daisy ain't going nowhere this time." She leered at the camera as if it were dripping with butterscotch sauce. "Up next, was it the vice president, global warming or both that was responsible for the recent near-flooding of New Orleans?"

A loud commercial came on and Remo was about to hit the remote control when he saw another familiar face.

"What the hell?" he said when he spotted Kitty Coughlin sitting on a tall stool surrounded by a wildly clapping audience. Strobe lights flashed crazily and the crowd applauded more urgently.

"You know it, you love it!" called an announcer's voice.

The word "Oopsie" splashed across the screen.

"See what all your friends are talking about!" yelled the announcer, whose voice Remo knew but could not place.

A rapid montage was next, with Kitty asking quick questions of contestants. Occasionally the audience would shout "Oopsie" at an incorrect answer and the camera would pull back to show a trapdoor opening and the contestant dropping through. But the legs of the male and female contestants were tied to bungee cords, so rather than fall to certain injury, they bounced helplessly in place.

"Good answers and you don't drop! But you don't want to see our splat round! And avoid the dreaded penalty whap! *Oopsie*! It's the new prime-time game show that's number one—that's right, number one—in the ratings!"

There was a final closeup of Kitty trying desperately to fake a sincere smile but looking utterly miserable.

"See what all your friends are talking about, tonight at eight on BCN," Kitty moaned.

Remo snapped off the TV. "I guess they found a use for Kitty after all. And that was Maddox doing the announcing. I knew I recognized that voice. And that was my game, Little Father. I invented that with Maddox on the roof of BCN. If they're not blowing smoke, this thing is going to kick ass in the ratings. Where are my residuals? When am I going to get my cut, huh? Tell me when?"

Chiun nodded firmly. "I will act as your agent," he said. "We will get what is rightly yours."

"You know what? Fine. There's no way Kitty Coughlin and Uriah Maddox get a number one show based on an idea they ripped off from me without paying me a damned dime."

"Yes, it is only fair. Fair is fair, Remo, and we want what is fair for you," said Chiun. "Ten percent." He rose from the floor and headed from the room.

"You got it," Remo said to his teacher's retreating back.

"Nail them to the wall, Little Father. Wait," he said suddenly. "You mean ten percent agent's fee for you. I get the ninety percent, right?"

Chiun's voice floated back from the depths of the condominium. "Have your people contact my people. Then we'll talk."